DOG ON COURSE

A Tori & Nick Adventure

P. J. Rich

Cover artwork and design by Daniel Greenhalgh

Interior illustrations by the author

ISBN 979-8-9945963-0-2 (paperback)

ISBN 979-8-9945963-1-9 (ebook)

Formatted using Lacuna

For Emma

CHAPTER 1

JANUARY

Tori's fingers drummed on her knees as she stared blankly out the side window of the old minivan. With an off-beat rhythm, the wipers swept the cold drizzle from the windshield. Squeak. SQUEAK. Squeak. SQUEAK. She stole a hopeful look at her dad in the driver's seat. He continued staring straight ahead.

For as long as Tori could remember, a tiny orange flame of hope had flickered inside her, a flame that flared blue whenever she saw a dog, any dog. It kept her warm when everything around her was cold and colorless. *Today,* she thought, *if all goes well, I will glow like the sun.*

Her father had promised that as soon as they moved to Maple Valley and lived in a house with a yard, she could finally have a dog. But he had broken promises before, promises like getting her a new bike or taking her to an amusement park. Those things didn't really matter though, not compared to adopting a dog. Would Dad come through this time? She glanced hopefully at him again. He continued staring straight ahead, so Tori watched their new neighborhood glide past—mostly small older homes surrounded by neatly mowed lawns dotted with hundred-foot Douglas-firs and cedar trees. Homes filled with strangers.

As they passed Maple Valley Middle School, Tori turned her eyes forward, through the drizzly windshield. She didn't want unpleasant thoughts of school in her head today, and anyway, she didn't need to worry about being the new kid in seventh grade until eight days, fifteen hours, and—she glanced at her watch—forty-seven minutes from now.

They entered a compact business area, where a few trendy restaurants and boutiques interrupted rows of tired shop fronts. Small groups of people in dirty, ragged clothing huddled in the entryways of vacant stores. Workmen removed the holiday decorations wrapping the old-fashioned light posts. Tori tapped her knees even faster.

Once, a long time ago, her dad had promised that her mother would get well. But she didn't. Back then, when Tori was just a little kid, she was angry that he didn't keep that promise. Now she was thirteen years old, and she understood that his promise had been more of a wish. Her father could build anything with wood, could fix any engine, but he couldn't cure cancer. Tori knew that he wished desperately that he could. That he had. She stopped tapping and her hands curled into fists.

Downtown gave way to open fields of weeds and tall grass. Tori nudged her eyeglasses into place and peered through the rain-streaked windshield to see an old concrete-block building with peeling paint and a moss-covered roof. The shelter! She had half expected the minivan to end up at the nearest hardware store or lumberyard instead.

Ancient letters hung precariously over the front door: Franklin County Animal Shelter. A large sign next to the door read "Please Contribute to Our Building Fund!"

Her father slowed and swung into the parking lot. Tori sat on the edge of her seat and gripped the door handle, ready to jump out. She glanced at her dad and smiled. Dad caught her eye. Tori thought she saw the corners of his mouth turn up, just a little.

In the front office, Tori spotted the "Dog Adoptions—Wait Here" sign and headed straight for it, her dad trailing behind her. She stopped at a piece of ragged yellow tape that stretched across the floor. The room was empty except for a young man with spiky bleached-blond hair and tattoos marching up his arms and neck. He sat at a desk and frowned at a computer screen. Tori watched as he tapped the return key five times in a row. Slowly. Soooo slowly. Then she couldn't wait any longer.

"Excuse me?"

Bleached-blond guy tapped once more, then looked up. "Oh, hi. May I help you?"

Dad touched Tori on the shoulder, a touch she knew meant *let me do the talking*. She pressed her lips together to contain her excitement.

"I'm Jim Leonhart, and this is my daughter Tori. We have an appointment to look at the . . ."

"Dogs!" Tori blurted. She couldn't help herself. Patience had never been one of her virtues. She quieted her voice. "Sorry, Dad."

Her father continued as though Tori hadn't spoken. ". . . to look at the dogs."

Bleached-blond guy smiled at Tori. "OK! I can see that you are rarin' to go." He picked up an official-looking clipboard and stood. "My name's Jordan. Right this way."

Jordan headed down a long hallway and Tori followed, a step behind him. Her dad brought up the rear. Tori patted her right front pocket. Yup, she had remembered to bring dog treats.

Jordan turned his head toward Tori. "What kind of dog are you hoping to find?"

Tori had prepared for such a question. "Maybe a border collie, if it's small. Dad wants to get a small dog," she said. "But the breed isn't important. I think I'll know when I see the right dog."

Jordan nodded as though her answer was perfectly reasonable. He led them around a bucket collecting water that dripped from the ceiling. "I'm sorry the building is in such bad shape. We're raising money for a new facility. We hope to move soon." He opened a door marked "Dogs Available for Adoption" and they stepped through.

The barking of what seemed like a thousand dogs and the pungent smell of wet concrete, disinfectant, urine, and poop filled the air. Dad wrinkled his nose. Tori's eyes searched the long, dark aisle and the rows of chain-link enclosures. Dogs of all colors, shapes, and sizes paced around their kennels and jumped at the wire gates. One of those dogs could be hers.

Tori took a deep breath. Her whole body tingled with the feeling that her life was about to change.

The three of them walked slowly down the aisle, pausing in front of each kennel. Jordan consulted his clipboard and told Tori and her father a little about each dog. Dad nodded and glanced at the dogs, but the phone in his hand drew most of his attention. Tori was used to that—work always seemed to come first for him.

Tori peered into the kennels, sometimes kneeling and talking to the animals. "Look at you! What a beautiful boy you are," she whispered to a small scruffy terrier. "Hi, pretty dog! Wow, you are a big strong girl!" she said softly to a big white dog with Dalmatian-like black spots.

"Remember, the dog needs to be quiet," Dad reminded Tori, his eyes still on his phone. "We're new in town and we don't want to annoy our neighbors." They had talked about that requirement before, so Tori just nodded and kept her eyes on the dogs. At the next kennel, a medium-size black-and-tan dog pressed the side of his body against the wire barrier, as though, Tori thought, he was trying to get as close as possible to his visitors.

"This is Dexter," Jordan said. "He's a German shepherd mix, about a year and a half old, and he weighs about fifty pounds. He was found as a stray, so we don't know much about his history."

The dog's medium-length fur was mostly black with silver highlights, and his legs, chest, and face were golden tan. His ears began as upright German shepherd ears, but after a couple inches they gave up and flopped over to the side. The black fur between his tan ears extended down his forehead in a V-shape that stopped between his eyes and pointed to his sensitive nose. Soft feathers of blond fur swung from the underside of his fluffy black tail.

And he was quiet! While the other dogs barked and hurled themselves against the kennel gates, Dexter just slowly wagged his long thick tail, thumping a steady rhythm against the wire. The corners of his mouth turned up into a silly grin.

Tori looked into the dog's eyes. He looked straight into hers. And her heart melted all over the cracked concrete floor. Stars— no, *constellations*—sparkled in his golden eyes. Eyes that could reach inside, grab and hold a girl's soul. The eyes of a best friend, a friend who would never leave her.

Tori sank to her knees and gripped the chain-link fence with all ten fingers. The world shrank to the five square feet that encompassed just her and the black-and-tan dog. He was all she saw, and the beat of his tail against the wire was all she heard.

Dexter turned and ambled to the back of the kennel and through a small swinging door. A few seconds later the door swung in toward Tori, and the beautiful dog stepped through carrying a soft pink toy in his mouth. Tori's eyes welled. "Hey, buddy. What is that? A pink elephant? Is that for me?" Dexter faced her, his golden eyes locked onto hers, his tail swinging softly from side to side.

For a moment, Tori became acutely aware of the smell, the noise, the dark dank air, and, most of all, the cold chain-link fence separating her and the dog. Then her focus returned to Dexter.

"I'll get you out of here," she whispered to him. "I promise."

CHAPTER 2

Tori cleared her throat and hoped the steady din of the kennel hid the thick emotion in her voice. Still kneeling in front of the kennel, she said, "Dad, I like Dexter. Can we meet him? Outside of the kennel, I mean?"

"Sure." Her father looked up from his phone. He folded his arms and stepped closer to Dexter's kennel. "Hmmm. We talked about getting a small dog, didn't we?"

Tori drew in a quick, noisy breath. She chewed her lower lip and looked up at her dad.

Dad's eyes shifted from Tori to Dexter, Dexter to Tori. "Well, OK. He seems quiet."

Tori exhaled. She smiled at Dexter. The dog dropped his pink elephant toy in front of her. He opened his mouth in a friendly smile, his brilliant white, pointy teeth framing his pink tongue.

Tori and Dad followed Jordan as he walked Dexter to the shelter's big fenced yard. Well, walk wasn't really the word. Dexter danced, pranced, bounced, and leaped to the yard while Jordan stumbled along behind. Dad opened the gate, they all entered, and then Jordan removed Dexter's leash. Without hesitation, Dexter took off and circled the entire yard at a wild, excited run.

Tori clapped her hands. "Hey, Dexter! C'mon over here!" The dog pivoted and galloped toward Tori. He skidded to a stop in front of her, slid his muddy paws down her jeans, then leaned and rubbed against her legs. Tori ran her hands in long sweeping strokes through the soft black and silver fur on Dexter's back. She couldn't stop smiling.

Through her rain-speckled glasses, Tori spotted a tennis ball in the mud and gingerly picked it up. Dexter's eyes sparkled with excitement. She drew her throwing arm back, and he spun around and ran before the ball even left her hand. She tossed it ahead of him. The ball bounced, and Dexter leaped into the air, snapped it into his jaws on the rebound, and landed lightly on all four paws. He trotted back to Tori, head high, teeth chomping on the yellow-brown ball, eyes on her.

She dared to think it: Her dream of owning a dog—a sweet, beautiful, playful dog who would be her best friend—was going to come true. If Dad agreed.

Jordan and Dad watched Tori and Dexter play in the light rain. Tori heard her father say, "We just moved here about a week ago. I'm a carpenter, and I got a new job designing and making cabinets . . . Anyway, it's just the two of us in our family, and I promised Tori we would adopt a dog." Dad's phone beeped, and he tapped the screen. He read something, then looked up and continued. "She's been asking for a dog for years. She's thirteen now, old enough to be responsible for it. And maybe a dog will help her make friends here."

"Well, Dexter seems to be a good match for your daughter," Jordan said.

Tori dug a small piece of beef jerky out of her pocket and placed it in her palm. Dexter's velvet-soft muzzle and damp nose snuffled at her hand. Quick blasts of dog breath warmed her skin, silky-stiff whiskers tickled it. Then his rough pink tongue gently lapped up the treat.

Electricity surged through Tori, from her muddy hand straight to her open heart. *This is my dog. We're meant to be together.*

Tori kneeled on the wet grass near her dad and stroked Dexter's buttery-soft ears. Dexter half-closed his eyes and leaned against Tori's chest, and his warmth fused with hers. Dad set his mouth in a thin line and scanned Dexter up and down and from head to tail.

Jordan consulted his clipboard. "Let's see . . . hmmmm . . . well, it looks like some other people are interested in adopting this dog, so if you wait too long he might be . . ."

Tori snapped to attention and stood, keeping a hand on Dexter. "Please, Dad? Can we take Dexter home? He's the one. I know it."

Dad met Tori's eyes. "This is a big decision, Tori. We should look at some other dogs too," he said. "Maybe a German shepherd isn't the right kind of dog for a girl. Don't the police use German shepherds to track down criminals? He might be hard to handle."

Dexter looked up at Dad's face and lowered his rear end. He opened his mouth in a wide smile and his long drooly tongue escaped out the side. Bubbly warm saliva dripped to the ground. *See how nice I am?* he seemed to say.

"But . . . but . . ." Tori's brain scrambled for a comeback. Dexter turned his head toward her and his eyes searched her face. She kneeled, put one arm over the dog's shoulders, and patted him gently. Dexter gave her face a sloppy lick. "Dexter's not a *purebred* German shepherd. He doesn't look like the police dogs I've seen in movies."

Dad folded his arms across his chest, one hand clutching his phone. "Still . . . let's look at some smaller dogs."

As Jordan leashed Dexter and led him away, Tori felt her chest rip open and the leash yank out her heart. Dexter walked with his head turned back, his eyes on Tori, as though he sensed and shared her pain.

CHAPTER 3

Tori and her dad walked up and down the rows of chain-link kennels. Like a robot following orders, Tori peered into each one. Raucous barking rose and fell as they passed. The sharp scent of dog waste was inescapable.

Four fat black Lab puppies tumbled over each other and played tug-of-war with their blankets. A tan terrier mix, wiry fur bristling from his muzzle, jumped endlessly at her kennel door. A tiny, gray-faced Chihuahua stared at her visitors and didn't move from her soft cuddly bed. The brilliant blue eyes of a fluffy white husky followed Tori and her dad as they passed.

Tori hoped that somewhere there was a family for each dog, people who would want them as much as she wanted—no, *needed*—Dexter.

Finally, Dad suggested they go home and think about all the dogs they had seen. They could come back tomorrow, he told Tori.

"OK," Tori said flatly. But what if the promise of a dog was one of those promises Dad wouldn't keep? What if they never went back to the shelter? She couldn't bear to think about Dexter being in that kennel for one more day. She watched her feet move across the sidewalk as she followed her dad to the minivan.

As they drove home, Tori told herself she was too old to throw a tantrum or whine or complain. Even if she were the sort of girl who threw tantrums or whined or complained, which she wasn't.

She imagined scenarios where she stole Dexter from the shelter and ran off with him and they wandered the country as fugitives and then Dad was sorry he said no. Or she taught Dexter all kinds of tricks and they competed in a talent show on TV and they won and became famous and then Dad was sorry he said no.

She was too old for ridiculous fantasies, Tori told herself. Even if she were the kind of girl who would run away to make her dad feel bad, which she wasn't.

Downtown, Dad braked for a red light. As they waited for it to change, Tori watched workmen strip away the last of the cheerful holiday decorations.

Then Dad rubbed the back of his neck, sighed, and looked at Tori. "You're sure?" he said. "About Dexter? Taking care of a big dog like him will take a lot of time. He'll need lots of exercise, every day. You'll have a lot to learn."

The inside of Tori's head hissed and buzzed like the car radio when it lost its signal. She didn't dare move in case she was dreaming. She kept her eyes on a man in a brown jumpsuit reaching for a strand of red and green lights. "Yes, I'm sure. I can take care of him."

Dad took a long deep breath. His back straightened so that his head almost touched the car's ceiling. The squeaks and shudders of the windshield wipers filled the silence.

Tori forgot to breathe. She could guess what her dad was thinking. She had once asked for clarinet lessons, but she soon quit because she wasn't a good player right away. And there was the time she insisted on learning archery, but she was too impatient to properly aim the arrow. She was older now, though. And a dog was different from learning clarinet or archery. She wouldn't need a lot of patience to have a dog.

Dad exhaled. "OK. He's your responsibility. You're going to clean up after him and teach him manners, right?"

Tori filled her lungs as though for the first time in her life. She turned to her dad and the words erupted from deep inside her. "Yeah. Heck, yeah!"

Dad sighed. "OK." The light turned green and he accelerated, drove around the block, and headed back to the shelter.

Tori hands drummed a quick excited rhythm on her knees. Dad pulled into the shelter parking lot. Before he had even turned off the engine, Tori jumped out and ran into the office. Her sneakers squeaked on the shiny floor as she rushed to Jordan's desk.

"We're back!" she exclaimed. "We're back for Dexter!"

While her father paid the adoption fee and completed the paperwork, Tori waited in the reception area. She perched on the edge of a hard plastic chair and stared down the hallway toward the kennels. Dexter wasn't the perfect name. For years, she had been thinking about what she would name her first dog. Now that the time had come, she couldn't decide. What name would fit such a special dog? Alexander—like Alexander the Great? Something full of energy, like Flash? Rocket? Jet? A strong mythological name? Zeus? Apollo?

A few long minutes later, the kennel door flew open and Dexter pulled Jordan into the hallway. Dexter saw Tori, pulled the leash out of Jordan's hand, and galloped toward her, scrabbling on the slick floor. He plopped his front end on her lap. His elbows dug into her thighs and his warm tongue reached toward her face. Tori wrapped her arms around his shoulders and giggled as he licked, again and again, coating her eyeglasses with a thick layer of drool.

Suddenly, she knew the perfect name. "Nick! Hi, Nick!" She buried her face into the thick fur of the dog's neck. *Her* dog.

Nick panted and gazed at Dad and Jordan. *Hi! Hi! Hi! Hi! Hi!* he seemed to say with every breath. He closed his smiling mouth for a split second. SLURP. Then, *Hi! Hi! Hi! Hi! Hi!*

"Nick?" Dad asked. Tori lifted her head. Her glasses tilted at a crazy angle and were covered in slime and fur. She peered through them at her dad. *Is he actually smiling?*

"Yeah. Nick! That's his name. Cause we got him in the 'nick of time.'"

"He's all yours," said Jordan. "Here—you can take his favorite toy." He handed the pink elephant to Tori. "He'll need a little training. But you'll learn as much from him as he learns from you."

Tori wrinkled her nose. *What does* that *mean? What can I learn from a dog?*

Jordan turned to Dad. "You said your yard is fenced. That's good. Be sure to keep the gate locked."

Dad nodded, then he told Tori, "That'll be your responsibility, Tori. OK?"

Tori nodded yes. She wondered why Jordan had made such a point about locking the gate, but guessed it was just one of those dog ownership things she had to learn about.

Jordan spoke to Tori. "You'll probably want to give Nick a bath. We keep the place as clean as we can, but the dogs can get pretty stinky."

Tori leaned over Nick and sniffed. Her nose twitched at the sour stale-urine odor. No, he did not smell good. Well, how hard could it be to give a dog a bath?

CHAPTER 4

What a disaster. Tori scanned the bathroom and gave a heavy sigh. Brown muddy spots sprinkled the walls, dog hair clogged the tub drain, and wet dirty towels covered the floor. Nick wouldn't stand still while she tried to shampoo him. He kept shaking off the sudsy dirty water and it flew all over the bathroom. Then Tori tried to lead him outside before he could shake again, but he managed to splatter the kitchen too before they made it to the back door.

She ran her hands through her straight brown hair and adjusted her ponytail. The dog care videos she had watched online didn't mention how much house cleaning was involved. Now Nick lay on the living room rug, licking his wet fur. The distinct scent of wet dog wafted through the house. Tori caught her reflection in the mirror and saw clumps of black-and-tan dog fur sticking out of her hair. She frowned at herself and sighed again.

"How ya doin'?" Dad called to Tori from his office.

Tori glanced down at her wet jeans and t-shirt. "Oh, fine." She tried to keep her voice light. "Ummmm . . . it's kind of a mess in here, but I'll clean it up."

"OK. See that you do. I have to get these designs finished today." Tori heard the scrape of a chair on the floor, footsteps, and Dad's office door swing shut. She got to work.

Finally the bathroom walls and floor were spotless, the drains were clear, and the dirty towels were whirling around in the washing machine. "C'mon Nick! Let's go outside!" Tori pulled on a jacket and rain boots, and she and Nick headed to the backyard.

Raindrops from the morning cloudburst glistened on the green lawn, even though the sun had made a cameo appearance. Tori watched Nick explore the yard. He glanced at Tori every minute or so, as though making sure she hadn't disappeared.

Tori's smile grew by the second. Her heart swelled as she watched Nick enjoy his freedom from the shelter. How many years had she waited for this day? She jumped up and down like a five-year-old, then glanced at the house. *Hope Dad didn't see that.*

While Nick continued sniffing every shrub and blade of grass, Tori walked the fence line and checked for holes and weak spots where Nick might escape. Not that he would ever want to escape, of course. The five-foot-tall wooden fence seemed secure, and the gate at the side of the house was even locked with a padlock. The key hung in the kitchen by the back door.

Nick danced over to Tori. He pounced down on his front paws, his rear end in the air, and grinned a huge open-mouth grin. His whole body said, *Let's play!*

Tori imitated Nick. With a big grin, she leaned over, stuck out her rear end, and slapped her hands against her knees. Nick took off running in a big circle around the yard, his tongue flapping out the side of his mouth. His feet pounding against the ground sounded like a herd of stampeding buffalo. Tori clapped her hands. "Go, Nick, go!"

With no warning, the rain returned. The heavy, dense drops stung Tori's face. "Aack! C'mon, Nick, back inside!" They ran to the house and up the steps. Tori swung open the back door, and Nick trotted into the kitchen. And promptly shook himself from head to tail, sending second-hand rain all over the floor and cupboards.

"Nick!" *Uh-oh. Dad won't like this.* Tori grabbed a towel and soaked up most of the water from Nick's fur. He shook himself again as soon as she was done. She mopped up the mess with the towel, while Nick lay on the floor and licked himself. *I should keep some towels by the door for drying Nick off* before *he can shake himself,* she thought.

Tori peered through the kitchen window. The rain showed no signs of letting up. On rainy days she usually curled up on the couch and watched TV or read a book, so she grabbed a can of sweet tea from the fridge and headed to the small living room. "C'mon, Nick," she said. "Let's get comfy." She tapped her leg to invite Nick to follow her.

Moving boxes filled with Dad's stereo equipment and music collection were stacked along one wall, but the couch and coffee table already sat against another wall, with the TV against the opposite one. Tori plunked down on the couch and picked up the remote control. But when she aimed it at the TV, all she saw was a damp black-and-tan dog blocking the screen. Nick shook himself, sneezed, and stared at Tori.

"Woof!"

"Ha! You still want to play?" Tori set her tea on the coffee table. "OK. I know. Clicker training. Let's try it. Whaddya say?"

Tori went to her room and found her small metal clicker, her treat bag, and some training treats. She clipped the treat bag around her waist and hurried back to the living room. Nick smelled the treats and was instantly, intensely, interested in doing whatever he needed to do to get one. Or ten. Or a hundred.

Tori tried to imitate the dog trainers she had seen in online videos. In one hand, she held a treat over Nick's nose and moved it toward his back, so that he had to sit down to keep watching it.

At the instant his rear end hit the ground, she was supposed to press the metal clicker, which was in her other hand. The quick, clear *click* would signal to Nick that he had done the correct thing, and he would get the treat. It sounded easy, but it wasn't.

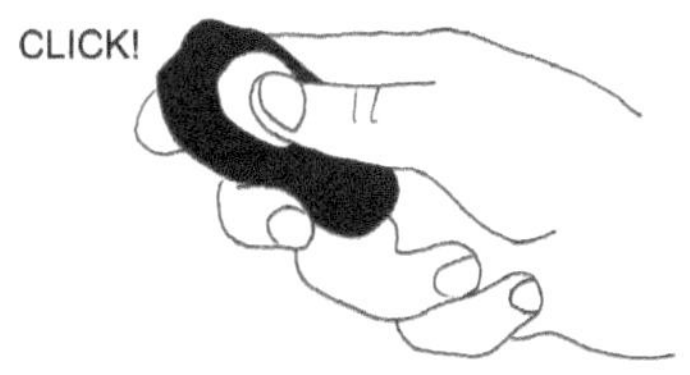

At first, Tori kept clicking at the wrong time, dropping the treats, and getting her clicker hand and her treat hand confused. "Grrrrrrr," she growled to herself. Finally, Nick sat when she asked him to. Tori clicked at the same time—well, almost ––and Nick stared at her treat hand. Tori gave him a treat. Then she said, "OK," to tell Nick he could stand up. She tossed another treat a few feet away, and Nick scrambled after it.

"Good work, buddy!" Now let's work on 'stay.'" With Nick sitting in front of her, Tori took three steps back and said "stay." Nick stood up and followed her.

"Oops. Let's try again." This time she took two steps back. Nick stood up, followed her, and nuzzled at her treat hand.

Harsh impatience crept into Tori's voice. "Stay means 'don't move,' Nick."

Nick lowered his head, looked sideways at Tori, and sidestepped away from her.

"I'm sorry!" Tori's heart sank into her stomach. Images of faceless people yelling at Nick flashed through her mind. Who knew what he had endured as a stray or from a previous owner? She ran a gentle hand down his back and lightened her voice. "You're doing great, buddy. I'll work on being patient, OK?"

Tori put a treat on the palm of her hand and offered it to Nick. He raised his head, took a step toward Tori, then, with one front paw raised, he gently lapped up the treat. Tori offered him another. Nick moved closer to Tori, stood confidently on all four feet, and gobbled the treat. He wagged his tail as though to say, *you're forgiven*, then his eyes searched Tori's face. *Got more treats?*

"Wheeeew." Tori exhaled in relief. She never wanted to make Nick feel bad or scared again. "Such a good boy. Let's try 'stay' once more." This time Tori took one baby step back and clicked. Nick didn't move! She stepped toward him and gave him a treat. Then she took a regular step back, clicked, and said "stay." Nick stayed. She stepped toward him and gave him a treat.

"Woo-hoo!" Tori ruffled the thick fur on her dog's neck. "Good boy! So I think you just taught me that I need to start with short distances and work up to longer ones. Right?"

Then Tori said "OK" and scattered a few treats on the living room rug. Nick bounded toward them and snuffled at the rug, right and left, up and down, his big fluffy tail wagging back and forth— and right across the coffee table.

Like a miniature tsunami, Nick's tail swept away Tori's tea, the TV remote, several guitar picks, and Dad's handwritten music journal.

"Nick!" Tori grabbed Dad's journal and, pinching a corner between a finger and thumb, held it up and away from her. Tea dripped onto the rug. "Ohno, ohno, ohno . . ." She ran into the kitchen with Nick close behind and patted the journal dry with a towel. Just a few pages looked damp. It could have been worse. Nick stood at her side and watched, his tail wagging slowly.

She couldn't help skimming the pages as she dried them, though she knew the journal was full of Dad's private thoughts. One page made her pause. *Song for Malia,* it said, and a simple melody with guitar chords was notated beneath the title. *Malia*. That was her mother's name. She shut the journal and stared blankly at the plain gray cover.

Tori missed her mother. But Mom had been gone so long, more than three years, that the picture of her in Tori's mind was blurry and faded. In her last memories of her mother, Mom was in a hospital bed with lots of tubes going in and out of her body. But for Dad, Mom hadn't faded at all. She seemed to be alive in his mind. Tori sometimes wished she could be more like her mother. Then maybe her father would be happier.

The rug. The mundane thought jerked her back to the present. She left the journal on the kitchen counter, grabbed a dry kitchen towel, and ran into the living room, with Nick trotting after her. Tori patted the rug dry and picked up the now-empty drink can. Good thing the plain brown color of the rug matched the tea. She sat back on her heels and surveyed her work. All back to normal, except . . . she had to tell Dad about his journal.

Tori stood at Dad's closed office door. She curled her fingers into fists, shook them out, and curled them again. She filled her lungs, then let the air escape with a rush.

Knock. Knock. Knock. "Dad? We had a little accident . . ."

She heard Dad's chair squeak and rattle as he stood up, then footsteps. The door opened. "What happened?"

In a few words, she told him.

With just five strides of his long legs, Dad was in the kitchen. Tori and Nick followed. Dad gingerly picked up the journal and turned the damp pages.

Tori rubbed the back of her neck, where her muscles were as taut as the strings on her father's guitar. Nick sat beside Tori, and his eyes moved from Tori to Dad, Dad to Tori, as they spoke.

"It was all my fault," said Tori. "Please don't be mad at Nick." Her hand automatically reached for her dog, and she stroked his neck and shoulder.

"He's a big dog to have in the house." Dad peered into the living room. "You did a good job cleaning up. Just be more careful."

"Yes, we will."

Dad cradled the journal in his arms, carried it back to his office, and shut the door.

Tori stood in the kitchen, listening to the hum of the refrigerator and the rain beating against the window. Nick nuzzled her hand. She kneeled beside him and buried her face into his thick fur.

🐕 🐕 🐕 🐕 🐕

That evening, Tori lay in bed with Nick beside her. He was supposed to be in his own bed on the floor, but he wouldn't settle there. Instead, he stood beside Tori's bed, tail wagging gently, and nuzzled her face with his cold wet nose. *Please let me sleep with you on your nice soft bed,* he seemed to say. She couldn't resist.

"Big day, huh Nick? Our first day together! I'm so glad you're here." She stroked his silky-soft—and still fairly clean—fur. "One little accident, and it wasn't your fault. I'll make sure everything goes smoothly from now on."

Nick put his muzzle on Tori's stomach. His eyes searched Tori's, as though he was trying to see right through them into her mind and understand her. Tori gazed back at him and imagined the questions that Nick might ask, if he could. She answered him with mind-messages. *Yes, you live here now. You'll never have to go back to the shelter. You'll never be a stray and have to scrounge for food again. I'm going to take care of you. We will be—I mean we are—best friends. Forever.*

Friends. Would she make friends at her new school? She wasn't sorry to leave her old school in Portland, where kids had treated her like the resident weirdo, the friendless girl with the sick mother who died. Would she fare any better at Maple Valley Middle School? She had one more week of vacation before she would have to go and find out.

Nick groaned contentedly and closed his eyes. His head, resting on Tori's stomach, rose and fell in sync with her breathing. His warmth filled the bed, filled the room, filled Tori.

Exhausted from the eventful day, Tori fingered Nick's floppy velvety ears until, seconds later, she fell sound asleep.

CHAPTER 5

T he next day after breakfast, Tori helped Dad unpack boxes in the living room. She kneeled on the floor and carefully placed her father's collection of vinyl records—in alphabetical order, by artist—on shelves, while Dad set up his vintage stereo equipment. Nick wandered around the room and stuck his nose into every box Tori opened.

"Where should we hang your mother's portrait?" Dad held up a large, framed photograph of a smiling woman with long, dark hair. The woman kneeled on one knee next to a black-and-white border collie. She held a fancy blue ribbon with one hand and hugged the dog with the other.

Tori sat back on her heels and scanned the bare walls. She pointed. "There, near your favorite chair, where you play your guitar. Maybe Mom will hear you. She liked jazz too."

Dad nodded. "Good idea." He rummaged in his toolbox for a tape measure, measured the wall to find the exact center, and marked it with a pencil. He picked up a small hammer, tapped in a bright new nail, and carefully hung the photograph. Briefly, gently, he touched the woman in the photo, then stepped back. Tori glanced away and pretended that she didn't see the tears welling in Dad's eyes as he turned and bent over to fiddle with his stereo.

She dusted off her hands on her jeans and scanned the room. With the music and stereo in place and the photo hung on the wall, the living room was starting to look and feel . . . like home. Like *Dad's* home.

Tori's eyes settled on her mother's photo. Tori didn't look much like her. Her mother had been thin and pretty in an athletic kind of way. Tori was short and a little plump, wore eyeglasses, and metal braces covered her teeth. What they did have in common, though, was a love for dogs. At least Tori assumed her mother had loved dogs, judging from Dad's favorite photo of her.

She looked at Dad, who was still busy with his stereo. The words "tell me about Mom and her dog" almost came out of her mouth. But instead, she heard herself say, "Is it OK if I take Nick for a walk?"

"Sure. Have fun." Dad studied the back of his amplifier and scratched his stubbled chin. Then he pulled a cord from the amp and plugged it into a different port.

Tori watched her father for another moment, then headed to the entry, patting her leg to tell Nick to follow her. He licked her face as she slipped the new hunter green harness on him and attached the matching leash. "You look so handsome in your new harness! Do you like it? Who wants to go for a walk?"

Nick's flashing eyes spoke to Tori. *PickMePickMePickMe!* He danced around her and his tail whacked her shins. Excitement overflowed out his nose and he sneezed, twice, his head bobbing up and down each time. Tori giggled.

"OK, OK! Here we go!" Tori opened the front door and Nick charged out. The leash snapped Tori's arm forward and she stumbled down the steps. "Nick! Wait!" She yanked the leash. Nick slowed for a millisecond, then all 50 pounds of eager dog leaned into the harness again.

Tori shifted her weight back. Nick's paws clawed at the concrete to gain some traction. She used both hands to pull him to a stop. Nick turned and took one step toward Tori, then surged forward again.

Tori gave in and let Nick lead the way down the sidewalk. She leaned back and held the taut leash with both hands. Her feet slapped the ground with each step. *And Dad says* I'm *impatient!* she thought. *He'll wear out eventually, right?*

Nick veered right to sniff a fire hydrant. Tori stumbled to the right. He pulled forward to pick up a candy wrapper. Tori jogged forward and pried the wrapper from his mouth. Nick stopped short to check out an irresistible scent on a dandelion. Tori fell over his rump and just about face-planted on the concrete.

Once around the block was enough for Tori. Nick, as happy to return home as he had been to leave it, pulled her up the front steps.

Inside, Tori shut the front door and leaned against it until her breathing slowed. Nick pranced around her, his tongue lolling and eyes shining. *What's next?"* he seemed to say. Tori tugged off Nick's new harness, now damp and stained from his habit of rolling in the grass.

Dad called from his office. "How was the walk?"

"Great!" Tori replied. *How much should I tell Dad?* "Nick is really . . . Nick really had fun."

"Good. Good." Dad said absently. Tori could tell that he had already moved on from their brief conversation. For once, that was a good thing. *I can't even walk my dog properly! I bet my mom didn't have that problem with her dog. I've got to figure out this dog training thing before Dad finds out how out of control Nick really is.*

CHAPTER 6

The rest of the winter holiday week was a blur of activity. Tori and her dad unpacked more boxes and stocked the kitchen with groceries. They discovered the best pizza place in town. Dad got his backyard workshop in shape and already had some carpentry jobs to work on.

Tori learned that taking care of a dog was a full-time job. Nick needed breakfast and dinner every day, at least two walks, and plenty of play time in the backyard. *Life has changed, all right,* thought Tori. No longer did she spend hours in front of the TV or computer. And she found that she LOVED taking care of Nick. She loved how he wanted to be with her. She loved the sight of him bounding toward her with a ball in his mouth, turning his ears to listen to her speak as they walked together, or just resting his head on her lap as they sat on the couch. He always brought a smile to her face.

She did her best to train him to walk nicely, sit, stay, and come, but he still pulled the leash and often decided he had better things to do, like chase a squirrel, when she wanted him to stay or come. In those moments, it was hard to keep from getting frustrated. But then she pictured Nick in the shelter behind the chain-link gate, alone and unwanted, and she couldn't blame him for wanting to have fun. Even if his idea of fun wasn't always the same as hers.

Nick chewed on the furniture, put his front paws on the kitchen counters and licked them, shook rain all over the floors, tracked in mud, napped in places where Dad was sure to trip over him, and scratched at any closed door, especially the bathroom door when

Tori was in there. Dad suggested leaving him in the yard, so Tori reluctantly tried, but Nick just barked and scratched at the door so she had to let him inside. She was secretly happy about that. What was the point of having a dog if he couldn't be with her always, inside and out?

Several times a day, Tori heard her dad call "Tori! Take care of your dog!" And she would find Nick licking crumbs off the kitchen counter or trying to dig a hole in the couch cushion or chewing a paperback book. Once she found him standing on top of the coffee table, for no apparent reason. Tori wanted to believe Nick's behavior was improving, but Dad seemed to be calling her name more and more every day. By Saturday, the calling had turned to yelling. Tori had become so jittery that she flinched whenever Dad spoke, no matter what he said. Worse, she was afraid that Dad regretted adopting a dog.

On top of all that, Tori had noticed a couple of disturbing posters while walking Nick. They featured big photos of cute dogs and the word LOST! The posters said the dogs had gone missing from their yards. Tori remembered how Jordan had warned her and Dad about keeping their gate locked. Maybe that was just a coincidence. But maybe not. Maybe Jordan knew something about how the dogs were getting lost. *Great. Something else to worry about,* Tori thought. *Maybe Maple Valley isn't such a nice place after all.* She didn't have room in her brain to think about anything but Nick, so she tucked those thoughts into a far back corner of her head.

But on Sunday, another worry began to balloon in her mind. School. Tomorrow. As bad as it was to start seventh grade at a new school in the middle of the year, even worse was that she would be away from Nick. "Tomorrow you'll be here with Dad all day," she told him. "You'll have to be on your best behavior. Let's practice that today."

At one o'clock, while Tori was getting a snack in the kitchen, Nick found Dad's favorite mechanical pencil and chewed it to bits. "Tori! Look at what Nick did!" called Dad.

"I'm sorry," Tori said. "I took my eyes off him for just a minute. He didn't know that was your favorite pencil."

At two o'clock, while Tori was in her bedroom picking out clothes for her first day of school, Nick knocked over the kitchen trash can and scattered stinky food scraps all over the floor. "Tori! Take care of your dog!" called Dad.

Tori ran to the kitchen and saw Nick smacking his lips over some delicacy he had extracted from the mess. I'm sorry, Dad. I'll clean it up. I guess I didn't do a good job covering the trash."

At three o'clock, while Tori worked on clicker training with Nick in the living room, some neighbors rang the doorbell. Nick ran to the door and barked like crazy. Dad sprinted into the living room. "Tori! Take Nick to the backyard," he growled, and pointed toward the back door. "Remember what I said about barking? Neighbors don't like noisy dogs."

Tori's face sagged and she felt the blood drain from her face. Silently, she grabbed Nick's collar and led him through the kitchen to the back door and into the yard. "I guess you're not as quiet as we thought you were, Nick." Nick smiled at her, and Tori couldn't stay upset with him. She had to figure out how to teach him not to bark.

At four o'clock, Tori took Nick for a walk and he rolled on a dead bird. As soon as they came into the house, Tori heard Dad yell from his office, "Tori! What is that smell?" Tori had to agree that the stench of decaying bird was stomach-churning. She gave Nick a bath, shampooing and rinsing him twice.

At five o'clock, while Tori was trying to dry him, Nick escaped the bathroom. He trotted into Dad's office and shook bath water all over Dad's desk. "Tori! Get your dog out of here!" Tori ran into the room and saw Dad waving his latest drawings in the air to dry them. He scowled at Tori.

"I'm really sorry, Dad. He got away from me. It won't happen again." Tori grabbed Nick's collar, led him into the bathroom, and shut the door. She sat on the floor next to him and gulped back tears. Thoughts and emotions ricocheted through her: *I'm not smart enough to take care of a dog. I've disappointed Dad. Nick deserves a better owner.*

Then Nick set his chin on her shoulder and licked her ear. Tori's mind cleared. She ruffled the thick fur on Nick's shoulders. "We'll figure it out, won't we?" she whispered into his ear.

At six o'clock. Nick paced around the big kitchen island as Tori prepared his dinner. He sniffed, nose high, nostrils flaring, to take in the cheesy aroma of the freshly baked casserole—Dad's favorite zucchini-tomato-parmesan-pasta casserole—that sat on the counter.

"Nick, I forgot your vitamins! I'll be right back. Don't do anything bad, OK?" Tori went to her room to get the supplement for Nick's dinner. A few seconds later, she walked back into the kitchen—and stopped short. *Something's wrong.*

The clacking of dog nails on the tile had been replaced with licking and slurping noises. *The casserole. Where's the casserole?* Tori stood on tiptoe and peered over the kitchen island. The casserole dish was on the floor, and Nick's muzzle was buried deep into it.

"Nick! No!" Tori cried.

Dad stepped into the kitchen, saw what was happening, and in one long stride reached Nick. He shoved the dog away from the casserole and picked up the dish. "Nick, how could you?" he scolded, his voice sharp.

Nick lowered his head and looked at Tori, then Dad. His big tongue flicked over his lips, collecting the crumbs stuck to his whiskers. Then he lay on his belly and licked stray chunks of casserole from the floor.

"That's the last straw, Tori." Dad's voice was harsh. "Nick needs to learn manners. You're going to train him, right?" He examined the casserole dish in his hands. It was licked almost clean. "I don't want to have to take him back to the shelter, but . . ."

. . . *back to the shelter.* The words gut-punched her. Tori lowered herself to the floor next to Nick, and he lay his muzzle on her outstretched leg. His eyes rolled upward to watch her face, and she watched his. *This past week has been the hardest—but the BEST—week of my life,* thought Tori. *I can't lose you, Nick.* Nick pulled his whole front end onto Tori's lap and reached his tongue to Tori's cheek and licked. Tori lowered her face to his and stroked Nick's side. She waited for her brain to stop spinning.

I'm such a failure. It was one thing to read and watch videos about how to train and take care of a dog, and quite another to try it in real life.

She raised her head. "I'm sorry. I should have been watching him," she croaked. Her throat was too dry and her eyes too wet to say any more.

Dad's jaw muscles tightened and popped as he tossed the casserole dish into the sink. It clattered against the metal sides, then slid to a stop in the center. With slow, deliberate motions, he squirted soap into the dish and filled it with water.

If he was a cartoon character, steam would be blowing out of his ears, thought Tori. Dad was usually distant, distracted. She was used to that. But angry? That was rare.

Nick gazed from Tori to Dad, Dad to Tori. His brow wrinkled, and his ears stiffened and stuck out to the sides like airplane wings. His expression said, *I'm confused. Is something wrong?*

Still at the sink, Dad exhaled a long "whew," and his shoulders dropped as the tension drained away. "Sorry Tori, I know we haven't had Nick long." He turned to face her, leaned against the sink, and crossed his long arms across his chest. "Jordan mentioned that new adopters can get a free dog training lesson at a place called the Dog Sports Center. Maybe you should do that. What do you think?"

School wasn't Tori's favorite place. She was always in the classes for kids who had trouble learning, so the other kids thought she was dumb. She hadn't been any good at clarinet or archery lessons. *But maybe lessons in dog training will be different. And if it means Nick can stay with us . . .*

"OK. Yeah." Tori plastered a fake smile on her face. *Look enthusiastic,* she told herself. "I mean, yes. A lesson sounds like a great idea."

Dad gazed wistfully at the empty dish in the sink. He really liked zucchini-tomato-parmesan-pasta casserole. "I'll call for a pizza delivery. Remind me—what's your favorite topping? Green peppers?"

"No, my favorite is mushrooms," said Tori. Green peppers had been Mom's favorite.

After their pizza dinner, Tori helped her dad clear the kitchen table and wash the dishes. They chatted awkwardly about the new house, Maple Valley, the neighbors, and Tori's new school, almost anything except the topic of Nick. Tori sensed that Dad was trying to be nice after his blowup earlier that evening. Nick sensed the undercurrent of tension and stayed out of the way.

Then Dad went to the living room and picked up his guitar, and Tori got out the laptop computer she and her dad shared and sat down at the kitchen table. She typed *Maple Valley Dog Sports Center* into the search field and pressed Enter. She clicked on the first match and a simple webpage loaded onto the screen. *Learn how to train your dog with positive reinforcement techniques!* the page read.

Tori scrolled down to a section with the title "What is Positive Reinforcement?"

She had heard of positive reinforcement dog training, but she had never really understood it from books and videos.

Well, I'll read about it again. Maybe this time it'll make sense, she told herself.

What is Positive Reinforcement Dog Training?

Positive reinforcement training is also called *reward-based* dog training. When you give your dog something they love, such as a tasty treat, when they sit, they'll sit more often in the future. The treats are called *rewards* or *reinforcers*.

A focus on rewards encourages your dog to learn new "good" behaviors, such as greeting a person by sitting in front of them, that can replace "bad" behaviors, such as greeting a person by jumping up on them. It also teaches dogs to love training. Without fear of being punished for doing the wrong thing, your dog can become an active participant in the training process. They'll start to try new things, get plenty of mental exercise, and look for ways to earn rewards. Plus, instead of just learning what *not* to do, they learn what you expect them to do in each situation and they are happy to do it. Finally, your dog learns to associate you with the wonderful rewards you provide, strengthening the bond between you and your dog. [adapted from www.akc.org]

She read the explanation three times but still couldn't imagine how just giving rewards to Nick could help him behave. She gave him rewards all the time, but he still got into trouble. She learned better by *doing*, not reading. Maybe that's why she sometimes struggled in school. But if she wanted to keep Nick, she would have to learn. She clicked on "Make an Appointment."

"Dad?" she called.

The guitar music that drifted in from the living room stopped. "Yes?"

"How about next Saturday at one o'clock? Can you take us to the Dog Sports Center?"

"OK. I think I'll be free that day." A few guitar chords sounded. Then, "Thanks for making the appointment." The guitar music started up again.

Tori clicked Submit. Done. She and Nick were officially enrolled at the Maple Valley Dog Sports Center. For one lesson, anyway. She hoped she wouldn't make a fool of herself.

Tori browsed back to the search results page and scrolled down, curious to see what other websites her search had found.

"Lost & Found Dogs in Oregon" read one search result. She remembered the lost-dog posters she had seen in her neighborhood and clicked on the link. The website loaded, and Tori scrolled down the page to see photo after photo of dogs, all reported missing in the last few weeks.

Beloved family pet missing!

Help us find Blinky!

Lost older dog, needs medication!

Our family is heartbroken without Mickey!

In the website search filter, she entered Maple Valley and set the distance to 10 miles.

Four dogs had gone missing from that search area in the past few weeks, three from nearby towns and one from Maple Valley: a Yorkshire terrier, shih tzu, poodle, and a Chihuahua. In the photos, the cute little dogs sat on couches or played in yards or chewed on bones in their comfortable homes. Kids with broad smiles, some about Tori's age, posed with the dogs.

Tori leaned over and stroked Nick, who sprawled on the floor next to her chair. She remembered Jordan telling her and Dad to keep their yard gate locked. *Nick will never go missing. I'll make sure of that,* thought Tori.

I already lost my mom. I can't lose Nick too.

🐕 🐕 🐕 🐕 🐕

As Tori lay in bed that evening with Nick beside her, all the worries and emotions from the past week cartwheeled through her mind: memories of losing her mother, fears of losing Nick too, her dad's disappointment with her, the photos of lost dogs on the website, dog training lessons . . . oh, and going to a new school. Tomorrow.

Tori had filed that little detail of her new life at the very back of her brain. Now visions of all the things that could go wrong paraded through her head. *Wrong clothes . . . wrong hair . . . wrong desk . . . wrong lunch table . . .* Her chest tightened and she felt her heart beating against her bones.

She threw an arm over Nick's shoulders. Being close to him always made her feel better. "I'll miss you, Nick," she whispered into his ear. "You have to behave, OK? Dad's really not so bad. He's just got a lot of work to do. I'll be back around three."

Nick rubbed his muzzle deeper into the blankets and gave a deep contented groan.

Tori lay back and her shallow breathing slowly deepened. She stroked Nick's velvety ears until she drifted into a fitful sleep.

CHAPTER 8

Tori gripped her blue plastic lunch tray and froze in the doorway of the school cafeteria. She had made it through her morning classes without drawing too much attention to herself. But it might be harder to stay under the radar in the cafeteria.

She scanned the big room and tried to look as though she knew exactly where to go. Kids of every size, shape, and color headed toward long tables lined with benches. They flowed around her, like a river parting around an island. The blend of high and low, loud and hushed voices created a constant buzz. A bouquet of steamy tuna casserole, buttery chocolate chip cookies, and spilled milk hung in the air.

Tori spotted some open seats in a quiet corner. Head down, she carried her tray to the table. Four other girls already sat at one end, chatting. They glanced at Tori as she slipped quietly onto the bench at the other end of the table, but they didn't say anything. Tori opened her milk carton and set it down on her left, arranged her French fries into a neat pile, and separated her carrots from the celery. Then she moved the milk carton from left to right.

From the corner of her eye, Tori saw a tray clatter onto the table next to her and a girl sit down. "Hi," said the girl.

Tori slid her eyes left. The girl was pretty, with a mass of curly chestnut-brown hair, about the same color as her skin. Tori tried to get her dry mouth to work. She finally managed to croak, "Hi."

"You're new, right?" said the girl, her deep brown eyes gazing at Tori. She wore an expensive-looking baby blue sweater with puffy sleeves.

Tori glanced down at her old green t-shirt. She pulled her shoulders forward and hunched her back. "Yeah."

"Where are you from?"

"Portland," said Tori.

"Oh. I'm Laura." Laura worked at opening her milk carton.

"Hi. I'm Tori." Tori didn't know what else to say, so she stabbed some lettuce with her fork and stuck it into her mouth. She noticed that Laura's rough scratched hands didn't match her neat clothes and hair. *Wonder what the story is there*, she thought.

Two girls plopped their trays down next to Laura and sat down. The first girl had long black hair and wore a flowered silk scarf around her neck. "Hi, Abby," Laura said to her.

Abby ran a hand through her dark hair and tossed it over her shoulder. "Hey, Laura," she said, without looking at either Laura or Tori. She carefully adjusted her scarf so that it laid evenly on her shoulders.

"Hi, Gisele!" Laura greeted the other girl with a little more enthusiasm. Gisele had cropped auburn hair and the tiniest nose Tori had ever seen.

"Hi, Laura!" said Gisele in a high, squeaky voice, which somehow matched her nose. Gisele glanced curiously at Tori but didn't say anything.

Tori kept her eyes on her lunch tray but couldn't help glancing at her tablemates. They chatted to each other like they were all old friends, although Laura soon opened a worn paperback book and began to read. Not one of the other girls wore braces on their teeth, as far as she could tell. A few of the girls stared at her, then whispered and giggled to each other. Tori hunched forward even more.

No problem, she told herself. *Never had friends, don't need them now.* In Portland, she had been the weirdo with the sick mother.

Then she was the weirdo with the dead mother. Kids didn't know what to say to her, so they said nothing.

Tori reached for her milk carton . . . and somehow, instead of grabbing it like a normal person would, she bumped it. SPLAT. The carton pitched onto its side and milk flowed in every direction. Tori froze and stared at the milk-lake in disbelief. Then she quickly righted the carton, picked up her napkin, and started to wipe up the mess.

Complete silence fell over the table. Tori raised her eyes. Every girl at the table was staring at her. Some even held their forks or spoons in midair where their hands had stopped when the milk spilled. *Maybe I'm in a time warp and this hasn't really happened,* thought Tori. She felt her face heat up.

Then someone coughed and the spell was broken. The other girls exchanged sideways glances among themselves and the chatter started up again.

Tori exhaled. She began to scrub the table again, but the soaking wet napkin fell apart in her hand. Laura handed her some dry ones. "Thanks," muttered Tori. She finished mopping up the milk.

"Nice shirt." Tori looked up to see Abby toss her long black hair over her shoulder and, in the process, literally look down her nose at Tori. Tori dropped her eyes to her plate and pretended she hadn't heard the comment. She had always liked the bright green t-shirt. Until now.

"Abby!" Gisele whisper-scolded Abby and elbowed her in the ribs. Then she turned to Tori and spoke in her squeaky voice. "Hi. We have social studies together. I'm Gisele." Gisele grinned. Her teeth were brilliant white and perfectly straight. She pointed at the other girls and said their names. Tori immediately forgot them.

"I'm Tori. Nice to meet you," she said. Sometimes the manners that Dad insisted she learn came in handy. Like when her brain wasn't working and she couldn't think of what to say. Like now.

The other girls went back to their conversation.

Laura glanced at them and then at Tori. She held up her book to shield her face from the others and whispered to Tori, "They're OK. Usually. Just give them a little time." She tilted her head. "Well, except for Abby. She thinks she's *special*. Just ignore her." She gave Tori a quick grin, then lowered her book and resumed reading.

"OK. Thanks." Tori turned her attention back to her lunch. She picked up a carrot and, with a firm grip on each end, snapped it in two. She bit off a piece and crunched it between her metal-clad teeth. Tori peeked at the cover of Laura's book. The title was *Young Detectives: Mystery at the Castle*.

She glanced at Laura. *Be normal. Try to make friends*, she told herself.

She searched her brain for something to say. "Is that a good book?" she asked. She immediately wanted to kick herself. What a lame question.

Laura raised her eyes and met Tori's. "Yes. I like mysteries." She absently flipped the pages of the book, back and forth. "Why did you move here?"

Tori shifted her eyes to her food. She pushed her French fries around the plate. "My dad got a new job. He designs and builds cabinets and stuff."

"I'll bet you think there's not much to do here, compared to Portland," said Laura.

"Living in a small apartment isn't much fun," replied Tori. "It's better here, in a house, in a small town." Tori imagined herself playing ball with Nick in their new yard. *Yes, it's a lot better here.*

"Oh." Laura nodded, then went back to reading her book.

Tori glanced at Laura and sat up a little taller. That wasn't a terrible first conversation, she thought. Maybe it was the start of a friendship. She had so little experience with such things, it was hard to tell.

Tori picked out an extra-big French fry, bit off a piece, and chewed thoughtfully. She had spent a lot of time indoors in Portland. She had been too young to go places by herself in the city, so she stayed home and watched TV and played video games and read books, mostly dog and horse stories. When her dad wasn't too busy taking care of her mother or working, he took her places like the skating rink or the swimming pool or museums, where she entertained herself while he worked on his computer. Here in Maple Valley, Tori could walk almost anywhere or ride her bike by herself. She liked how grown-up that made her feel.

What was Nick doing at home? She hoped he was behaving himself. He was probably napping in her room, she thought. Dad said he would let Nick into the backyard when he needed to go potty. The backyard gate was locked, so he couldn't wander away and get lost like all those poor dogs on the Lost Dogs website. She told herself to check the lock when she got home, just in case.

Tori thought about her upcoming lesson. What would the Dog Sports Center and the teacher, Min Qi, be like? She had to learn how to train Nick. Nothing was more important than making sure that she could keep him.

In her mind, Tori called Nick, and he ran toward her with bright eyes and floppy ears. She said "sit" and "down" and he obeyed instantly. They ran together, Nick staying right at her side . . .

CLAAAAAANG! For a split second, the bell lifted Tori right off the bench. She was alone at the corner table. She hadn't even noticed the other girls leaving. Tori picked up her tray, swung her legs over the bench, and walked over to the clean-up area. She glanced down at her left side and wished that her friend—her best friend, her only friend, Nick—was there.

Chapter 9

Tori survived the first week of school. She practically sprinted home every day to see Nick. He greeted her each time as though she had been gone seven years rather than seven hours. They went on long walks, even though Nick pulled and stopped to sniff a lot, and Tori continued trying to train him to do what she asked. She told him about each class, the homework she did or didn't understand, and the kids she was slowly meeting.

At lunch, she managed to have conversations about food or school events with Laura, before Laura opened her book of the day. The girl was obsessed with mysteries! But Tori liked her. She still wondered what Laura did to make her hands so rough and scratched. Tori sat next to Gisele in social studies and they rolled their eyes at each other when the teacher told corny jokes. Abby, on the other hand, was a puzzle. What had Tori ever done to make Abby pick on her so much? Maybe just being the new kid was enough.

Nick survived staying home with Dad, and hadn't done anything *too* bad while Tori was at school. Nothing too bad other than stealing Dad's sandwich off the kitchen counter, digging a big hole in the backyard, eating grass and throwing up on the living room rug, chewing big holes in the quilt on Tori's bed, and drinking out of the toilet and then dripping toilet water down the hallway. Both she and Dad were learning to cover the trash can securely, keep food off the counters, and dry Nick off before he entered the house. Dad called it "not tempting fate." Tori thought it was like Nick was training *them* to behave differently, so that he could stay with them.

Saturday came, and with it, Tori and Nick's first dog training lesson. It came not a moment too soon. Dad hadn't complained too much about Nick's behavior over the past week, but his deep sighs, heavy footsteps, and door-slamming told Tori he was running out of patience. She found herself looking forward to the lesson because learning new ways to train Nick might help her make peace with Dad. But at the same time her insides tensed and churned at the thought of spending an hour as the only student with a new teacher in a strange place. At least at school, she knew from experience what to expect in math class. Math. What would a dog training lesson be like?

As she rode in the gray minivan to the Dog Sports Center, her fingers drummed a nervous rhythm on her knees. She stopped tapping long enough to turn and check on Nick in the backseat. He sat up, stretched his nose over the seatback, and nuzzled Tori's cheek. She gave him a kiss and went back to tapping.

Dad peered through the minivan's windshield at a big barn-like building. "This must be the place. The sign says Maple Valley Dog Sports Center. I'll pick you up in about an hour, OK?" Dad's phone beeped, letting him know he'd received a text.

Tori opened the car door and paused, one foot out the door. She tried to hide her anxiety behind her blank face, but she couldn't control the tremor in her voice. "We can walk. Home isn't that far away."

Dad didn't seem to notice her shaky voice. He glanced at the overcast sky. "No, it's supposed to start pouring rain soon." He tapped his phone, read his text, then looked up at Tori. "I'll come back here after my meeting."

"OK. See ya later." Tori opened the back door to let Nick jump out and slammed it shut. The minivan crunched over the wet gravel, gained speed, and turned onto the main road. She surveyed the large building. *This is the Dog Sports Center?*

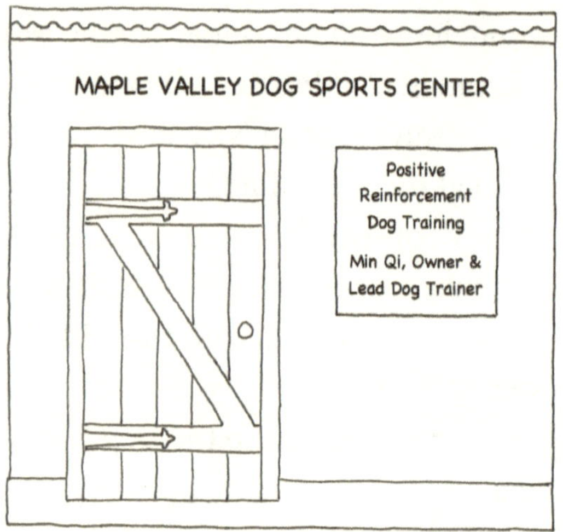

She had imagined a gym, something like the YMCA in Portland. This place looked like an old barn. The faded red walls held up a rusty corrugated metal roof. Tall oak trees occupied most of the surrounding property, their gnarled limbs covered with pillows of emerald green moss and dripping with pale green lichen. If not for a faded compact car parked outside, she would have thought it was abandoned.

Nick sniffed the air and pulled Tori to the door. "You want to go in? I guess that's a good sign." Tori checked the treat bag at her waist. *Yup, full of dog cookies, several different kinds.* She patted her right front pocket. *Yup, got the clicker.* She took a big deep breath and exhaled slowly. Then she pulled open the heavy door and they stepped inside.

Tori's chin dropped. Nick's eyes went wide and his nose wiggled and bobbed up and down. To their right, on the other side of a tall wooden fence, they saw a brightly lit arena. Colorful jumps and tunnels and a see-saw, dogwalk, and A-frame were set up at various angles, creating a huge agility course. Until now, Tori had seen agility obstacles only in online videos.

A young woman and a black-and-white border collie ran around the course. "Jump, tunnel! Climb! Climb! Jump . . . jump . . . jump! SeeeeSaaaw!" The woman called to her dog and directed him with her hands and arms. It was like human and dog were connected with an invisible, very long leash. Tori's heart skipped a beat as she realized the dog looked a lot like her mother's dog in the photo on her living room wall.

The border collie flew over the final jump near Tori, and the woman threw a long fleecy toy ahead of him. He rushed to retrieve it, tossed the toy into the air, then caught it with a snap of his jaws. Nick, who had stared silently at the dog as he sprinted around the course, started to bark.

The barking caught the woman's attention. "Hi! You must be Tori, right? I'm Min."

Tori gawked at the woman and her dog. The border collie ran circles around Min and shook his toy back and forth as he and Min walked toward Tori. "Wow," she murmured. *I'm getting a lesson from* her? *Nick and I are still working on "sit" and "down." Maybe I'm in the wrong place.*

Min's tight-fitting running clothes showed off her petite figure. Her short black hair was streaked with pink, and a small gold ring pierced one eyebrow. Nick filled the silence with deep "woofs." His front feet lifted off the ground with every bark.

"Yes, I'm Tori." She raised her voice to cover Nick's barking. "And this is Nick. We've got a lesson at one o'clock." Then she raised a finger to her lips and whispered to Nick, "Shhhhh." Nick whined, but at least that wasn't as loud as his barking. She gripped and regripped his leash. Her toes curled and uncurled inside her sneakers.

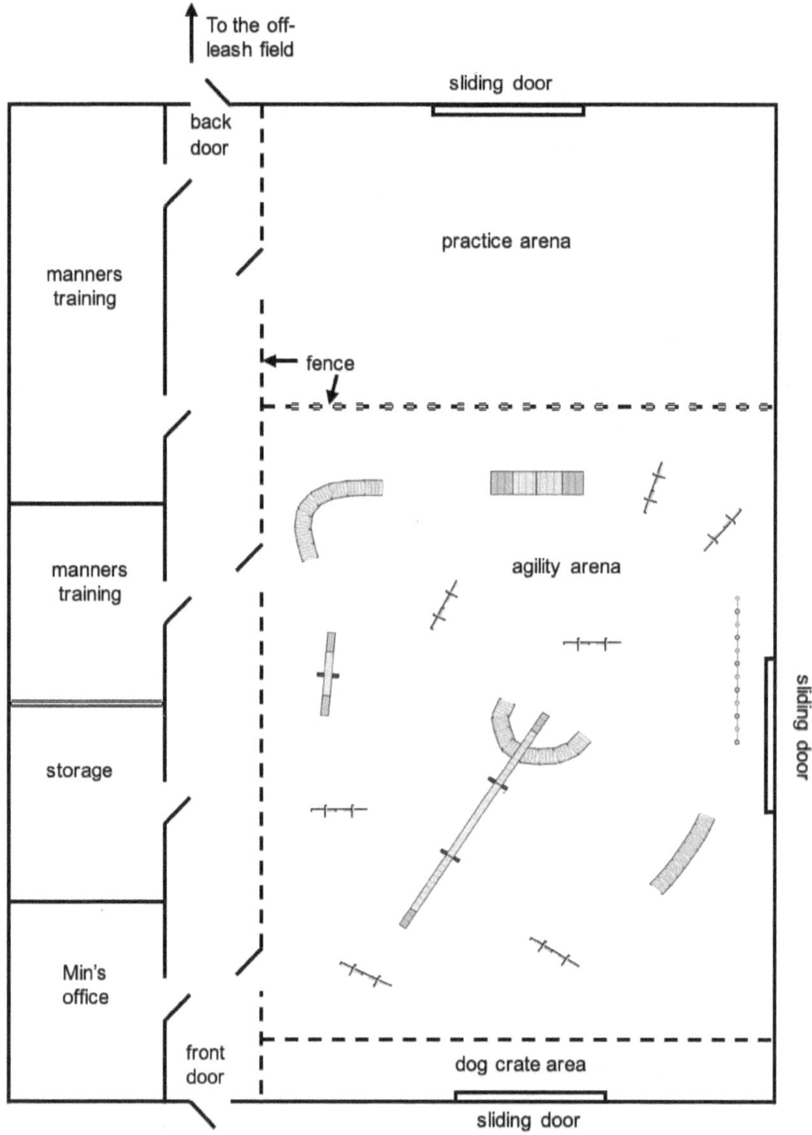

Maple Valley Dog Sports Center

Min opened a gate near Tori and she and her dog stepped into the aisle. "Nice to meet you both. This is Zen." She leaned over and patted the dog's shoulder. "Let's go to the training room." Min, with Zen trotting by her side carrying his toy, led the way up the aisle. Tori craned her neck to look at the agility ring as they passed it. She tried to imagine herself directing Nick around an agility course the way Min had. No way. Impossible.

Old horse stalls lined the left-hand side of the aisle, and Tori and Nick followed Min into one of them. It seemed to be two or even three stalls combined because it was so long and narrow. The walls had been painted yellow, but the paint couldn't completely disguise all the scars left behind by horses that had kicked and chewed the wood.

Blue foam mats covered the floor, and shelves held boxes of mysterious things that Tori supposed were for dog training. One whole wall was decorated with fancy ribbons from agility trials and photos of Min and Zen running agility together and standing on award podiums. *I am definitely in the wrong place,* thought Tori. *Someone who's won all those awards won't want to teach a shelter dog and a dumb kid like me.*

"Zen, kennel-up." The border collie trotted to a wire crate in the corner, quickly turned, lay down, and began to chew on a bone. Min smiled at Tori and ruffled the fur on Nick's back. Nick smiled up at her. "So, you adopted Nick recently, right? Tell me about that."

Tori nudged her glasses and ran her tongue over her braces. Nick pulled toward an invisible scent, so she loosened his leash and let him wander around her and sniff the floor. With her eyes on her dog, Tori told Min about Nick's adoption, her attempts to train him, and the events that led to her signing up for a lesson. She listed so many failures, she decided not to mention what her father had said about returning Nick to the shelter if Tori couldn't teach him to behave. That proved that she was a complete failure at dog training, and it was too embarrassing to mention.

But Min didn't seem surprised or concerned about Nick's behavior, even his tendency to help himself to food from the kitchen counter. "He's still getting used to his new life!" she said. "He just doesn't know any better. So let's teach him, OK? Show me what you've done so far."

Tori stuck a sweaty hand into her pocket and pulled out her clicker. She showed Min how she had trained Nick's *sit* cue. With Nick facing her, she said "sit" and clicked when Nick sat. Her shaky hand fumbled around in her treat bag and pulled out a small cookie. She gave it to Nick and told him, "Good boy!" Then she said "OK" to tell him it was all right to get up, and she tossed another cookie on the floor. The treat flew sideways out of her nervous hand, but Nick tracked it down with his keen nose and swallowed it whole. He trotted back to Tori and looked eagerly at her face to find out how to get another treat. His tail never stopped wagging.

"Nick, down." Tori did the same steps with the cue to lie down. Her hands didn't shake quite so much for that cue.

"That's great, Tori. You've made a good start in just a few days." Min nodded and smiled.

A small wave of pride swept through Tori. She glanced at Min and caught her eye for a moment. Lots of practice over the past few days had helped. Maybe she didn't look as awkward as she felt.

"The technique you used is called *luring*, did you know that?" Min continued. "The dog follows the treat in your hand until he's in the position you want, like a sit or a down. And that's a great way to start training.

"But here at the DSC, we like to go a little deeper into dog training, more than just luring. We teach people how to encourage their dogs to make good choices. That way, training—really, we should call it *teaching*—seems like a game to the dog. The dogs *want* to do what we ask, because it's so fun and rewarding for them when they do so. You two learn to work as a *team*. How does that sound to you?"

For the second time that afternoon, Tori's chin dropped to the floor. Min had just described exactly how she wanted to—that is, *teach*—Nick, but hadn't been able to put into words. Tori looked right into Min's eyes. She managed to get three words out of her mouth: "That . . . sounds . . . *perfect*!"

CHAPTER 10

The rest of the lesson flew by. Min explained things so clearly and patiently that Tori forgot to be nervous or worried that she wasn't good enough to be at the Dog Sports Center. She focused on absorbing everything Min said.

They practiced the art of clicker training. Min suggested a few adjustments in the way Tori held the leash, clicker, and treats, and gave Tori some tips about how to observe Nick's movements. Tori's timing improved, and Nick seemed even more eager to do the right thing. *Maybe because the treats get to his mouth faster,* thought Tori.

Then Min put a cardboard box on the floor. The box was just big enough for Nick to fit in, and the sides were low. In this game, she was supposed to be silent and let Nick start to interact with the box on his own. The goal was to have him place all four feet inside the box.

"You'll need to be patient with Nick in this game," said Min. "Wait for him to figure out what you want."

Min wasn't kidding, thought Tori. She stood with the clicker for what seemed like forever, waiting for Nick to do something, anything, with the box. Nick looked at her. He sat. He lay down. His eyes asked her, *What the heck? Whaddo I hafta do to get a treat?*

Tori knew that only a few seconds had passed, but she got tired of waiting. She pointed to the box and said, "Go to the box!"

"Patience," Min whispered.

Tori waited another forever. Nick paced back and forth. He circled around her and stared at her face. She folded her arms to keep from pointing and bit her lip to keep from talking. Then Nick happened to walk near the box.

"Click!" Min whispered to Tori. Tori pressed the metal clicker. CLICK. Nick swiveled his head toward the sound and saw Tori toss a small treat to the ground. He trotted to the treat, his tail swishing back and forth, and lapped it up. He opened his mouth in a big grin and swung his head back to the box, then to Tori's face. Tori could practically see the gears spinning in his head. He went to the box and touched it with his nose.

Tori clicked and tossed a treat. She felt the corners of her mouth reach for her ears, and Nick's face echoed hers. Or maybe it was the other way around. She imagined what Nick might be thinking—that he wasn't just following commands. Nobody was making him do anything with the box; it was his decision to interact with it. That he was smart enough to make decisions and figure out which decisions earned a treat. And maybe he even liked making her face light up the way she liked lighting up his.

Nick pushed at the box with his nose, then with a front paw. Tori clicked and tossed a treat whenever he got closer to getting his feet into the box. The game tested her patience. Min reminded her to let Nick think it through. Nick needed to learn patience too.

Finally, Nick put his two front feet into the box. CLICK! "Good boy!" said Tori. Her whole body felt light, like she might float right up to the ceiling. Teaching Nick, and learning to teach him, was fun! She patted and fussed over Nick and told him he was the best dog in the whole world.

"Nice job, Tori!" said Min. "That's a good stopping point. We don't want him to get frustrated." Tori's homework was to continue the stand-in-a-box game—and to be sure to let Nick figure out the game on his own. No hints from Tori.

"That kind of game, where the dog figures out what to do to earn a reward, is called *shaping,* said Min. "Let's think of some other fun behaviors to shape. For example, I've noticed that Nick likes to back up. So start to click and treat for that behavior. Then when he understands that's what you want, you can use a cue word, like 'back,' to ask him to back up."

"Now, it sounds like your dad is not at all pleased with Nick's counter-surfing habit," Min continued. She held out her arms and shimmied her hips. Her pierced eyebrow went up as she grinned. Tori chuckled, both at her teacher and at the mental image of Nick surfing down a kitchen counter, gobbling up every crumb of food. It was not far from reality. "So you should work on some impulse-control games with Nick, so he learns to wait for permission to do or take anything."

Impulse control, thought Tori. *Sounds like another way to say* patience.

Min held a treat in her fist and let Nick sniff it. Nick nosed at her hand and then pawed at it, trying to get the hand to open so he could eat the treat. Finally, when none of his begging techniques worked, he backed up, sat down, and eyed Min's face. Min opened her treat hand and, with her other hand, gave Nick the treat. Nick's eyes lit up. *I can figure out this game too!* he seemed to say.

Min started the game again. This time, Nick didn't lick and paw at her hand as much. After just a few licks, he sat back and looked at her. Again, she opened her hand and gave him the treat. Nick's sparkling eyes said, *I love this game!*

"He's learning that he gets the treat only when he doesn't try to grab it out of your hand," said Tori.

"Right . . ."

"Hi, gang!" A familiar voice interrupted the lesson. Jordan with his hard-to-miss bleached-blond hair and tattooed arms walked into the room.

Words tumbled out of Tori's mouth. "Jordan! Hi! Remember me? I'm Tori. This is Nick. I mean Dexter. I mean he used to be Dexter, now he's Nick... and I'm Tori..."

Jordan laughed. "Of course I remember you, from the shelter." He put an arm around Min's waist, and Min leaned into him.

Tori glanced from Min to Jordan, then lowered her eyes and fussed with Nick's collar, which already fit him perfectly. *Looks like Min and Jordan are more than friends.*

Out of the corner of her eye, she saw Jordan whisper into Min's ear. The words *stolen* and *dogs* jumped out at Tori. Min's eyes widened and she gave Jordan a worried look. Tori's thoughts leaped to the Lost Dogs website and she remembered Jordan's warning about keeping the yard gate locked. *Maybe the dogs on the website didn't just wander away. Maybe they were stolen! Are Jordan and Min connected to the missing dogs somehow?*

Jordan took a step away from Min. "So how is Nick doing?" he asked Tori.

Tori wanted to ask what was stolen, but she chickened out. They were adults; she was just a kid. Instead, she petted Nick and slowly started to tell Jordan about some of the struggles she had with Nick's behavior. Jordan gave her his full attention and listened. She forgot about Jordan's whispers, and her words picked up speed. She met Jordan's eyes. "Ya know, the dogs in books and movies always seem perfect. Like they *know* how to behave like their owners want them to behave. And when they don't, it's just funny. But real life isn't like that."

"Right!" said Jordan. "Lots of people never get that. They think that dogs should automatically know how to behave. Or that they were born understanding English." He leaned over and patted Nick's shoulder.

"Really? But that makes no sense. Dogs can't know commands —I mean *cues*—unless someone teaches them," Tori said.

"Exactly right!" Min said. "You're a good student!"

Tori blinked. She stared at Min with wide eyes. Good student? No one had ever called her *that* before.

"Woof!" Nick barked and trotted toward the door. His tail picked up so much speed that his whole rear end waggled back and forth. Tori's father peered around the doorway and then took a hesitant step into the room. Nick smiled up at him. "Woof!"

"Hi, Nick." Dad leaned over and gave Nick a quick pat as the dog curled into him, grinning and rubbing his sides against Dad's legs.

Tori introduced her dad to Min. He remembered Jordan from the day they adopted Nick at the shelter. The three adults talked while Tori gathered her jacket and dog training treats and put them in her backpack. She hoped her dad didn't say anything embarrassing about her.

"Bye! Thank you!" Tori called to Min as she, Nick, and her dad left the training room and headed down the aisle to the front door. Tori's feet bounced off the floor with each step. Her brain whirled with all the new ideas she had just learned.

As they passed the agility arena, Dad peered over the fence and said, "Looks like they teach agility here too.

"Yeah." Tori marveled that her dad knew what dog agility was, then she remembered the photo of her mother with a border collie. Had Mom played dog agility with her dog? Border collies, like Min's dog Zen, made great agility dogs. She didn't dare ask. Dad seemed to be in a good mood now and she didn't want to ruin it.

Instead, Tori said, "You should see Min and Zen run this course! They are amazing!" She and her dad stopped, and Tori pointed out the different obstacles and described how Min and Zen had run the course.

Dad listened. Really listened. "Hmmmm . . . a lot of training is needed for agility. For the dogs *and* the people," he said. He studied Tori's face for a moment, then turned and pushed at the heavy door.

"Yeah, I guess so," Tori said. Her mind was still busy playing videos of Min and Zen running the agility course and Nick learning clicker training games. She followed her dad into the parking lot and eyed the overcast sky and drooping oak trees. "Funny. While I was inside, I totally forgot that it's one of those cloudy gray days." Raindrops began to spatter the gravel and multiplied with every step they took away from the Dog Sports Center.

As they drove home, the din of pounding rain and squeaky windshield wipers filled the minivan. Dad leaned forward and gripped the wheel tightly, as though that would help him see through the rain-blurred glass.

Tori barely noticed the storm outside, because inside, the rain was slowly drowning her good mood. She got only one free lesson with Min. She wouldn't be going back to the Dog Sports Center— or the DSC, as Min called it. With all the other expenses of owning a dog, she couldn't ask her dad to pay for lessons too. She stared blankly through the rain-streaked window, until the minivan pulled into the driveway of their small yellow house.

CHAPTER 11

FEBRUARY

Nick loved his backyard training sessions. Rain or shine, he was ready to play the training games Tori had learned from Min. To him, the games were just as fun as chasing his ball, playing tag with Tori, or sniffing out the treats she sometimes hid around the yard for him to find.

"Back, Nick! Back." Nick walked five steps in reverse. Click! Tori pressed the clicker and tossed a small piece of beef jerky to him. Nick's front feet left the ground as he caught the treat in midair and gulped it down. "Good boy!" Tori said. She couldn't help laughing at Nick's enthusiasm.

In the last couple of weeks, since their lesson at the DSC, Tori had worked with him as much as she could around her school schedule. They had pretty much mastered the basic sit, down, come, and stay cues, at least in the backyard. In the kitchen, Nick had stopped putting his feet on the counters and licking, but if any food hit the floor he was on it instantly. Tori had to make sure he was well supplied with chew toys, because without them Nick didn't see any reason not to chew on the furniture and bedding. On their walks, the sight of a squirrel made him completely forget that she was on the other end of the leash. Tori was developing very strong shoulder muscles from trying to keep him under control.

"Come!" Nick trotted to Tori and sat beside her. Tori gave him another piece of jerky. She had discovered that giving him treats when he was at her side, instead of in front of her, helped him understand that he should WALK at her side too, where he couldn't pull her forward. Tori leaned over and rubbed the wet fur on his neck. "A little rain doesn't bother you, does it?" Nick licked her face.

"Let's try the jump again, OK?" Nick followed Tori to the middle of the backyard, where she had fashioned an agility jump by placing each end of a broomstick on a milk crate. She stood next to it, facing the direction she wanted Nick to go.

"C'mon, Nick! Jump!"

Nick looked at Tori as if asking, *Are you crazy?* He lowered his nose, sniffed the wet grass, and wandered around the jump.

"You're probably thinking 'why jump this thing, when I can just walk around it!'" she said to Nick. "I know, it doesn't look much like a real jump, not like the jumps at Min's place." Tori kicked the broomstick and it fell to the ground. She looked up at the gray sky. "Let's go in, Nick."

Tori's father stood at the sink, looking out the window to the backyard, as she and Nick entered the kitchen. *Crunch.* He bit into an apple and watched Tori as she toweled the rain off Nick and then peeled off her jacket.

Dad leaned against the sink. "How did the training go?"

Tori hung the damp towel on a wall hook. "Good. Kinda wish I knew a little more, though."

Nick trotted to Dad and nuzzled his hand. "Hey, buddy," Dad's voice was light and affectionate. Nick rubbed against Dad's legs and Dad petted him as he spoke to Tori. "You've been training Nick every day since your lesson at the Dog Sports Center."

Tori smiled at the sight of Dad and Nick together. Nick's magic was starting to work on her father. "Yeah. It's fun. And Nick thinks it's fun too." Tori slipped off her rain boots. "We're gonna watch a little TV. C'mon, Nick." She padded into the living room in her socks, and Nick trotted after her, tail wagging.

Guilt gnawed at her insides. She wanted more dog training lessons, but she *should* be satisfied with just HAVING Nick. Dad hadn't yet told her that Nick didn't have to go back to the shelter, so that was a constant worry. Still, she yearned to give Nick the life he deserved, a life filled with learning and running and jumping and having fun.

Tori plopped onto the couch, picked up the remote, and turned on the TV, while Nick lay on the rug and licked his damp fur. Tori previewed a few free streaming channels and finally settled on a show that featured a detective with a police dog. This episode was about some missing kids, and she had already seen it twice. The story made her think of the missing dogs in Maple Valley. She wasn't sure that any crime had been committed, but it WAS a mystery, to Tori anyway. The TV detective had created a crime board that showed the victims and suspects, and that gave Tori an idea. She got her school notebook and made a list.

Website:

    Yorkshire terrier

    shih tzu

    poodle (mini)

    Chihuahua

Posters:

    poodle mix

    terrier mix

She couldn't think of any suspects to add, but when she wrote down the dogs' breeds, she noticed a pattern: They were all small dogs. If the dogs were just lost, it seemed like quite a coincidence that they were all about the same size. *Maybe someone is stealing the dogs, and smaller dogs are just easier to steal because you can carry them away,* she thought. *So maybe I don't have to worry about Nick because he's pretty big.*

"Dinner's ready," called Dad, interrupting Tori's thoughts. She clicked off the TV, put her notebook in her backpack, and joined Dad in the kitchen. She sat down, and Nick lay on the floor at her side. "Good boy," Tori whispered to him. "You're keeping that nose off the table."

Dad handed her a serving bowl. "Have some vegetables," he said, and he slid into the chair across from her.

Tori's mouth watered at the savory aroma of hot olive oil and herbs. "Thanks." She spooned some of the sizzling roast carrots, potatoes, broccoli, and turnips onto her plate and passed the bowl to her dad.

Dad put two big scoops on his plate and set down the bowl. He sipped some water, carefully set down the glass, and cleared his throat. "So . . . I was thinking, would you like to take more lessons at the Dog Sports Center?" he asked. "And maybe learn agility? Sounds like fun. But challenging too."

Tori's head snapped up and she looked wide-eyed at her father's face. She gulped the carrots in her mouth. "Does that mean we can keep Nick? I'm doing OK, training him?" Her father hadn't brought up the subject of returning Nick to the shelter since that first time, weeks ago, and Tori hadn't been sure whether that was a good sign or a bad sign.

Dad put his elbows on the table, raised his hands and interlaced his fingers. "I can see how hard you're working. He's not doing as much barking and counter-surfing."

"Yeah, he *is* doing better!" Tori dropped her fork to her plate. The clatter woke Nick, who scrambled to his feet and sat at Tori's side. "Do you mean it? We can take more lessons?"

"I phoned Min today." Dad wiggled his fingers as he talked. *He seems to be excited about agility lessons too,* Tori thought. *Or maybe nervous.* Dad continued, "She says that she thinks both you and Nick will learn fast. And she says that agility training will help Nick behave better in the house too."

A smile split Tori's face. Her right hand automatically found the soft fur on Nick's neck. "Thanks. We'll work hard."

"You can have two more manners lessons this month. Then after that, you can join an agility class."

"I bet Nick will be an awesome agility dog," Tori said. An inner voice spoke to her: *But can I learn to be a good agility trainer?*

She shoved away the inner voice and turned to Nick. "What do you think, Nick? Do you want to play agility?"

Nick's nose reached toward Tori's face and his nostrils quivered, as though he could smell Tori's happiness. His tail beat a steady rhythm against the kitchen floor.

Tori grinned, first at Nick and then at her dad. "Nick says yes."

Dad kept his eyes on Tori and leaned back in his chair. "You'll need to keep your grades up. And part of the deal is that you keep a journal. A *handwritten* journal of your lessons and practice. OK?"

"A journal? No one writes *by hand* anymore!" As soon as she said it, Tori's mind flashed to her dad's handwritten journal and his Song for Malia, and she knew she would agree to write a journal.

"In our family, we do. It'll be private," said Dad. "You don't have to show it to anyone."

Sounds like schoolwork. But it'll be worth it. "Sure. It's a deal." Butterflies of anticipation and excitement began to fly in her stomach. "Thanks, Dad." She gave her dad a wide metallic smile. "Thanks a lot."

Tori turned to Nick. "Didja hear that, Nick? Agility lessons! We're going to play agility!"

CHAPTER 12

Tori held her lunch tray and scanned the big room bustling with students. It hadn't changed much since her first day. *Eau de school cafeteria* filled the air. A group of boys crowded around someone's phone. That wouldn't last long. Phones weren't allowed in school. The popular girls whispered and glanced at the boys.

Tori found a seat at her table of regular, average girls. They weren't popular girls, that's for sure, but they weren't exactly outcasts either. It was exhausting trying to keep up with the constantly shifting alliances and rivalries. As soon as she figured out who was best friends with who and who had a crush on who, new pairs would form, and she had to start all over. Part of her wanted to avoid all the drama and keep to herself, but another part wanted to take part in the conversations at the lunch table. That seemed to be the way to make friends here. It might be nice to have a friend. A human friend, that is.

She had made a few school friends—the kind of friends you talk with at school about classes, homework, teachers, and other kids. Laura was that kind of friend. Gisele too. She classified Abby, who was still quick with the insults, as a *frenemy*. It turned out that Gisele and Abby were cousins, that's why they hung out together all the time. The girls didn't talk about anything *too* personal. Tori told herself she was OK with that.

At her old school, Tori had grown a shell, like a turtle, that protected her from the furtive curious glances and pitying remarks from other kids. So far, at her new school, she hadn't been able to completely shed that shell because it had to protect her from Abby's snide remarks *and* contain Tori's secrets.

If the other kids found out about her mother, they might start treating her like a weirdo. Or if they knew she was obsessed with her dog, they would call her a nerd. So she chatted about English homework and complained about the food and listened to Abby tell ridiculous stories that couldn't be true and watched her flip her long black hair.

There was one thing the girls talked about a lot. Boys. Boys were still a mystery to Tori, but so were a lot of other things, like the current topic of conversation.

"Did you hear? Third Rail is going to play at Jen's party on Saturday!" Abby said dramatically. She scanned the table to be sure everyone heard her announcement. The girls oohed and aahed in a joking sort of way, probably because none of them had been invited to the party, thought Tori. Tori had learned that Abby fancied herself as an actress, which explained her constant desire for attention and her bad storytelling. She wore silk scarves around her neck in imitation of some famous actress that Tori had never heard of. Most of the girls thought she was entertaining.

Tori leaned toward Gisele. Gisele could be counted on to know all the gossip. She was a good listener. That was probably another reason that Abby hung out with her, because Abby was quite the talker. "Who, or what, is Third Rail?" asked Tori.

Gisele's hands were busy trying to hold onto a sandwich that threatened to fall apart. She lifted her chin toward a table of boys across the room. They wore baggy jeans and t-shirts with logos of bands, and most of them sported shaggy, unkempt hair. "A seventh-grade band," she said in her high Minnie-Mouse voice. "They're sitting over there. Mike plays drums."

Laura, sitting across from Tori, glanced up from her book and over to the boys' table. Tori thought she saw a spark of interest in her eyes.

One of the boys held up a spoonful of mashed potatoes and flung it at another. The second boy picked up a handful of peas and threw it back. The boys' table erupted into laughter and shouts.

"Yes. They look like sensitive artistic types," Tori said dryly.

"Hmmmph." A short, stifled giggle escaped Laura, although her eyes dropped back to her book. The other girls gawked at Tori.

Abby broke the spell. "Gisele likes Mi-ike," she said in a sing-song voice.

"Do not!" Gisele's voice rose into a range only dogs could hear, thought Tori.

"Yeah, you do!" Abby fired back.

"Well, I think he's *nice*." Gisele popped the last bite of her sandwich into her mouth. Her tiny nose wiggled as she chewed.

"Nice?" Abby lowered her voice. "*I* heard he's been in trouble with the police. For *stealing*." She fingered her blue-and-white striped scarf and straightened it.

Tori's ears perked up. A boy here at school with a record of stealing?

"That was a long time ago, when he was just a kid." Gisele glanced toward Mike, then back to Abby. "He's a really good drummer."

"Which one's Mike?" asked Tori.

Gisele pointed at a boy with deep brown skin, close-cropped curly black hair, and a Jimi Hendrix t-shirt. He was talking——in a friendly way, it looked like—to the lunch monitor while the other boys cleaned up the thrown food.

"What did Mike steal?" Tori asked, trying to sound casual.

Gisele started to say, "We dunno . . ."

"Hey!" Abby interrupted. "Did you hear about Taylor Swift? She's going to be in Portland . . ." Tori tuned out of the girls' conversation and turned her attention to her cheese sandwich. At the moment, she didn't care about Abby taking over the conversation. She had more important things to think about.

Tori took a big bite and chewed slowly. She eyed Mike. The words—*stolen* and *dogs*—that she had overheard at her first lesson gnawed at her. Jordan didn't actually say the words together, like *stolen dogs*, she reminded herself. He might have been talking about someone stealing dog food, or dog leashes and harnesses, or even money *for* the dogs from the shelter. Or maybe he meant . . .

"I liked your book report." Laura's voice broke through Tori's thoughts. Laura had laid down her book, spine up, and was looking at her over her milk carton as she sipped.

Tori gulped her food and focused on Laura. "Oh. Thanks." Tori's eyebrows lifted. "I was surprised that the teacher let me pick that book. I think the idea was to read a biography of a *person*. And Rin Tin Tin was, ya know, a *dog*."

"Exactly!" Laura tilted her head. "Well, I thought it was . . . lit." Laura stumbled a little over the slang. She picked up her book— today it was *The Hound of the Baskervilles*—flipped it over, and continued reading.

Tori didn't mind that Laura preferred reading to talking, although she was curious about Laura's life outside of school. She thought that someone who read so much might have some interesting stuff going on in her head. But this way, Tori told herself, she had time to daydream about Nick. She imagined herself and Nick running an agility course. Nick leaped effortlessly over jumps and Tori ran like a track star. But would she ever *really* be able to direct Nick through a maze of jumps, tunnels and other obstacles? Min seemed to think she could learn. So . . .

CLAAAAAANG! The bell broke Tori's daydream. The other girls had already left the table and headed to class. She gathered her things, picked up her tray, and headed to the clean-up area. The rank odor of food scraps hit her, and she sneezed. *Back to the real world.*

CHAPTER 13

T he day was unusually warm, dry, and sunny for February, but still cool enough that Tori wore a fleece jacket and cap for her and Nick's afternoon walk around Maple Valley. Tori wanted to work on Nick's leash walking and impulse control skills before their first agility lesson the next day.

Nick lifted his nose and pointed it toward the small burger restaurant that Tori and he were passing. The meaty aroma drew him in, and his legs couldn't help following his nose.

Nick's harness pulled on his shoulders as he reached the end of the leash. Tori imagined him thinking, *Oh, I remember. When I feel the tug of the leash, I should turn toward my girl. She wants me to walk beside her, not pull on the leash. I can do that!*

Tori was ready with the clicker. When Nick turned toward her, she clicked and started walking backwards. Nick followed. After a few steps, she said, "Good boy," and gave him a treat from the pouch at her waist. Then she pivoted 180 degrees so that she walked at Nick's side. They took a few more steps, then she turned again, this time with Nick staying at her side. They tried walking past the restaurant again. Nick ignored the meaty scent and kept walking beside her. The leash swung loosely between them.

Tori's back straightened and her chest swelled. She thought she would explode with pride. It had taken a lot of practice to get those steps right. If it hadn't been for Min's patient coaching over the last couple of weeks, she would have given up. The best part was the look on Nick's face when she did it right and Nick understood what she asked.

A squirrel taunted Nick from the branch of a hazelnut tree. Nick tugged the leash toward it, pulling Tori back to the present. She went through the loose-leash training steps with him again.

When he was back in step with her, Tori leaned over and patted Nick's shoulder. "You are really getting good at this loose-leash stuff, Nick!" Nick gave her a proud smile.

They walked another block, then Tori asked Nick to sit at her side. Nick's rear end hit the sidewalk and he looked up at Tori. *What's next?* his sparkling eyes said. Tori tossed a treat about five feet ahead of them. Nick's head snapped toward it and his hindquarters lifted three inches off the sidewalk. Then they slowly lowered to the ground as he stared at the treat and waited for Tori's cue. Big drops of dog saliva splattered the sidewalk.

"OK, get it!" said Tori. Nick rocketed to the treat and devoured it.

Tori giggled. "Sheesh, you only had to wait five seconds! You acted like it was five minutes! That was good impulse control though." She patted Nick's side.

Tori practiced the game a few more times as they walked. Sometimes she asked Nick to lie down instead of sit, or sit on her right side instead of her left, and she varied the number of seconds he had to wait. Between cues, she praised Nick and chattered to him. The silliest things came out of her mouth when she talked to him. "Yum, yum, yum in your tum!" "Hey, stinky, binky, boo!" "Tell me, Nick, is chewing your food an overrated skill, in your opinion?" She hoped no one heard her.

Nick wagged his tail and smiled at her. *I could do this all day!* he seemed to say.

Tori raised her head and looked around. She had been concentrating on Nick and their training so much she hadn't paid attention to exactly where they were going. Now she saw that they had entered a rundown area of old vacant buildings and liquor stores. She had seen neighborhoods like this in Portland but was surprised to find one in Maple Valley. Dad wouldn't like her to be walking there. She turned to head back home.

Out of the corner of her eye, she saw a tall young man with spiky bleached-blonde hair. His back was turned to Tori, but he sure looked like . . . could it be . . .? Yes, it was Jordan! He stood and talked with a group of older men outside one of the old shabby buildings. A small Jack Russell terrier mix hunched and shivered near the feet of one man, who held a frayed rope attached to the dog's collar.

Jordan's hair and clean clothes made quite a contrast with the other men, who wore dirty ragged clothing and gray beards. A couple of them seemed to have trouble standing upright. One man handed Jordan an envelope and said in a gruff voice, "You got the goods?" He chuckled. The chuckle quickly became a hacking cough.

Jordan nodded, stepped over to a green pickup truck parked nearby, and took a cardboard box, about the size of a shoebox, from the cab. He handed the box to the man with the gruff voice, saying, "I'll have more for you next week." Jordan bent over and patted the little Jack Russell mix. "Are the dogs OK?" he asked. The man holding the dog's leash nodded. Then Jordan waved to the men and drove off in the pickup.

Tori stood frozen on the sidewalk for a few moments, her mouth gaping, her mind treading water, as she tried to make sense of what she had seen. All she could think of were questions.

What was Jordan doing *here*? What was in the box? What dogs was he asking about? Did Jordan have dark secrets? Did Min know he spent time in this area of town? Why would a nice guy who worked at an animal shelter be doing some kind of business with people who looked like they might have serious problems?

Then Tori saw two of the men staring at Nick and her. Mostly at Nick. An electric charge coursed through her body, and under her warm fleece jacket her skin erupted in goose bumps. She shivered. Without making a conscious decision to do so, she turned on her heels and hurried away from the ramshackle building. "C'mon, Nick," she urged. Nick didn't argue. He stuck by her side, matching her quick pace.

When they finally entered their own neighborhood and home wasn't far away, Tori and Nick slowed. Tori tried to answer her own questions about Jordan. What was he doing? Only bad things came to mind. Criminal things, like drugs or stealing. She passed the lost-dog posters that she had noticed a month ago. They were tattered but still clung to telephone poles. She picked up the pace again and headed straight home.

Tori and Nick trotted up the steps to the front door of their house. Tori tried to shake off the memory of seeing Jordan and leave it outside. He was probably doing something perfectly innocent, she told herself. Her imagination was probably just running wild. She opened the door and let Nick go in. "We'll do some impulse control games in the kitchen after dinner, OK, Nick? We want to be ready for our lesson tomorrow. I better try to do a little homework now."

Tori got her schoolwork and the computer and sat on the living room couch. Nick jumped up, circled, then lay down beside her with a tired sigh. She started to open her school notebook, then hesitated. Homework could wait for a minute. First, she wanted to check the Lost & Found Dogs in Oregon website. She wondered whether she would find a Jack Russell terrier mix on the list.

Three more dogs had gone missing since the last time Tori had looked at the website. There was no Jack Russell terrier mix. But another Yorkshire terrier, a Maltese, and a French bulldog mix had been added to the list. The mixed dog looked like a purebred French bulldog in his photo. All four dogs Tori had read about a couple weeks ago were still missing. Including the two dogs from the posters, that made nine dogs, all small breeds, that had disappeared recently from the Maple Valley area. Was that a lot? How many dogs usually went missing in a month or a year? She didn't know. She opened her notebook and updated her data.

Website:

    Yorkshire terrier (2)
    shih tzu
    poodle (mini)
    Chihuahua
    Maltese
    French bulldog mix

Posters:

    poodle mix
    terrier mix

Total: 9 small dogs

Tori noticed that data about missing dogs from past years was available on the website, so she filtered for the Maple Valley area and the previous year. There had been just five missing dogs for that whole year. So nine in just the past few weeks was a big increase. Of course, her science teacher would tell her that that there were probably some "variables involved that made comparisons meaningless." In other words, other stuff might be affecting the numbers. Maybe more people had found out about the website and were using it now. Maybe there were more dogs living in Franklin County this year compared to last year, so more lost dogs might make sense.

An image flashed through her mind: Jordan in that rough neighborhood. Maybe he wasn't as nice as she thought he was. On TV, nice guys often turned out to be the bad guys. Maybe she should add a suspect—Jordan—to her list of missing dogs. Then it really would be a *crime* chart, not just a list of dogs.

An unsettled feeling came over her, as it did whenever she thought about the missing dogs in Maple Valley. She had no idea what she could do to find them, but she couldn't stop herself from checking the website every week or so. The photos of the dogs and their families, families with kids like her, tore at her heart.

Tori's eyes left the computer screen, roamed the living room, and found her mother's photo on the wall.

She knew what it was like to lose someone you loved.

CHAPTER 14

Nick's muzzle pushed at Tori's arm, and her hand fell away from the computer keyboard and onto the couch. She scratched him under his chin. "OK, OK. Homework."

Tori set the computer on the coffee table and picked up her notebook. Her English teacher had assigned a 500-word story. Tori wrote her name at the top of a blank page. Well, that was a start.

"Hi," said Dad. She lifted her eyes and saw him standing in the doorway holding a big book.

"Look what I found," he said quietly. He held up the book. "Do you want to see some photos of your mom and her dog?"

Tori's mouth fell open. She realized the book was a photo album. Her school notebook and pencil slipped to the floor. "Uh, yeah. Sure." She shoved her schoolwork under the coffee table.

Dad sat beside her, put the album in his lap, and carefully opened it. On Tori's other side, Nick sat up and rested his muzzle on her shoulder. She felt her t-shirt start to absorb his drool.

"Since you're going to be learning dog agility, I thought you might like to see some photos of your mom and Kahu." He pointed at a photo of her mother and the black-and-white dog Tori knew from Mom's photo on the living room wall. The dog flew over a jump and Mom ran beside her with a big grin on her face. "See? They used to play agility too, before Malia—your mom, I mean—got sick. Kahu died around the same time, when you were really small."

Tori touched the photo, as though it would help her get closer to the two figures. Mom looked a little like Min. Black hair, although Mom's was long and pulled back into a ponytail. Smallish.

Athletic. Tori could feel the joy radiating from her, right off the glossy photographic paper. Kahu's intense border collie eyes drilled into Mom's face. *If Mom asked Kahu to do a backwards somersault, Kahu would only wonder "how high? How fast?"* thought Tori.

Tori looked at Dad with wonder. "I never knew the dog's name. What does Kahu mean?"

"It's a Hawaiian word that means 'guardian' or 'protector.'" Dad turned to the next page. "But Kahu couldn't protect Mom from cancer."

Together, they paged through the photo album. Dad was mostly silent, but he sometimes remembered details about the photos and told Tori about them.

"Wow. Thanks," said Tori when they had turned the last page and closed the album. So many emotions bubbled inside her, she couldn't get her mouth to say any more. Finally, she said, "Can we keep this photo album out here, in the living room? So we can look at it again?"

"Sure," said Dad.

Tori's mind buzzed. For years, she had wanted to know more about her mother. And in the last fifteen minutes, she had learned more than she ever imagined. The memory of her mother now brought her and her dad closer, instead of keeping them apart. She watched Dad carefully place the photo album on a high shelf, next to his vinyl records. After looking at the photos, Tori felt like she could really talk with her father, almost like an adult would. Like adult to adult, not kid to adult.

Nick lay down, put his muzzle on Tori's leg, and rolled his eyes up to see her face. Tori ran a hand down his back and remembered how Dad had been annoyed at him during those first few weeks. "I hope Nick doesn't bother you too much. I know you have to work a lot to pay for everything," she said.

"Ya know what? I had forgotten how nice it was to have a dog around the house," said Dad. He chuckled. "Well, it was a little rough at first. But you're doing a good job teaching him how to behave."

Tori leaned over and kissed Nick's nose. "He *is* the best, isn't he?"

Dad sat on the couch next to her. "When you're at school, he likes to nap in my office while I work, and we walk around the backyard together when I take coffee breaks. He doesn't like the noise when I use the tools in the workshop, though."

Tori was relieved. She had hoped that Nick was behaving OK while she was at school, but she had been a little afraid to ask Dad for details in case the details weren't good. She figured that no news was good news.

Tori stroked the black V-shaped fur on Nick's forehead. *Thanks for taking care of Dad*, she told him silently.

CHAPTER 15

As Dad pulled into the DSC driveway on Saturday afternoon, an old green pickup truck whizzed past them on its way out of the parking lot. Tori noticed some agility jumps and blue-and-yellow dogwalk boards in the truck bed. She turned to see who was driving, but the truck had already passed and was accelerating down the main road. *Wonder who that was,* she thought. They were early for the agility lesson, so no other cars were in the parking lot, not even Min's. But when Tori tugged at the heavy door, it opened. She waved at Dad and he drove away.

Tori let Nick lead the way into the old barn. In one hand she carried Nick's foldable crate, made of canvas over a light metal frame. Min had told her to bring a crate so Nick had a place to take rest breaks during the 90-minute lesson. She surveyed the agility arena and tried to picture herself and Nick running the course. Unfortunately, in her imagination she tripped and fell on her face, and Nick ran around looking for things to eat.

She shook her head. How on earth could she teach Nick to follow her directions, off leash, the way Zen followed Min's? Min and Zen were just magical together. But at the same time . . . how amazing would it be if she and Nick could create even a little bit of that magic for themselves? She really wanted to try.

Tori set up Nick's crate in one end of the arena, then took Nick to go potty in the big field north of the building, where students could exercise their dogs. Then she walked Nick up and down the barn aisle and practiced loose-leash walking. Nick was more interested in searching the cracks and crevices for lost treats. Her mind wandered: Who moved all that heavy equipment around? Would Min notice if anything went missing? Why was that agility equipment in the truck and who was driving? With a start, Tori realized that Jordan drove a green pickup just like that truck. She had seen it the day she saw Jordan near the rundown building downtown. But Jordan and Min were together, so it made sense that he would help her move equipment. Right?

She wished she had a friend to talk with about Jordan and the missing dogs. Someone like Laura. She liked mysteries. But it was hard enough to talk to the other kids about regular school stuff. And what if Abby overheard? Tori's mystery, which was probably just a product of her imagination anyway, would be all over the school in minutes. No, right now it was up to her alone to figure out what was going on. Maybe she could visit the building where she saw Jordan and gather some clues that way.

Then Min and her dog Zen entered the barn, and the other students in the agility foundations class started to trickle in. *They're all adults! No other kids?* Tori ducked into a training room and scrutinized herself in a dusty mirror. Blue jeans, slightly tattered Converse sneakers, her old, but warm, green winter jacket. She checked her face. Braces clean. Glasses straight. Hair not a complete mess. "You're lucky, Nick. You're always so handsome in your fur coat." She sighed and patted her dog. Nick smacked his lips as he ate a wayward treat. They headed for the arena.

"Hi, everyone. Over here, please!" Min, looking athletic as usual in her running shoes, form-fitting pants, and fitted jacket, stepped out of her office and entered the arena. The students, wearing jeans and jackets much like Tori's, gathered around Min with their dogs.

"This is an agility foundations class, as you know. So you'll be spending the next few weeks teaching your dogs important skills they'll need to get around an agility course correctly and safely. And *you* need to learn a lot of skills too! So, and I know this will disappoint some of you, we won't be using real jumps and dogwalks and such right away. But you and your dogs will have fun, I promise!"

A small wave of disappointment swept through Tori. No real obstacles? She had been looking forward to seeing Nick race over the A-frame and fly over a jump *today*.

Min asked everyone to introduce themselves and their dogs. One by one, the students said their names and their dogs' names and a little about themselves. Harry was an engineer, about her dad's age but about twice as big around the middle. He owned a Labrador retriever named Gunnar. There was an older woman, a retired nurse, with a Shetland sheepdog, and a married couple who said they hoped to give their border collie an outlet for her energy. Two teachers said they wanted to compete someday with their dogs, a border collie and a whippet. Nick snuffled for lost treats around Tori's feet as everyone spoke.

Nick was the only mixed-breed dog, and the only shelter dog, as far as Tori could tell. *How can I possibly be as good a trainer as the adults?* When her turn came, Tori kept her eyes on her sneakers and simply said, "Hi. I'm Tori, and this is Nick."

Thankfully, Min started the lesson right away, taking the attention off Tori. Min explained that they would learn some games today. The behaviors the dogs practiced in the games would help them learn the skills they would need for agility. *More games!* thought Tori. *Nick likes games!*

Journal Entry, February 25

First agility lesson! It was weird being the only kid in class. But everyone was nice.

First, we learned restrained recall. Restrained means to hold back. Recall means to call your dog to you. Harry held Nick—he put his hands around Nick's chest—and I walked away dragging a long tug toy. Then I said "Break" and Harry let go of Nick. Well, Nick was supposed to run real fast to me to get the toy. But he is more interested in food than toys. So he just kinda trotted up to me and sniffed my treat bag!

So Min gave me a toy that holds treats. Nick was way more interested in the toy when he knew there were ~~delishus~~ tasty treats to be had. He ran real fast to me when I used the food-toy. Min says restrained recall teaches dogs to wait at the start line and break quickly and to want to follow you around the course.

Then we did something called circle work. Although it's not really work. And you don't always go in circles. Anyway, everybody took turns walking in a circle with their dog beside them, on the outside of the circle. Not as simple as it sounds. You have to hold the leash, have one hand full of treats, and with the other hand take one treat and give it to the dog every five seconds or so. You really need three hands to do that. Which I don't have.

So I dropped a lot of treats and Nick wanted to stop and search for each one (of course). I started to get frustrated, but Min told me to take a break before Nick got frustrated too. Our circles looked more like those weird shapes they make you study in math. Good thing I don't have to figure out the area or the ~~sirkumference~~ circumference.

But I did manage to teach Nick his first cue: "me-me-me-me-me." That tells him that I want him to stay at my side, like he does (or is learning to do) in circle work.

Min says circle work teaches the dog to follow your body (your shoulders and feet, mostly) so they turn with you. And they learn that being at your side is a great place to be because that's where they get treats.

Last, we got to send our dogs through a tunnel! A REAL tunnel! Min held Nick a few feet from one end of the tunnel, and I kneeled (knelt?) at the other end where Nick could see me. I showed him a big meaty treat. His eyes lit up. I said "Break," Min let go, and Nick raced through that tunnel. He ran into me and I fell over! He took the meatball right out of my hand anyway, while I lay there on the ground.

Everybody laughed. I wanted to dig a hole and disappear into it. Min said I shouldn't be embarrassed. People fall down all the time in agility. But at that moment, I thought that maybe I'm not smart enough to learn how to play agility. Then the same thing happened to Harry, who had a hard time getting up because he's kinda big and round, so I didn't feel so stupid anymore.

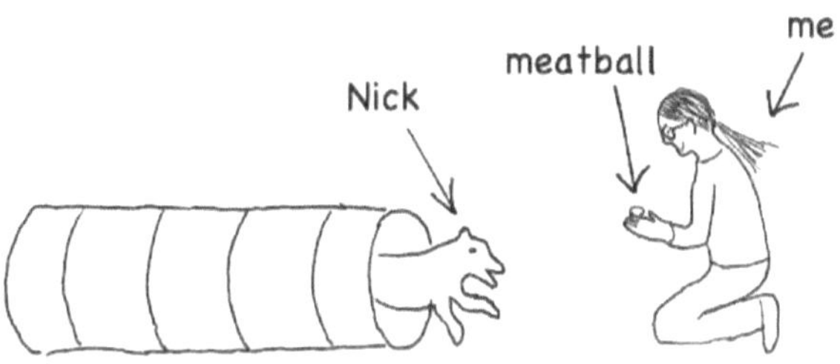

So homework for this week is

- Restrained recall. Maybe Dad can help hold Nick.
- Circle Work. Can do in backyard.
- Tunnel. I'll try to make a short tunnel out of a big cardboard box.
- Plus manners stuff: impulse control, loose-leash walking, clicker, shaping

My beautiful Nick. Hiking in Franklin County Park.
The wind made his ears stand up!

P.S. After class, some of the other students ~~comlemi~~
complimented me about my training and asked about Nick. I
was so surprised! At first, I thought they were just being polite.
But maybe they really meant it. Maybe we did OK. Nick and I did
all the same training games and exercises during the lesson
that the adults did, and sometimes Nick did them better than
anyone else. It was nice to be treated as though I am, or at
least could be someday, a real dog agility trainer.

CHAPTER 16

MARCH

T ori glanced right and left and slowly approached the old rundown building where she had seen Jordan last week. The last time she had been there, some men looked at Nick in a way that scared her, like they might be thinking about stealing him. So today Nick was safe at home. But he had become such a big part of her life that without him at her side, she felt small and vulnerable. Only her intense curiosity about Jordan had given her the nerve to walk this far, alone, into the seedy neighborhood.

This morning there were no old men hanging around on the sidewalk. If there had been, Tori might have turned around and gone back home. *This is a stupid idea,* she told herself. *Dad would NOT like me being here.* She climbed the two narrow steps that led to the front door, raised her hand, and knocked. No answer. *But If Jordan's got something to do with the missing dogs, I want to know.* She glanced right and left. Still no one about. She knocked again, louder this time, hoping that no one would answer and, at the same time, hoping that someone would. Bits of peeling gray paint fell off the door and landed at her feet. She heard approaching footsteps and the door suddenly creaked inward. Tori jumped back and stumbled down onto the lower step. She recovered and straightened.

In the doorway stood a middle-aged man with short salt-and-pepper hair, wearing blue jeans and a plain white t-shirt. He blinked at Tori through black-rimmed glasses. "Oh," he said. "Hello." His eyes swept up and down Tori, as though surprised to find her on his doorstep.

Tori had practiced what to say. She stared at the man's face and searched her brain. "Uhhhh . . ." Then the words came out fast. A little too fast. "I think I saw a friend of mine here. Jordan? He's a tall guy with blond hair and tattoos all over his arms and I was wondering if he lives here, or what he was doing here, and what kind of place this is . . ." She paused to take a breath.

The man held up one hand in a stop gesture. But his smile and the deep dimples in his scruffy cheeks were kind.

Behind him, Tori saw several people in ragged clothing lining up and shuffling into another room. The distinct smell of frying bacon wafted through the front door and hit her nose. Her nostrils flared involuntarily.

"I'm sorry, I can't give out information about anyone here," the man said. He followed Tori's eyes and glanced behind him at the line of people. "We provide a place to sleep and eat for people who need it. Why don't you talk to your friend and ask him your questions directly?"

Tori took another step back, and her feet slid off the step and onto the sidewalk. "OK. Thanks. Sorry to bother you." She turned and walked away, trying to keep her legs from accelerating into a run.

"Have a great day!" The man called after her.

Well, that was embarrassing, Tori thought. *And I still don't know how Jordan is connected to that place. I can't possibly ask him. That would be even more embarrassing.*

Jordan had a job at the animal shelter, so he must have some money. What was he up to? As she walked home, Tori thought about her clues. She had overheard Jordan and Min at the DSC whispering about something being stolen. She had seen Jordan at the sketchy building downtown exchanging something—*the goods,* according to one of the old men—for an envelope and talking about dogs, and the man she had just met there wouldn't tell her anything about him. Then she had seen Jordan's truck at the DSC with expensive agility equipment in the back. But she couldn't envision any clear connections between any of those things.

A couple blocks from home, a bright yellow paper fluttering from a telephone pole caught Tori's attention. "Have you seen me?" the paper said, and a small brown dog smiled at her from a photo. *Another lost—or stolen!—dog.* Tori quickened her pace and race-walked home.

At home, Tori greeted Nick, checked that the yard gate was locked, then opened the Lost Dogs website. One more dog was listed, a cocker spaniel. The dog's photo matched the poster she had just seen not far from her own house. She added the dog to her own list of dogs missing from Maple Valley.

Website:

 Yorkshire terrier (2)
 shih tzu
 poodle (mini)
 Chihuahua
 Maltese
 French bulldog mix
 cocker spaniel (website and poster near home)

Posters:

> poodle mix
> terrier mix

Total: 10 small dogs

It seemed odd that none of the dogs had been found yet. Tori figured that the owners would have deleted their listings if they got their dogs back. She focused on the word *small*. Then she typed a search into the browser: How big are cocker spaniels? The computer told her they were small- to medium-size dogs. On the list in her notebook, she changed the total:

Total: 9 small dogs and 1 medium dog

So it wasn't just small dogs missing now. A bigger, medium-size dog in her own neighborhood was lost. She remembered the old men at the rundown building looking at Nick, and her stomach tightened.

Were the dogs lost? Or stolen?

CHAPTER 17

Tori stilled her body and let her eyes roam across the big open field, the willow trees lining the riverbank to the east, and the big old barn nestled among the oak trees to the south. She glanced at her watch. Twenty minutes until her and Nick's lesson at the DSC.

Tori closed her eyes. *What does Nick hear?* The muffled, distant roar of the river. A meadowlark's liquid song. The high squeaks of a rodent. The wind weaving through the tall grass. A ground squirrel scrabbling at its burrow entrance. A hawk's wings brushing the sky. *What does Nick smell?* Damp earth. Pungent tarweed. Musty wild turkey poop.

Tori opened her eyes. She examined the soles of her sneakers. *I smell turkey poop because I stepped in it. Great.* She scraped her sneakers clean on a patch of weeds.

Ahead of her, Nick bounded over the tangle of grass and weeds as though he was on a trampoline. Then he arced over the tall grass and seemed to hang in the air as he aimed his muzzle and front paws downward. With laser focus he dove into the vegetation.

Tori tip-toed up to him and saw his nose buried deep into a ground squirrel's burrow, inhaling the delicious scent. Nick pulled his dirt-covered muzzle out of the hole, stepped back, and froze, with one front leg raised and eyes locked on the burrow. Without thinking, Tori stopped breathing and moving too. Nick cocked his head to the right, then left, at some squirrely voice beyond Tori's hearing. He dove into the hole again, this time up to his eyeballs, and snuffled. Tori exhaled in a rush.

With a final snort, Nick abandoned the burrow. He caught another enticing scent and paced back and forth, nose close to the ground. Then he slowly lowered himself, tipped onto his side and then his back, flung his legs into the air, and twisted back and forth, back and forth. With the odor thoroughly ground into his fur, he jumped up, shook himself from head to tail, and flashed Tori a joyful grin before trotting off to find the next irresistible aroma. Tori sighed and wandered after him. Another bath for Nick tonight. "I know *you* love the smell of wild-animal poop and dead things, Nick. But Dad doesn't. And—guess what—not my favorite scent either."

Nick stopped and held up a front leg. He licked at his paw, took a limping step, then raised the leg again. His eyes searched for Tori.

"Nick, what's the matter?" Tori lengthened her strides to reach him quickly and carefully lifted and folded his leg. A blackberry thorn protruded from the pad. She plucked it out, gently rubbed his paw, and let him set his leg down.

Nick took an experimental step. No limp. His sparkling eyes gazed straight into Tori's, his mouth turned up in his trademark grin. *He's thanking me, like I'm the most amazing person in the whole world. Just like in the fable, Androcles and the Lion, that we had to read in English class.* Tori rubbed Nick's shoulders and planted a kiss on the top of his head.

"Almost time for our lesson, Nick. Let's head back to the barn." She ran her fingers through Nick's fur. As the cold wet winter had given way to the not-quite-as-cold but still-wet spring, Nick's coat had changed too. No matter how much Tori brushed him, he had shed great handfuls of thick fur. For a while, vacuuming the house had practically been Tori's full-time job.

Now his coat was sleek and shiny, except for his black tail, which still sported delicate golden feathers that fluttered in the breeze. His muscular haunches and shoulders rippled as he moved. Tori didn't think it was possible to love him more, but every day she did. She could swear that her heart literally swelled whenever their eyes met. One day she would burst.

Love. Was that just a human concoction? Or could dogs really feel love? Tori had read somewhere that to a dog, love might be a combination of a lot of things: feeling respected and protected by a person and safe with them, having a comfortable place to live and play, feeling secure—like knowing they would always get food—and being able to trust a person. All those things packaged together and tied up with a red ribbon could be described as love, even though dogs don't have the language to think of it that way. *And really*, thought Tori, *human love is probably made up of those same good feelings. Our species just has to label everything and make it more complicated.*

Tori looked across the field to the Dog Sports Center, the one place where she felt she belonged. Schoolwork was still challenging, and she couldn't call any of her classmates *real* friends, not yet. Home was getting better though. A couple times, Dad had stayed to watch her agility lesson! And he had volunteered to help her practice restrained recall with Nick in the backyard. More than once, Tori had seen him secretly petting and talking baby talk to Nick. She barely managed to contain her giggling and pretend she hadn't seen him. She figured Dad wasn't quite ready to reveal that side of himself to her.

They reached the gravel road that led to the barn. Tori clipped Nick's leash onto his harness and they quickened their pace. The leash swung loosely between them.

Tori pulled open the heavy door, and she and Nick entered the DSC.

CHAPTER 18

Journal Entry, March 15

Who knew that running around a bucket could be part of agility training?

Today Nick learned to circle around a 5-gallon bucket. I have to remember to motion toward the bucket with the arm closest to Nick and say the cue "around." He's supposed to circle all the way around it, and then I throw his reward on the ground a few feet beyond the bucket. That way he learns to keep going instead of always looking to me for the reward.

Everybody did pretty well with one bucket, so we tried two. The dogs circled them in a figure 8 and got their reward after the second bucket. It was hard to get the arm motions right. Good thing we didn't spend too much time on the figure 8, cause I was starting to get confused and impatient. We'll work on it at home. Min says we'll use this skill in our jump training. I don't see how. But I'm sure Min has a plan.

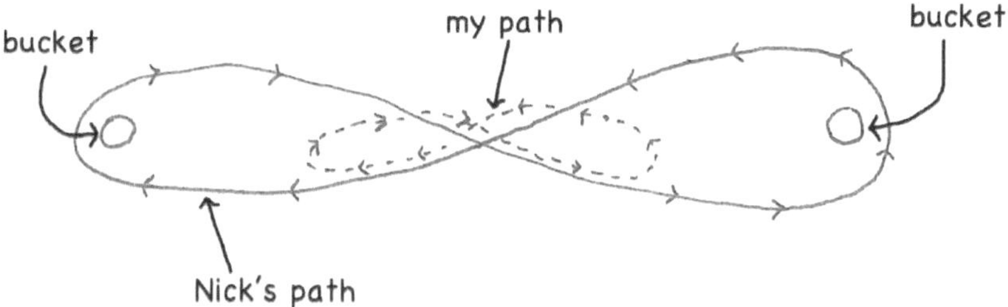

Then we used a lid from a yogurt container to help train contacts! The dogs are supposed to touch the lid with their nose. That's called targeting. The lid is called the target. Min said to SHAPE the behavior with clicker training. And she asked ME to explain shaping to the other students! I was kind of nervous, but I said what I know about shaping. Nick was curious about the lid, so he touched it right away. I clicked and gave him a treat. He learned really fast that targeting the lid was a good thing to do.

Finally, we got to start learning about REAL ~~OBSTIKELS~~ OBSTACLES. Min showed us a practice plank. It's like part of a dogwalk, but it sits on the ground. It's covered with a yoga mat, so the dogs don't slip. Everybody tried walking their dogs across it. Well, the person walks on the ground, the dog walks on the plank. (Ha! Walks the plank! Like a pirate!) Some of the dogs started OK, but they jumped off in the middle. Nick walked next to me across the whole plank the first time. I was proud of him!

It turns out that the yogurt lid and the plank go together. Min placed the lid on the ground near the end of the plank. She had her dog Zen walk across the plank and touch the lid with his nose. His front paws were on the ground, and his back paws were on the plank. That's called a stopped contact. The target helps the dog understand where to place himself at the end of the dogwalk. When you compete, it's a rule that the dog needs to touch the yellow end of the contact obstacles with at least one paw. Everybody tried it with their dogs, but we all agreed we'll need way more practice to get it right.

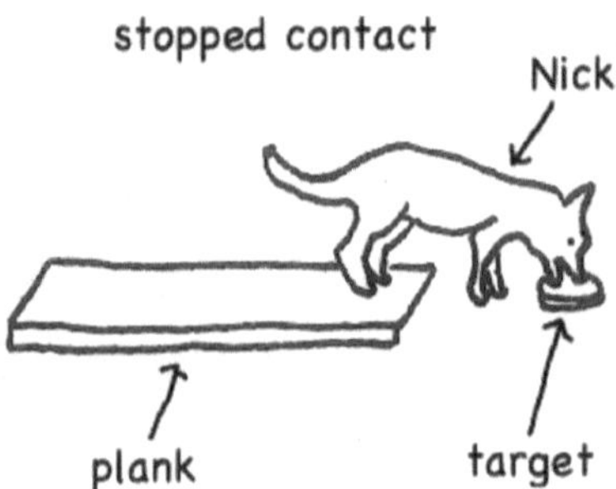

Then we did the same thing with a see-saw plank. It's like the dogwalk plank, but there's a round thing in the middle so it tips up and down a little bit.

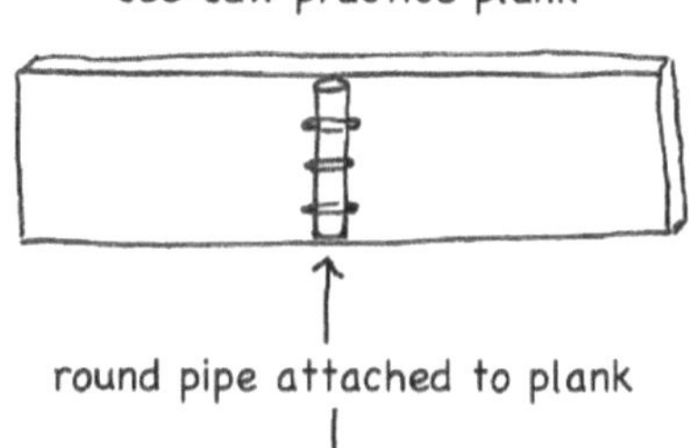

If our dogs weren't scared, we could walk them across it holding their leash. But if they WERE scared, we weren't supposed to MAKE them walk over it. That's not positive. Min said to shape it. (Glad I've already practiced shaping.) Nick wasn't scared though. He got right on the plank, sort of balanced himself in the middle for a second as it tipped, then walked off. Then he wanted his treat. Of course.

Homework

- Buy a couple of buckets and practice sending Nick to circle them. Try to increase distance I stand away from the bucket.
- Shape targeting the yogurt lid (target)
- Dogwalk plank and see-saw plank: Ask Dad to make them for me.
- Practice stopped contact behavior with the target.

P.S. I sure hope I can figure out a way to practice at the DSC. Min says that once we start our dogs on the real obstacles, we should schedule practice times AT THE DSC between lessons. We'll get better faster by practicing on our own, especially if we want to compete. Dad offered to pay for weekly lessons, but he doesn't know about the practice sessions. They cost money too.

Chapter 19

APRIL

Tori watched from her seat at the kitchen table as Dad stood, arms folded across his chest, head back, and frowned at the ceiling. Then he lowered his head and frowned at the bucket on the floor collecting the water that dripped from the ceiling.

Nick trotted around the bucket, his toenails clacking on the tile floor, then looked expectantly at Tori. *Do I get a treat?*

"Not now, Nick," Tori said quietly. "It's not that kind of bucket."

Nick stuck his head into the bucket and slurped.

"Over here, buddy." Tori patted her leg to get Nick's attention.

Nick pointed his nose at Tori, and water dripped from his muzzle onto the floor. He ambled over to her and, with a dramatic sigh, plunked down next to her chair. His bones clunked against the hard floor.

Dad didn't say anything about Nick dripping water onto the floor, so Tori knew the roof situation was serious. "Does a new roof cost a lot?" she asked.

"Yup." Dad sighed and looked up at the leaky ceiling again. The circle of wet, cracked plaster widened as they watched. "I can patch it myself, but we'll need a whole new roof soon."

Tori knew that the roof was in bad shape when Dad bought the house, but he hoped to get through the wet winter and spring without too much trouble. Tori had been gearing up to ask her dad about scheduling agility practice sessions at the DSC, but clearly now was not the right time.

With one foot, Dad shoved the bucket a few inches to the left. The dripping water began to hit it dead center. "You don't need to worry about the roof. That's my job," he said. He turned to Tori. "It's about time for your lesson, isn't it? Do you want a ride to the DSC?"

Tori glanced at the rain-battered kitchen window. "Yes, please. If you have time."

As Tori rode with her dad to the DSC, guilt wormed its way into her stomach and she squirmed in her seat. Dad wasn't exactly a billionaire, and agility lessons weren't cheap. She was serious about learning agility. For her, it had become more than just a weekly diversion from the routine of school and home. She wanted to compete someday. The least she could do was figure out a way to earn money for practice time.

🐕   🐕   🐕   🐕   🐕

Dad was late picking her up after the lesson, so Tori wandered down the aisle with Nick and practiced changing direction with front crosses—as they walked, she turned toward Nick and Nick turned toward her, so he ended up on her other side. She thought that the other agility students had already gone home, but when she got to the far side of the barn, near the small practice arena, she heard quiet words and muffled footsteps, the kind made by sneakers on dirt.

She looked to her right and saw a girl with a black miniature poodle. At least Tori thought it was a poodle. The dog's fur wasn't cut in the classic poodle style, with big balls of fur on its head and legs. Instead, the dog sported short black curls from head to toe. As the girl walked gracefully in a large circle, the dog twirled, pranced through the girl's legs, circled around her, then returned to a perfect heel position, all with her flashing eyes riveted on the girl and a huge open-mouth smile on her face.

Tori and Nick stopped in the aisle and watched through the fence. Tori had seen videos of dog training like this. She thought it was called dog *dancing*. Nick's eyes followed the small dog as she waltzed around the arena. He whined softly, then louder, and then the whines turned into excited barks. "Woof! Woof!" Nose in the air, his front legs lifted off the ground with every bark.

"No bark," Tori said softly. Nick knew his no-barking cue and quieted. "Let's go, Nick." She turned and headed down the aisle toward the main door. She didn't want to bother the girl, who was obviously a skilled trainer.

"Hey! Tori?" The voice sounded familiar. Tori had been watching the dog so closely she hadn't really noticed the girl's face. She turned back toward the arena.

Tori's eyes widened and she stepped toward the fence. "Laura? Hi! Oh my gosh, I didn't realize that was you."

To Nick, Tori said softly, "Sit." Thankfully, Nick sat. She wanted to look like she knew what she was doing in front of Laura. "I didn't know you had a dog. Or trained her to dance!"

Laura pulled earbuds from her ears and tapped her phone. She walked toward Tori. The poodle pranced beside her, still gazing at Laura's face. "Yes, this is Onyx. What are you doing here?"

"This is Nick. We take agility lessons with Min." Tori decided not to say that they were beginners. "You and Onyx are beautiful dancers!" Nick paddled his front feet and stared at Onyx, but stayed in his sit. His wagging tail made an ever-deepening semicircle in the dirt behind him.

Laura tilted her head. "Thank you. Ummm . . . it's called *freestyle*, not dancing," she said evenly.

Tori's face heated up. She lowered her eyes and started to gather Nick's leash. She knew the correct name. She had watched videos of freestyle performances but had never seen anyone perform live, in person. "Oh, yeah. Sorry. Freestyle." She faked a smile and aimed it at Laura. "Well, we hafta go. See ya." She and Nick continued toward the front door.

"See you later," said Laura. She put one knee on the dirt floor and patted Onyx. Then she peered through the fence and called to Tori, "See you at lunch tomorrow. OK?"

Tori raised her eyebrows. She smiled, a real smile this time, at Laura. "Uhhh . . . yeah, OK."

Dad pulled up to the barn just as Tori and Nick exited. They piled into the car and Dad headed down the driveway and turned onto the main road.

"Good lesson?" asked Dad.

"Yeah. And a girl I know from school was there, practicing dog dancing. I mean freestyle. She has a poodle!" Tori told her dad what she knew about the sport of freestyle.

As they passed the shelter, Dad slowed the car to allow a dirty blue van to turn into the driveway. Then he sped up and continued toward home.

Tori thought about Laura. The mystery of her scratched, rough hands was solved—working with dogs would do that. And she wondered: *Does Laura want to be* real *friends? More than just lunch friends? But why would Laura want to befriend* me, *a total beginner at dog training?*

Chapter 19

As Tori thought about tomorrow's lunch period, she felt a sunny glow inside that had nothing to do with the warming April weather.

CHAPTER 20

Tori and Laura began to chat at lunch every day, and not just about homework or pizza, but about their families and dogs. Mostly dogs. Laura had lived in Maple Valley her whole life, and her big newer home was only about a half mile from Tori's, but in a far fancier neighborhood. Laura was a serious sort of girl, and she sometimes came across as mean or stuck-up because of her business-like way of talking. She probably couldn't help it—her dad was a lawyer and her mother was a doctor.

But when she talked about dogs, Laura was different. Interested and interesting. Very proud of Onyx. And she was nice enough to ask Tori about Nick. The girls agreed, in an unspoken way, that the other kids would think they were nerds for their consuming interest in dogs and dog training, so they tried to keep it quiet.

"My grandmother used to say that it's *mean* to train a dog. She didn't know about positive reinforcement," said Laura. She and Tori sat across from each other, a little apart from the other girls, although by now Tori could more easily joke and talk with them. Well, except for Abby. Laura's current mystery book stayed in her backpack.

"Really? I'm glad somebody thought of that positive training idea before I got Nick. He thinks all the training is just play." Tori stuck her fork in her mashed potatoes and swirled them around the plate.

Laura placed a pat of butter in the center of her neat mound of potatoes. "It's important to teach dogs how to live with humans. That way, they're happy. No one's yelling at them to behave all the time."

"Yeah, imagine if we humans had to live in dog society and follow their rules!" Tori gazed blankly at the light green wall behind Laura for a moment, thinking. "I guess our parents and teachers are training *us* to live in human society." She shifted her eyes down the table and lowered her voice. "Not sure they're being very successful with Abby."

Laura slid her eyes sideways toward Abby and, to Tori's surprise, grinned. Abby was telling the other girls a story, complete with lots of hand gestures and hair tossing. Her neighbors had to duck to avoid getting smacked in the face.

Tori and Laura looked at each other, rolled their eyes, and giggled. It was nice to know someone who was on the same wavelength, Tori thought. Maybe Laura could help with her problem.

"I've got to figure out how to pay for practice sessions at the DSC. Any ideas?" she asked Laura.

Laura looked into the distance, past Tori's left ear. "Hmmmm . . . Then she met Tori's eyes. "I know. Ask Min if you can help her somehow. Maybe you could swap work for practice time."

Tori's face brightened. "Why didn't I think of that? Yeah, Min has to move all kinds of stuff before and after my lesson. I bet she would love to have someone help her. I'll call her tonight!"

Tori began to sculpt her mushy pile of potatoes. "So, I was wondering. Do you *compete* in freestyle?"

Laura sat back on the bench. "Oh, no. Training Onyx is just fun. For both of us. Min helps me with training, but mostly I learned on my own by watching videos." Laura silently sipped some milk, then continued. "I think if we had the pressure of competition, it wouldn't be fun anymore."

"Really?" said Tori. She arranged the green beans on her plate in a line, as though they were agility jumps. Then she speared them, in order, and stuffed them into her mouth. She chewed slowly and stared into the distance.

"Agility is a little different, I think. The fun, and challenge too, is figuring out how to run the different courses that are set for you. And I kinda like winning. Or *trying* to win. Not that I've ever won anything yet." Tori picked up her milk carton and noisily slurped at the straw. "In freestyle, you get to make up your own routines. It's more . . . well . . . *free.*"

"Yes, I guess so. I don't really care about winning ribbons. The important thing is, you're working as a team with your dog and doing what your dog wants to do, right? Nick likes to run fast and jump. Onyx likes to dance!" Laura placed one green bean in her mouth, chewed, and swallowed.

Tori had built a lumpy white A-frame from her mashed potatoes. Butter-yellow contact zones covered each end. She dug out a giant spoonful and slid it into her mouth.

"I saw that," said Laura. "You're obsessed with dog agility, aren't you?"

"Yeah," said Tori, her voice muffled by potatoes. She gulped them down. "Heck, yeah, I am."

Training with Nick—just *having* Nick—these past few months had made such a difference in her life, thought Tori. She was feeling closer to her dad, and the girl sitting across from her was turning out to be a real friend. Those things wouldn't have happened without Nick. She couldn't imagine life without him. She thought of the photos of kids and dogs on the Lost Dogs website. What were those kids feeling?

She should tell Laura about the missing dogs. Laura had a small dog, and she should know about all the small dogs that were missing. It would be nice to share her concerns with someone too. She shifted her eyes right and left, leaned toward Laura, and spoke quietly. "Have you ever seen the Lost and Found Dogs in Oregon website?"

"No. I've never lost or found a dog in Oregon." Laura lifted the bread of her sandwich and examined the egg salad underneath. Then she replaced the bread and took a bite.

Laura's distracted response annoyed Tori. "Seriously. A lot of dogs are going missing around here. More than usual, that is. I've been keeping track."

Laura swallowed and leaned toward Tori. "Wow. Really?" Her forehead wrinkled in concern.

Tori pulled out her notebook and showed Laura the list of missing dogs. Laura stared at Tori's list and tapped it with one finger. "Onyx weighs only about 20 pounds. Almost all the dogs on your list are about that size or smaller." She raised her eyes to meet Tori's. "And a couple of them are miniature poodles. What makes you think the dogs might be stolen, not just lost?"

"Well, for one thing, there are so many of them compared to previous years and, for another, they never get found," Tori said quietly. "And for another . . . another, I know of someone who's been acting suspiciously lately." Tori told Laura about Jordan—how she had overheard him whisper about something being stolen, saw him downtown interacting with the group of men at the old rundown building, and saw him driving his truck with agility equipment in the back.

"But I'm not sure what all that means," Tori continued. "Except he seems to be up to something. Why do people steal dogs?"

"I read somewhere that testing laboratories buy stolen dogs," Laura said slowly. "You know, places that test medicine and other stuff on animals before they sell it to humans."

Tori wrinkled her nose. "Ewww. Boy, I hate to even think about that. Are there any labs around here?"

"I have no idea," said Laura, shaking her head. "I suppose people could try to sell dogs online as pets." She pressed her lips together and frowned. "I saw a news story on TV about stolen dogs being used for dog fighting too."

Tori couldn't imagine the kind of person who would make dogs fight each other.

Laura continued, "I'm going to be super careful with Onyx from now on, that's for sure." There was a fierceness in her voice that Tori had never heard before. But she understood it perfectly, because she felt the same way about Nick.

CHAPTER 21

T ori and Min stood in a corner of the big agility arena at the DSC and studied a piece of paper in Min's hand. "It'll be nice to have a helper," said Min.

To Tori, the map looked like a random jumble of shapes and numbers. She looked up and out at the arena. Somehow, she had to place the obstacles in the arena so that they matched the map. The placement numbers on the map made her think that math might be involved. She hoped not.

Min explained that the numbers beside each obstacle told her exactly where the obstacle should be. If the numbers for a jump were 15 and 20, that meant the jump should be 15 feet from the south wall and 20 feet from the side wall of the arena. Min showed Tori how to measure distances so she could match the map to the arena and place the jumps and other obstacles in the correct places. *I like this kind of math,* thought Tori. *It's useful. It's not just book math.*

Min showed her how to set the tunnels correctly and to be sure they were secure by placing heavy bags filled with sand on both sides of them. It was important that the tunnels didn't move when the dogs ran through them. The bags were so heavy, Tori could carry only one at a time.

A separate map showed the obstacles with a different, simpler set of numbers: one through twelve. Tori placed small plastic cones, numbered one through twelve, beside the obstacles to create a path. Then the obstacles seemed to lose their randomness and transform into a real agility course. She and Min stood in the middle of the arena and admired their work. Min stuck out her hand. "Congratulations, Tori. You built your first course. Good job!"

Tori grinned up at her and shook her hand. She looked forward to telling her dad that she got the job and would be able to exchange work for practice time. She pictured herself and Nick running through the newly built course. They weren't quite ready to run this one, but with a few more lessons and practice they would be.

Min showed Tori the storage area, which was an old horse stall where she kept equipment that wasn't being used. The stall was filled with towers of five-gallon buckets, tunnels that were collapsed to save space, weave poles and their metal bases, jumps, an extra dogwalk that had been taken apart into three pieces, plus stuff that Tori didn't even recognize. "If you need more equipment, this is the place to find it," Min said.

Tori wondered how Min could keep track of everything and even notice if anything was missing. She remembered seeing Jordan's truck packed with jumps and a dogwalk. "Does any of the equipment ever go missing?" Tori blurted without thinking. She continued slowly, "I mean . . . do people ever borrow things and forget to return them?"

"No, I don't think so. To be honest, it's kind of hard to keep track. Let me know if you see anyone taking things, OK?" Min looked away and frowned.

"Well . . ." Tori began. She fidgeted with a stack of dog toys to hide her uncertainty about mentioning Jordan's truck.

Min gave her a sharp look.

Go for it, Tori told herself. "One time, a few weeks ago, I saw a truck leaving your parking lot with some jumps and a dogwalk in the back," she said quickly.

"Was it a green pickup?" Min's face softened. "That's Jordan's truck. He helps me move things sometimes."

"Oh, good." Tori smiled in relief. At least she knew now that Jordan wasn't taking equipment from the DSC.

But Min seemed to be concerned about *something* being stolen. Did she know about the unusual number of lost dogs in Maple Valley? Did she think—or know—that the dogs were stolen, not lost?

Journal Entry, April 9

Nick's doing real well going over low jumps. He keeps his head low and pointed forward, and he lands softly. Min says he is a naturally good jumper. Wish I was a natural runner. All the training with buckets is coming in handy now. Today I started learning to cue Nick to turn right and left after taking a jump, and it's like he already knows how, because the upright part of the jump is sorta like a bucket.

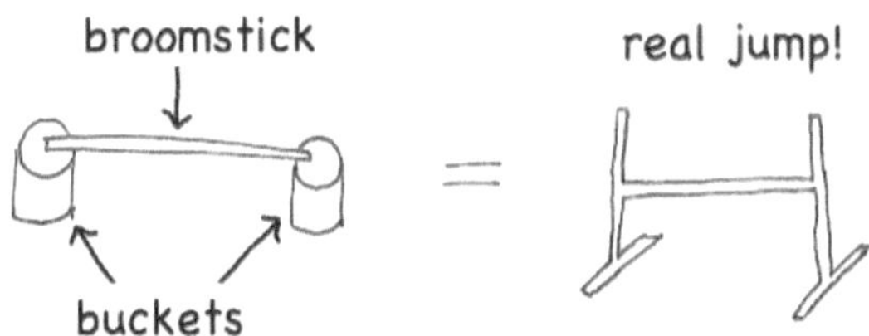

And because Nick practiced running around several buckets in different arrangements (SEQUENCES), like in a triangle and a square, he can go over several JUMPS set in a sequence too. WE'RE REALLY PLAYING AGILITY NOW!

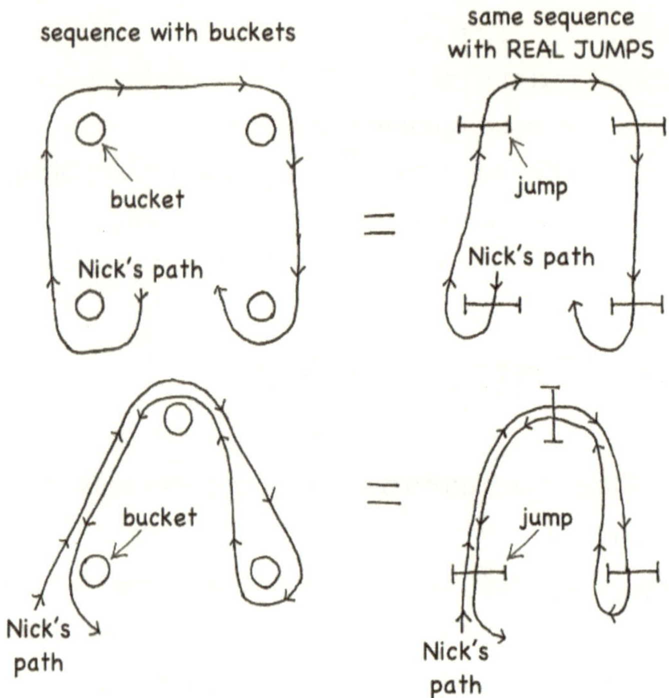

I love how Nick looks to me for directions with those happy eyes and his tongue hanging out. He loves getting treats, but he loves getting praise too. When I praise him, he knows he's made me happy, and maybe that makes him happy.

Homework

- Make some jumps out of hard plastic poles (called PVC poles). (Need to buy PVC and glue at hardware store.) Ask Dad to help. He likes it when I ask for help now, ~~espeshially~~ especially help with building stuff!
- Practice jumps. Make sure Nick jumps with good form.

- Practice sequences with buckets and jumps.
- Work on left and right cues.
- Don't forget all the stuff from previous lessons.

P.S. It feels like Nick and I are connected somehow, even though there's no leash between us. Or maybe BECAUSE there's no leash between us. Sometimes it seems like he can read my mind. Like Min said, we are becoming a TEAM. I can't wait to COMPETE in a real trial someday and have Dad watch us WIN, just like Mom did.

CHAPTER 22

MAY

The week's lesson had finished and everyone was packing up and getting ready to leave the barn. Min pulled Tori aside. "Tori, can I talk to you for a minute? Come with me." Min led the way to her small office near the barn entrance.

Tori had never been in that room before. She stepped through the door and stopped, mouth open. Photos, ribbons, and awards covered the walls. A shelf held several trophies topped with tiny golden dogs in various poses. Tori resisted the urge to examine each one. She wasn't sure whether getting called to the office at the DSC was good or bad. Maybe she wasn't doing a good job setting up the lesson courses, and Min had bad news for her.

Min sat down behind a small desk that faced the door, where Tori stood trying not to gape at Min's awards. "I know a lady who needs a dog walker a few times a week. Would you be interested in the job?"

Tori straightened in surprise. She hadn't expected to hear *that*. *Min thinks I'm good enough to walk someone else's dog?* She pushed up her glasses and swept a stray lock of hair off her face. Dad was trying to save money for a new roof, and the dog-walking earnings could help pay for agility lessons, dog food, vet bills . . . "Yes! Thank you! I'll have to ask my dad, but I think that'll be OK."

"Good! Let me find Mrs. Johnson's phone number." Tori watched as Min began to sort through some papers on her desk.

She noticed a paper with a photo and the words *Come to Our Fundraiser! Support the Main Street Help Center!* The building in the photo looked familiar. She moved closer to the desk and leaned over for a better look. It was the rundown building where she had seen Jordan!

A yelp of surprise escaped Tori's mouth. "Oh!" The memory of standing on the doorstep and talking with the salt-and-pepper-haired man played in her mind. "What is this place?" she asked Min.

Min glanced at the paper. "That's the Help Center. I volunteer there. They help a lot of people who are struggling with their living situations."

Should I ask her about Jordan? Tori thought. She summoned her courage. "Does Jordan go there too?"

"Yes, both of us volunteer there. Jordan especially likes to help people out by making sure they have enough food and other supplies for their dogs and cats."

A wave of understanding swept over Tori. Jordan had been at the Help Center because he was doing volunteer work. The cardboard box had contained pet supplies. That made sense. She should have known he wouldn't do anything criminal. She would call Laura tonight and update her on Jordan.

When her father arrived to pick them up, Tori and Nick hopped into the back seat of the minivan. Nick licked the back of Dad's neck, then—*KERCHEEEEW*—Nick sneezed. An enormous, explosive sneeze. A couple months ago, Tori would have braced for an annoyed reaction from Dad. But today, he just wiped the dog snot off his neck and said, "Ewwwww." Tori chuckled.

She told her dad about the dog walking job. "My job helping Min is great so I can practice there, but if I have a real paying job, I could help pay for agility lessons and all the stuff that Nick needs. What do you think?"

"I think . . ." Dad spoke slowly as he steered the car onto the street. ". . . I think that would be fine. You'll keep up with your schoolwork, right? Summer's almost here. You'll be out of school soon. I'll call Min and get the details."

Summer! Tori imagined hanging out with Laura and playing with their dogs. They hadn't managed to spend much time together outside of school yet. The other girls at the lunch table had noticed by now that Laura and Tori talked about dogs. A lot. Some of the girls called them nerds, but . . . *who cares? Everybody's a little nerdy about something,* thought Tori.

Tori watched a dirty blue van turn into the shelter parking lot. *That's funny. The shelter's closed by now,* she thought absently. Then she began to imagine what walking someone else's dog, as a real paid job, would be like. Fun? Hope so. Terrifying? Maybe. She had learned from Nick that dogs weren't automatically well behaved.

Dad cleared his throat and spoke. "You're doing a really good job of training and taking responsibility for Nick. And you do a lot of chores around the house too, more than most kids." He glanced at Tori and smiled. "I *do* notice things like that, you know."

Tori smiled back. "Oh. Thanks." She knew it was hard for him to talk about feelings. She was starting to think of her father not as just Dad, but as a *person*, with strengths and flaws like everyone else. She thought for a few moments. He liked it when she asked for help. "Can you help me figure out what to say to Mrs. Johnson? I don't know how much to charge, or what she expects exactly . . ."

"Sure. We can talk about that at dinner." He paused. "How was your lesson?"

Remembering, Tori smiled. "Nick ran over a full-height dogwalk *and* see-saw! I was so proud of him. I hope you can see us run in a real trial someday . . .

Journal Entry, May 5

Min said Nick was ready to try a full-height dogwalk today! That means the middle plank is about four feet high. The sequence was jump, dogwalk, jump. I put the yogurt lid in place at the end of the dogwalk, although he doesn't need that all the time anymore. Nick sat and stayed perfectly at the first jump. I called his cues, and he jumped, ran up and across the dogwalk (I ran alongside him the whole way), stopped in his two-paws-on, two-paws-off position, and touched the yogurt lid with his nose. I rewarded him there. Then I said "break, jump," and he took off fast and went over the second jump. I threw a toy for him to run after. He got the toy and ran back to me, and we played tug. Perfect!

Then we did the same thing (except instead of "climb" I said "see-saw") with a full-height see-saw. Perfect again! Everybody clapped for us.

We learned about endorphins in science class the other day. Endorphins are chemicals that make you feel good, and your body releases them when you exercise (or eat chocolate!). I feel a rush of endorphins when Nick and I run well together. I think he does too! I wonder what it'll feel like if we ever WIN at a trial.

Journal Entry, May 12

Nick was the star of the class today. We practiced the A-frame with a running contact. He really understands his cues. I called "climb," and he ran toward the A-frame and up the first side. I called "run, run, run," and he ran down the second side—with all four paws touching the yellow part of the ramp. I called "jump" for the next obstacle, and he jumped ~~beatefully~~ beautifully. Some of the other dogs leaped right over the yellow zone and onto the ground! Harry joked that Gunnar just needed a red cape and he would look like Superman! (I think he meant SuperDOG!)

Then we worked on weaves. The weave poles have been the hardest obstacle for Nick to learn. I really have to watch myself so I don't get impatient with him. I've got to keep my voice light, or Nick gets scared. Jumping and running over things are natural movements for dogs, cause their wolf ancestors do those kinds of things when hunting, but there's no reason for a wolf to weave around poles.

Nick is working on six poles now. We practiced them with the first two poles opened up a little. Then Min said Nick was ready to try six in a straight row.

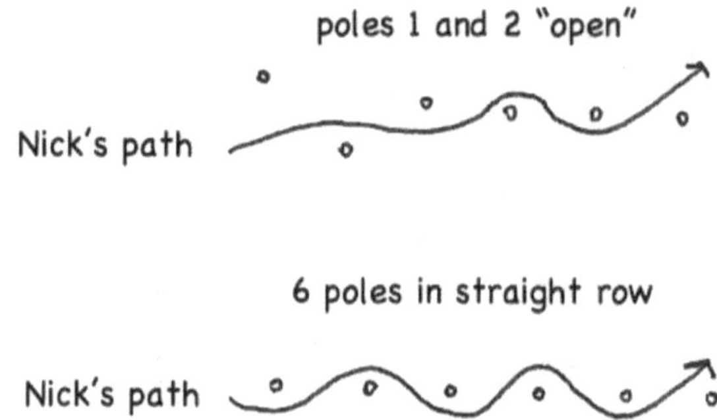

We tried three times, but he kept entering between the second and third poles, not between the first and second like he's supposed to. So I'll have to figure out what I can do to help him understand. He's so good at the contacts, but it's gonna take a while to master the weaves.

Nick flying over the A-frame

CHAPTER 23

JUNE

Tori and her dad had met Mrs. Johnson, and Tori was walking the elderly woman's stout French bulldog, Francois, for the first time. Mrs. Johnson was recovering from hip surgery and couldn't walk very well yet. She lived a few blocks away from Tori, in a neighborhood she had not explored on foot yet. Francois was proving to be a fun, and funny, little dog to walk.

Francois snorted, then sneezed such a mighty sneeze that it tossed his whole front end upward. As his front feet came back to earth, his back feet left it. Somehow, he managed to continue his brisk walk through all of it. He lifted his heavy head to show Tori both his proud smile and his expertise at licking the snot off his face.

"Good job, Francois! I admire your personal hygiene habits." Francois' oversize upright ears swiveled back to hear Tori's compliment.

Tori put her hand on the back pocket of her jeans and, for the tenth time, felt for her new phone. It wasn't fancy—she couldn't even get on the internet—but she could call and text. Dad had bought it "for safety," he said, although Tori thought of it as a good way to keep in touch with Laura. Yup, still there. She nudged the phone further down into her pocket.

Light rain began to spatter the sidewalk. Tori zipped up her jacket and flipped the hood up over her head. Francois wore a bright yellow raincoat. He walked steadily beside her, unlike Nick a few months ago when he was pulling Tori around like crazy. A smile tugged at the corners of her mouth as she thought of the progress she and Nick had made.

A dirty white two-story house with peeling paint and a weed-filled yard came up on their left. Compared to the other houses in the neighborhood, it was huge and much older. A thin gray-haired woman in sagging jeans, an oversized t-shirt, and work boots unloaded a big bag of dry dog food from the back of a dented green hatchback. She flung the bag over one shoulder and, as she straightened up, caught sight of Tori and Francois.

Tori smiled and nodded at the woman. Did professional dog walkers smile and nod at strangers? She thought they probably did, and she wanted to look professional. Francois snorted and wagged his nub of a tail. Through thick glasses that magnified her eyes, the woman looked with interest at Francois and smiled at Tori, but then she quickly turned and carried the dog food up the driveway toward the big old-fashioned porch. *Oh, well,* thought Tori. *I guess I just look like a kid.* Tori turned her attention back to Francois and gave him a pat on his round rump.

A few houses down the block, a woman in a red and white polka-dot jacket kneeled in her flower garden near the sidewalk and worked at the soil with a small spade. Inside the house, a terrier began barking and jumping against the big picture window. The French bulldog just kept trotting and snorting. Business as usual. The woman sat back on her heels and yelled at her dog, "Jerry! Quiet!" The windowpane shuddered as the terrier jumped even higher and barked even louder. "I wish my dog was as well-mannered as yours," the woman called to Tori.

"Oh, this isn't my dog," she said. "I'm walking him for the owner. But thank you!"

The seed of an idea planted itself in Tori's brain. She had taught Nick to walk nicely on leash. Maybe she could walk other people's dogs and help the dogs with their manners too. "What do you think, Francois? Can I be a professional dog walker?" Francois sneezed and grinned at her.

The photo of the French bulldog mix on the Lost Dogs website flashed into Tori's mind. If someone thought a Frenchie *mix* was worth stealing—*if* the dog had really been stolen and not just lost—then a purebred like Francois might be valuable. And here she was, walking a purebred. It was her job to keep Francois safe.

I better keep my eyes open for potential dog thieves, Tori thought. But what did dog thieves look like? On TV, the bad guys didn't always *look* like bad guys. Tori turned her head left and right and looked down the block behind her. No one there, except the woman in the polka-dot jacket in her garden. The woman stood up and flipped the hood of her jacket over her head. As she did, she caught Tori's eye and waved.

Tori hesitated, then waved back halfheartedly. She turned and led Francois away, her eyes scanning the neighborhood as they walked.

By the time they returned to Mrs. Johnson's house, the rain had eased and the sun had broken through the clouds. The humid air was downright warm. Steam rose from the wet street. Mrs. Johnson thanked Tori several times and then pressed some rolled-up dollar bills into her hand.

Tori recited the polite language Dad had suggested. "Thanks, Mrs. Johnson! I'll be back tomorrow. It's a pleasure to walk Francois."

Outside, she peeled off her rain jacket and pulled her t-shirt away from her sweaty skin. She counted her first payment for dog walking. And counted it again. She straightened to her full five-foot height and, for just a moment, raised her face to the sun. Then she stuffed the bills into her pocket and raced to where her bicycle leaned against the house. *I'll keep track of my earnings in my journal . . .*

Tori grabbed the handlebars and pulled the bike away from the house. "Arghh!" She scrunched up her face and absently pumped the handbrakes. *My journal.* She had forgotten her training journal at the DSC yesterday. Well, it wasn't far by bicycle. She swung onto the bike and started pedaling.

🐕 🐕 🐕 🐕 🐕

The barn was oddly quiet, the arena dark and empty. Tori inhaled the familiar smell of damp earth and wood, human sweat, and dog feet, and headed down the long wide aisle toward the manners training room. When she got close, she heard two people talking in the room, and she stopped to wait for a pause in the conversation. She didn't want to be rude and interrupt. *That sounds like Min and Jordan.*

". . . if you need money, maybe I can help." Min was saying.

"Thanks, but I'll figure out how to raise the money somehow," said Jordan. "The reason I stopped by is to tell you that it's happened again. A couple more dogs have gone missing from the shelter. We can't figure out how it happened. The building is locked at night. The dogs were in their kennels at six in the evening. Then at seven the next morning they were gone."

Tori froze. She was probably not supposed to hear this conversation. She should probably turn around and leave. But her feet wouldn't move.

"I'll keep an eye out for them," said Min. "What do they look like?"

"Bernie is a young beagle. He's small, with tan and white patches. Cindy is an apricot-colored miniature poodle. Both are really nice dogs," Jordan said. "We don't want the general public to know about this, at least not yet. We're just telling a few local people who work with dogs."

"I'm so sorry, Jordy," said Min.

Tori's feet unglued themselves from the dirt floor and she tiptoed back down the aisle toward the main door. So that's what Jordan and Min had been concerned about all this time. Dogs were being stolen from the shelter! If someone wants dogs badly enough to steal them from the shelter, any dog in town could be in danger too. Even Nick.

CHAPTER 24

T ori sat at the desk in her room, her training journal open in front of her. Yesterday she forgot the journal after hearing Min's and Jordan's conversation, so she retrieved it from the DSC during today's agility lesson. Her hand was motionless, poised over the page, not quite ready to put pencil to paper.

Dogs are missing from the shelter. Tori still couldn't decide what to do with that information. She wasn't supposed to know about it. She might tell Laura—or Dad—but neither of them could really help find the dogs anyway. She decided to sleep on it. Again. Maybe she would think more clearly tomorrow. And anyway, school, her jobs helping Min and walking Francois, Nick's training, and her chores around the house kept her busy. Especially Nick's training. The DSC was holding a practice agility trial—a "fun match" Min called it—later that month. "You should enter," Min had told Tori several weeks ago. "You and Nick are ready. You're a great team. A fun match isn't that different from a lesson."

Tori had hesitated. Trying new things, like dog agility, on her own or with a teacher was one thing. Performing in front of an audience was entirely different. In fact, it was terrifying to even think about. When she had dreamed of competing, she hadn't thought about how agility trials are public—other people can watch! But she had to start somewhere, as scary as it might be, so she had finally agreed to take part in the fun match.

Now the match was only a few days away, and it seemed *real*. Not just some blurry faraway thing. Tori focused her mind on today's lesson. Min had taught some important skills that would help her run the courses at the fun match. She lowered the pencil to the blank page.

Journal Entry, June 8

Now that we are practicing sequences, Nick doesn't get a treat for every obstacle. He does three or four or five and then gets a treat. And he loves doing each obstacle anyway! I was afraid he wouldn't want to run with me unless he got treats all the time. Min says the food and toy rewards build VALUE for the obstacles. ~~Evenchu~~ Eventually the dog finds the jumping and weaving and running across contact obstacles rewarding on their own. That's how positive reinforcement works. It's sure working for Nick! He looks like he's having so much fun.

Min is so smart. I want to be like her someday and know EVERYTHING about dogs! I like what she said today about mistakes: When things go wrong, think of it as your dog's feedback on your handling. Then analyze what happened and adjust your training or handling to improve.

The sequences we're practicing are getting more complicated. Sometimes when I'm running with Nick, I have to stop because I can't remember where to go next. Grrrrr. And on top of remembering the correct order of the obstacles, I have to remember what cues to say, what motions to make with my arms, how to place my feet to cue Nick to go in the right direction—and I have to do all of that at the right time and in the right place. Sometimes I have to switch Nick from running on my right to running on my left, or from left to right. (Once, in the middle of running a sequence with Gunnar, Harry yelled "My brain hurts!" And he's a grown man, an engineer!)

Min said to look for patterns and shapes that the obstacles form. If you see a circle, a figure eight, or even just a straight line, it can be easier to think of running that SHAPE instead of running from one obstacle to the next. Min also said to have a plan for our walkthrough (that's when you walk around the sequence or course without your dog). So everyone tried it with this sequence:

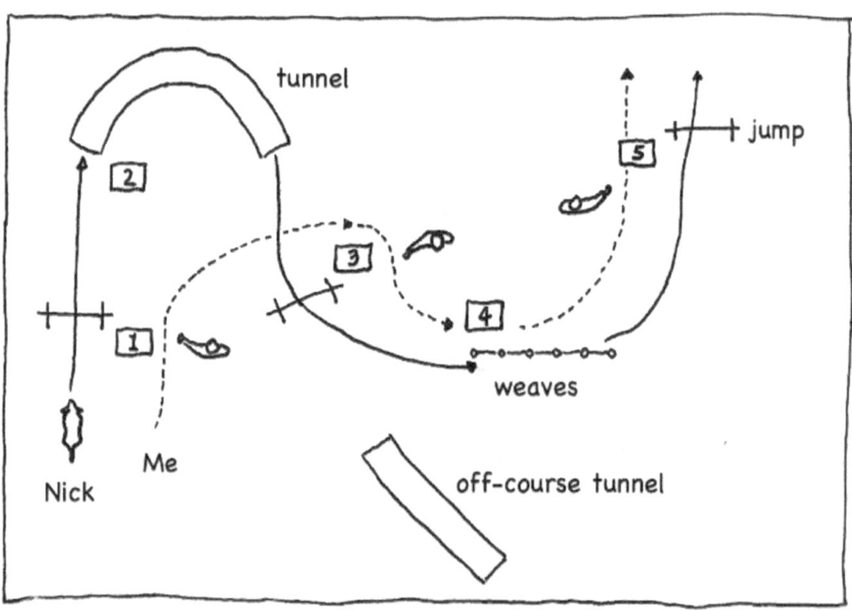

Walkthrough Plan

First time walking the sequence: Learn the order of the obstacles. Figure out the shape or shapes the obstacles make.

Jump 1, tunnel, jump 3, weaves, and jump 5 form an S shape.

Second time walking the sequence: Focus on the difficult spots.

At jump 1, Nick will be on my left. But while Nick is in the tunnel, I need to get to the other side of jump 3 and turn so that the jump, weaves and Nick will end up on my right. Remember to say the weaves cue in time for Nick to collect himself, so he can enter correctly. He might want to go straight into the off-course tunnel, so be prepared to call his name. (The extra obstacles that aren't actually part of the sequence can make things harder. Nick might want to go to them, especially tunnels!)

Third time walking the sequence: Run the sequence and say the cues.

Break. Jump. Tunnel. Jump. Weave. Jump.

Using the plan really helped. I was kinda slow getting to the other side of jump 3 (for some reason I waited to watch him go into the 2 tunnel), so Nick almost went into the off-course tunnel. But at least I remembered where to go! We tried the whole sequence a second time and Nick was perfect! I gave him extra treats after that.

Min says: Give your cue, then run. Don't wait and watch your dog! Trust that he knows your cue and he'll do it. TRUST YOUR DOG!

Chapter 25

The sun disappeared behind dark clouds and the gnarled oak trees that grew to the west of the DSC barn. Tori and Nick climbed into the minivan, and Dad headed down the driveway. He switched on the headlights to see better in the dusk. Nick gave a tired groan as he lay down on the back seat.

"How was practice?" Dad stopped at the end of the driveway, looked both ways, then turned the car onto the main road.

"Fun. The weaves are still hard. But Nick's contacts are really good." Tori peeked over the seatback to smile at Nick.

As they passed the animal shelter, a blue van—with no lights—suddenly veered into their lane. Dad jerked the steering wheel to the right, and their car lurched away from the van. Tori pitched to the left, while her stomach heaved to the right. She gave a small involuntary scream. The blue van careened into the shelter driveway. Dad corrected his steering and their minivan lurched back into its lane. "Whew!" he exclaimed. "Is everybody OK?"

Tori willed her insides to stop spinning. "Yeah. I think so." She loosened her grip on the armrests and took a shaky breath. She turned and looked at Nick. "Are you OK, boy?" Other than raising his head, Nick hadn't moved from his napping position on the back seat. His trusting eyes showed no concern. He lowered his head and went back to sleep.

I've seen that van around here before. I wonder who it belongs to, thought Tori. Nick meant everything to her. And he trusted her to keep him safe. That was a huge responsibility. What if he was hurt in a car crash?

Or stolen by the dog thief?

🐾 🐾 🐾 🐾 🐾

The kitchen radio played quietly in the background, the solemn voice of the news announcer no match for the clatter of Dad's cooking. The refrigerator door squeaked open and slammed shut. A knife sliced through a zucchini and hit the cutting board with a *thunk, thunk, thunk*. Spaghetti sauce bubbled and popped on the stove.

As her dad prepared dinner, Tori sat at the kitchen table and opened the computer. She typed "car safety for dogs" and pressed the return key. She scrolled, clicked, and read . . . scrolled, clicked, and read . . . scrolled, clicked, and read.

"Dad, can we put a crate in the back of the minivan for Nick? One made of hard plastic, so it won't crumple in an accident. That's the best way to keep Nick safe. Oh, and he should have a ramp that goes from the ground to the car, so he won't hurt his legs by jumping in and out."

Dad gave his daughter a curious glance. "Good idea. That's grown-up thinking. You pick out the crate—not too expensive, I hope—and we'll set it up this weekend. I can probably build a ramp. OK?"

"OK, but the fun match is this weekend, remember?"

"Oh, the fun match! How could I forget? Well, let's aim for Friday then."

Tori looked at the back of Dad's threadbare plaid shirt as he rinsed the cutting board in the sink. "OK. Thanks." Having a dog, especially an agility dog, wasn't cheap. Now they needed a new crate. The expenses were adding up. She turned back to the computer and started a new search: How to start a dog walking business.

🐕 🐕 🐕 🐕 🐕

That evening, Tori and Nick sprawled on Tori's bed, Nick on his side, Tori on her stomach. Quiet guitar music from the living room drifted into the bedroom. Tori was watching agility videos on the computer, but the conversation she had overheard between Min and Jordan and images of the missing shelter dogs replayed again and again in her mind.

"Hmph! Can't concentrate!" She closed the computer. The sudden movement woke Nick, and he raised his head and looked at her with sleepy eyes. "Hey, buddy. Want to show me your new trick?" Tori pointed to the open bedroom door. "Push!" Nick, now wide awake and eager to earn a treat, jumped off the bed, trotted to the door, and pushed the door shut with his paw. "Lock!" said Tori. He placed his nose on the small lock button on the doorknob and nudged it in. Then he turned toward Tori with his *I get a treat now, right?* expression. Tori dug into her pocket and found a stray piece of beef jerky. "Good job, Nick. Thanks!"

Nick gulped the treat and jumped on the bed. He circled, pawed at the quilt, and lay down with a grunt.

Tori picked up her phone and tapped Laura's number.

"Hello," said Laura. "What's up?"

Tori took a breath. "I heard something the other day. A secret. But I have to tell you."

Then Tori told Laura about the missing shelter dogs. Nick rolled onto his back, his rear legs flopped to each side, his front legs folded.

"Wow, it's like a real mystery," said Laura. Tori heard a hint of excitement in her usually even, quiet voice. "But why would anyone steal shelter dogs? It doesn't cost too much to adopt them."

"Well, they don't let just anybody adopt a dog." Tori remembered waiting impatiently in the shelter office while her dad filled out the application form for Nick. "They call you later to check on the dog. And if one person tried to adopt a bunch of dogs, they would get suspicious and wonder what was happening to the dogs."

"Oh, yeah, you're right. I knew that," said Laura. "My family adopted Onyx from the shelter a few years ago. She looks like a purebred poodle, but she's probably not."

"Really? I just assumed that Onyx was . . ." Tori stopped herself. She had *assumed*, just because Laura was pretty and rich, that Onyx was an expensive purebred. Her voice softened. "I'm sorry, I never thought to ask where you got Onyx."

"We didn't want to buy a purebred puppy, the way you buy a . . . a new car," Laura continued. "We wanted to adopt a dog who needed a home."

"Shelter dogs are the best, aren't they?" Tori scratched Nick's chest and admired his soft black-and-tan fur. "Well, I just thought I should tell you what I heard about the missing shelter dogs. We're just kids. We can't really do anything about it."

"I don't know, Tori. We could investigate, like the kids in the Young Detectives books. People don't pay attention to kids when they're poking around. They think we're just playing, so it's easy to get into places and talk to people. We could identify suspects and figure out who has the motive, means, and opportunity to steal dogs. That's how you figure out who the culprit is."

Tori was impressed. Laura seemed to know a lot about detective work. "Well, maybe. It sure would make me feel better if the thief was caught. What if the shelter dog thief is also stealing other dogs, like the dogs on the Lost Dogs website? I worry about Nick and Onyx."

"Me too," said Laura. "Let's get together and talk about it."

"Tomorrow afternoon I'm going to walk Francois for Mrs. Johnson. Do you want to go with me?" asked Tori. Tomorrow was also the last day of school, so it would be fun to talk about that and their summer plans too.

"Sure. Good idea. See you tomorrow."

Tori ended the call. Nick lay upside down on the bed, oblivious to Tori's—and now Laura's—secret. Gravity made his black-lined lips slide back, baring his pearly white teeth in a comical grin. As Tori rubbed his belly, he sighed, stretched his legs toward the ceiling, then relaxed and folded them.

Laura was right. They had to do something. Most people didn't value shelter dogs, so they wouldn't care about finding the thief. But Tori cared, and Laura cared. Maybe together they could solve the mystery.

CHAPTER 26

Francois turned his head and rolled his eyes at Tori and Laura. *Hey, this is fun! Are you girls keeping up? Let's go!* he seemed to say. He panted, his spoon-shaped tongue lolling up and down. His oversize ears flicked back and forth. He snuffled and snorted through his pushed-in nose, and his round body rolled back and forth as he walked. Even serious Laura had to laugh at the French bulldog.

"Whew!" The girls took a minute to recover from the giggles. For a few minutes they chatted about their morning at school, how glad they were that summer vacation was beginning, and the gossip about their school friends' summer plans. Abby told everyone, several times, about her drama camp. Gisele was going to Girl Scout camp. Tori would be building her dog walking business and helping Min at the DSC, and both Laura and Tori planned to spend lots of time with their dogs and train them to do some fun tricks.

Then Laura dove into the main topic on their minds: the dog thief. "Who do you think it could be?" she asked. "How are they getting the dogs out of the shelter? And where are they taking the dogs?"

"Wellllll," said Tori, drawing out the l's to give herself time to think. But all she could say was, "I have no idea. Yet." She kicked absently at a small rock on the sidewalk. It spun away, startling Francois. "Sorry, Francois." She bent down and gave him a quick pat. "Ya know, I've noticed a blue van parked by the shelter sometimes, in the evenings, when my dad drives me home from the DSC. And yesterday, it just about hit us." Tori related yesterday's incident.

Laura scrunched her face in concern. "That sounds scary. Are you OK?"

"Yeah, now I am. I screamed a little bit, I admit." Tori lowered her voice. "Maybe the thief is the person who drives that van."

"Hmmm. Maybe," said Laura. "In murder mysteries, the culprit is always the person with motive, means, and opportunity. Motive is the why. Like maybe the criminal will inherit lots of money if the victim dies."

"Right," said Tori, thinking about the detective shows she watched on TV. "Means is the how. The murderer has a gun, or he can get ahold of poison, for example."

Laura continued. "Yeah, and opportunity is the way that the murderer can get to the victim. If the culprit knows that the victim will be all alone one night, and he has a key to the house, that's a good opportunity."

As they passed a small rundown apartment building, Tori noticed a dented gray minivan in the driveway. The tailgate was open and two empty plastic dog crates sat inside. Tori slowed and studied the crates. She took a step toward the car to see how the crates were tied down.

"Hey, wh . . . what are you doing?" The voice came from a tall skinny guy who was rummaging through a nearby dumpster. He looked about 18 or 19 years old. Not a boy, but not a man.

Tori jumped back. "Oh, sorry. Nothing. I was just interested in your crates. My dad and I are going to get one for our minivan. It looks a lot like yours."

The skinny guy started to walk toward the girls. He ran his palm over his buzz cut and scratched. Tori couldn't help staring at his nose. It formed a long thin zigzag down his face. She felt in her pocket for her new phone. It was programmed to call 911 with one push of a button.

But the skinny guy just passed by them on his way to the minivan and reached into it with one long tattooed arm. The words "Mac'n'Cheese" covered his forearm in a fancy font. He pulled one of the crates forward. With the other bony hand, he waved at the girls to come closer.

Tori and Laura shot each other concerned looks. "Umm, that's OK. We have to get going," said Tori. The girls and the little dog hurried down the sidewalk.

Laura glanced behind them. "He's not watching us. He went back to the dumpster," she said quietly.

They walked silently for a while. "I hate to say it, and I know we shouldn't judge people by how they look, but the dog thief could be someone like that guy, Mr. Mac'n'Cheese," said Tori.

"Mac'n'Cheese? Oh, yeah, the tattoo," Laura said. "Well, maybe. He acted kind of funny."

The old, dilapidated farmhouse that Tori had noticed during her first walk with Francois came into view. After the scary encounter with the skinny guy, maybe it would be nice to speak to the old woman who lived there. Tori told Laura about her.

"I thought that house was empty," said Laura. "It's the original farmhouse from before this part of town even existed. That's why it's different from all the other houses around here. The little kids think it's haunted."

"Shhhhh. There she is," whispered Tori.

The woman sat on the top porch step, her legs splayed out in front of her. She wore the same saggy blue jeans, oversized yellow t-shirt, and work boots Tori had seen her wear a few days ago. She took a sip from a coffee mug.

"Hi!" said Tori with a smile.

Laura echoed her. "Hi!"

The woman pushed her shortish gray hair out of her face and nudged her thick glasses further up the bridge of her nose. "Oh hi, girls," she said. "How are you?"

She's friendlier today, thought Tori. "We're great. How 'bout you?"

"Good. Good." She stood up, leaned back and twisted her torso back and forth, then on wobbly legs she walked down the steps. One hand gripped the coffee mug, the other the stair rail. "Is that your dog? I've seen you walking him recently."

"No, we're just walking him for one of your neighbors. She can't get around very well right now, so I'm helping her out."

"That's nice. My name is Marion, by the way. Do you girls have your own dogs at home?" Marion sipped her drink. The words "World's Best Mom" circled the mug.

"Yes, I adopted a dog from the shelter, and my friend Laura has a dog too. I'm Tori."

"I heard that someone has stolen dogs from the shelter, can you believe it?" said Marion. "A poodle and a beagle."

Tori stared at her. How did Marion know about that? Wasn't it supposed to be a secret? Tori wasn't sure what to say.

Laura came to her rescue. "Really? That's awful. How did you find out about it?"

Marion took a long sip from her mug, peered closely at its contents, then looked up. "I volunteer at the shelter."

Tori realized she had been holding her breath. She exhaled. "Oh, then you know Jordan."

"Yes," Marion said quickly. "I sure hope they don't blame him."

"Yeah," Tori agreed. She and Laura exchanged glances. Was it weird that Marion told them about the dogs? She probably shouldn't have. Jordan didn't want the public to know.

"I hope no more dogs get stolen," Laura said.

Marion nodded and took a step back. "Well, I better let you get on with your walk. Have a nice day!" She waved and sipped her drink as she watched the girls walk away.

Francois, who had been getting restless while the humans talked, eagerly led Tori and Laura down the sidewalk.

When Marion was out of earshot, Tori spoke. "I suppose it could be—whaddya call it—an *inside* job. For a while I thought Jordan was a little sketchy, but all my suspicions of him turned out to be wrong, like I told you before. And it's Jordan who told Min about the missing dogs. Although . . ." She hesitated.

"Although what?"

"Jordan is having money problems. I heard him say something about needing to raise money." Tori moved Francois' leash to her other hand.

"Ahhhh. Motive." Laura held up her index finger. "Maybe he plans to sell the dogs to raise money, even the small amount of money that a shelter dog might be worth. Although some shelter dogs *are* purebred, or they look purebred." She held up a second finger. "And maybe he has the means, a way to get to the dogs, because he might have a key to the building." She waggled three fingers in the air. "And he has opportunity, because he knows how the shelter works, like when no one will be inside so he won't get caught."

"But . . . Jordan?" Tori didn't want to think of Jordan as a dog thief. "I don't think so. He's Min's boyfriend. And Min would never date a criminal!" In Tori's mind, Min could do no wrong.

Laura wrapped her fingers into a fist and lowered her hand. "Ohhhh . . . I didn't know they were together. Well, let's keep him on our suspect list."

"Our suspect list? We have a suspect list?" Tori wrinkled her nose at Laura. She hadn't written down any suspects alongside the list of missing dogs in her notebook yet.

"Well, it's a short list. Just Jordan so far. And maybe Mac'n'Cheese. And maybe the guy who drives the blue van, whoever that is."

Francois stopped to sniff and pee on a telephone pole that was covered with old and new paper posters. They fluttered in the light breeze. Tori absently scanned the concert announcements, ads for gutter cleaning, lost cat notices, and . . .

She gulped. "Lost or Stolen" read the bright yellow poster. "German shepherd puppy. Six months old. Beloved family pet. Needs daily medications!" The dog in the photo looked like a younger version of Nick.

Bigger dogs were missing now. Not just small or medium dogs. Dogs almost as big as Nick.

With her eyes glued to the photo, Tori spoke to Laura. "Let's go to the shelter and look around. Tomorrow. They open at eleven. There won't be many people there in the early morning. Are you in?"

Laura's mouth fell open, and she stepped back to stare at her friend. Tori imagined what Laura was thinking. Yesterday, Tori had been reluctant to get involved. They were just kids, she had said. They couldn't do anything about stolen dogs.

Then Laura saw the poster. She looked at the photo of the German shepherd puppy, then at Tori's determined face. "I'm in," she said.

CHAPTER 27

"The game is afoot," said Laura, in an exaggerated English accent. At her side, Onyx raised her delicate nose and sampled the aromas in the crisp morning air.

"Shhhh. Quiet, Sherlock." Tori looked at her, one eyebrow raised. *Laura's really loosening up.* Next to her, Nick sniffed the overgrown grass and weeds that served as the front lawn of the shelter. The four of them stood on the sidewalk, facing the front door of the old building. To their right, the sun broke free of the horizon and began to warm the cool air.

Laura whispered, "Well, actually, that's a quote from a Shakespeare play, but everyone thinks it's from Sherlock Holmes." She tilted her head. "Sorry, I get chatty when I'm nervous."

And I thought I *was weird.* Tori adjusted her ponytail with one hand and glanced to her right, then to her left.

"We don't have to be quiet," Laura whispered. "The shelter's closed, and anyway, people walk their dogs around here all the time." Laura had tied her hair back into a ponytail too, and her curly chestnut hair fanned out behind her.

"Then why are you whispering?" whispered Tori. The girls' eyes met and they broke out laughing. Nick and Onyx stopped sniffing the weeds, turned their noses to their owners for a moment, then lowered their heads to the scent-filled weeds.

"What did you tell your dad?" asked Laura in her normal voice.

"The truth. Going for a long walk with Nick,'" said Tori. "Let's look around."

"What are we trying to find?" Laura squinted into the sun, shading her eyes with one hand.

Tori put a hand on her hip. "I thought *you* would have ideas, Ms. Mystery Expert."

Laura turned away from the rising sun and looked at Tori. "I like mysteries on paper. I've never investigated a *real* mystery. But maybe we'll know what we're looking for when we find it."

Tori gathered Nick's leash. "Well, OK. That's a plan. Sort of." She took a breath and headed east, with Nick beside her.

With their leashed dogs, the girls began to circle the old concrete-block building. Over the years, it had been painted several different colors so that now the peeling paint and chipped concrete created a kaleidoscopic effect. A thick layer of moss covered the roof. Remnants of the early morning rain dripped from broken gutters and downspouts.

A chain-link fence on the east, north, and west sides of the building created a fifteen-foot border that bristled with huge thorny blackberry bushes. No normal human would enter it, thought Tori. The prickly vines reminded her of alien monsters, reaching for and grabbing anything in their path.

Both girls wore jeans, rain jackets, and tall plastic rain boots. They took long, high steps through the wet tangle of grass and weeds outside the fence. Occasionally they had to stop and free themselves or their dogs from clingy blackberry vines that snaked along the ground.

They reached the back of the building. Nick pulled Tori toward a large hole in the fence. There were probably lots of mice living among the blackberries, thought Tori. Nick loved rodents. Tori didn't.

"Hey look, Laura. Someone's made a hole in the fence. And they trimmed the blackberries to make a trail to the building."

"Yes. And look at the window." Through the bushes, at the end of the trail, they could see a warped window that didn't fit properly in its frame. There was a gap of several inches in one corner. "If that window opens, I bet someone could get in and out pretty easily. And no one can see back here from the road."

While Laura held Nick, Tori ducked through the hole in the fence. She twisted and shimmied her way down the narrow trail lined with prickly berry bushes. A vine snagged her boot and she hopped on one foot as she pulled it away.

"Nice dance moves!" said Laura. "Look for clues. Like footprints. Or pieces of clothing stuck in the bushes. Can you reach the window?"

Tori scanned the wet ground under the window. Sure enough, footprints. Lots of them. Made by shoes with waffle-like soles. Her dad wore work boots with soles like that. She saw some smaller square impressions in the wet ground too. Tori couldn't think what they might be. "There are footprints here, all right."

"Try not to tromp all over them, OK?" called Laura.

"OK. I'll check the window."

The windowsill was right at Tori's eye level. She reached up, stuck her hands through the small open area, and tried to push up the window. "Ugh. It's too hard. At this angle, I can't push with any strength. You're taller. Wanna give it a try?"

The girls switched places. Laura was able to move the window up a fraction of an inch. "Oooof. If we had a ladder, we might be able to open it," she said. She studied the soft wet ground.

"Hey, I bet those square prints are from a ladder!" Laura fished her phone out of her pocket. "I'll take photos. All these prints are evidence. We can compare the prints to different ladders. And compare the bootprints to people's boots." She dug into her jacket pocket, pulled out a pencil, and placed the pencil beside a bootprint. She held her phone over some of the square prints and two different bootprints and snapped photos.

Laura made her way through the blackberry bushes and the fence to where Tori held the dogs. "What's the deal with the pencil?" Tori asked.

"It gives the bootprint some scale. It's hard to know how big the print is from the photo, unless there's something to compare it to, like the pencil."

The dogs had been snuffling in the weeds and pawing at the ground. They started to pull on their leashes toward the field behind the shelter. Their noses quivered as they picked up a scent. The girls turned to face the same direction.

A boy and a dog walked toward them. Tori noticed the dog first. It looked like a beagle, with the typical tan, white, and black coloring. The dog's nose hovered over the ground.

One of the missing shelter dogs is a beagle. Tori tried to remember what Jordan had said about the stolen beagle. Was it tan and white? Or did he say black, tan, and white? She couldn't remember.

Laura's attention went first to the boy. He wore a baseball cap, a tan rain jacket, and baggy blue jeans tucked into tall black rain boots. He held one end of a long leash and trailed his dog by about fifteen feet.

The boy was focused on his dog and hadn't seen the girls. Then Nick barked, his excited *I see someone who might pet me and give me a treat* bark, and the boy raised his head and spotted the girls. He stopped and stared at them for a moment, then he continued through the grassy field toward them.

"It's Mike, from school," Tori whispered. "Didn't he get into trouble for stealing? One of the stolen dogs is a beagle!"

"Oh, that's right!" Laura whispered back. She pursed her lips. "Let's see what he says. Shhhhh."

Laura ran one hand through her curly hair, pulled out a sticky piece of blackberry vine, and threw it behind her with a quick turn of her wrist.

Mike stopped about fifteen feet from the girls and reeled in the beagle. His eyes took in Nick and Onyx but avoided the girls. Laura spoke first. "Hi." She elbowed Tori in the ribs.

"Hi," said Tori. She glanced at Mike, then shifted her eyes back to Mike's dog.

"Hi," Mike said in a deep voice. He took off his Seattle Seahawks baseball cap, wiped his brow and ran a hand over his short, tightly curled black hair, then replaced the cap. Finally he looked up at the girls. "Is it OK for my dog to meet yours?" he asked.

Laura and Tori exchanged glances, silently asking each other, *Is that OK with you?* Tori nodded. "Sure," Laura said to Mike.

Mike and his dog stepped closer to the girls, and Nick, Onyx, and the beagle sniffed each other's rear ends. Their tails wagged softly back and forth. The beagle's wide brown eyes were rimmed with black, as though he wore eyeliner. His long jowls made his face look dignified, like an old English gentleman, thought Tori. He seemed perfectly comfortable with Mike.

"Whachya doin' here?" said the boy.

"Oh, nothing really. Just walking our dogs," said Laura. "You're Mike, right?"

"Yeah, and you're Laura and . . . Tori?" Mike gathered up most of the long leash. "This is Chase. We're practicing for a tracking test that's coming up soon. This is a good place to lay track."

Tori only knew of Mike from the cafeteria, where he sat at the music boys' table. He seemed different out here with a dog. She was surprised he knew her name. She searched his face, looking for . . . she didn't know what. Anything that didn't ring true, she supposed.

Tori finally found her voice. "This is Nick, and that's Onyx," she told Mike, indicating each dog.

"Beauties," Mike said simply. "Hey, Nick. C'mere boy." Nick's whole body wiggled and he curled into his new friend, asking for attention. A smile grew across Mike's face as he ran his hands down Nick's back. Tori noticed that his hands were big, almost man-size.

Onyx, not quite as outgoing as Nick, just watched from where she stood at Laura's side. Chase stared at Nick. When Nick returned to Tori, Chase instantly moved next to the boy, where Nick had been.

"What do you mean by *tracking*?" asked Laura. Her careful voice carried a hint of suspicion. *She's testing him,* thought Tori. *Is he really here to practice tracking? Or is he up to no good?*

Mike kept his eyes on Chase and, as he spoke, deliberately folded the long leash back and forth into one big hand. "I'm training Chase to follow a scent trail to find articles—that's something a person might drop, like a leather glove. We're working toward our Tracking Dog title." The words *Tracking Dog* came out in a high squeak. He cleared his throat, kneeled beside Chase, and checked the fit of the beagle's harness. Chase gazed at Mike's face with half-closed adoring eyes.

"Actually, Chase is a *trailing* dog. He uses both ground and air scent to find the article. Someday I want to work with search-and-rescue dogs to find lost people and . . ." Mike's voice faded and he looked up at the silent girls.

Tori and Laura stared wide-eyed at Mike. *He's as much of a dog nerd as we are,* thought Tori. The tension in her body drained away. Chase couldn't be the stolen shelter dog. The beagle had been stolen just a few days ago, and Chase and Mike had clearly spent a lot of time together training. They had a bond.

"Wow!" Laura's face lit up. Her wide smile showed off her perfect teeth. "I bet you're really good at tracking. I mean *trailing*." Her enthusiasm told Tori that Mike had passed her test.

Mike lowered his eyes and continued checking Chase's already perfectly fitted harness. "Uhhhhh . . . well, I'm just . . ."

The rumble of an approaching car engine and the grinding of shifting gears got too loud to ignore. Tori and Nick ran to the corner of the fence and peeked around it. The blue van! It was turning off the main road onto the shelter driveway that led to the small parking lot at the front of the building. "Laura! Look! It's that van I told you about."

Laura with Onyx joined Tori. Mike got to his feet, watched the girls, then walked over to them. "What's going on?" he asked.

"Shhhhh!" In unison, Tori and Laura shushed him. "Tell you later," whispered Tori. Finally, she would see who drove the blue van.

The girls and their dogs crept along the west side of the building toward the parking lot. Mike followed, whispering, "What the heck? And why am I whispering?"

"Shhhh!" said Laura. Mike sighed and followed the girls.

At the corner, peeking through the blackberry bushes, they saw the parked van. A man with a bushy black moustache wearing tan work clothes and big work boots exited the driver's side. He slammed the door shut, then opened the rear door of the van, pulled out a toolbox, and walked toward the east side of the building. He disappeared around the corner.

Uh-oh. He might walk all the way around the building—and maybe see us here! Watching the man walk through a muddy area gave Tori an idea. "Hey, let's go! Follow me!"

She bent over at the waist and ran through the parking lot, past the van, and stopped where the pavement ended at the east end of the lot. Laura and Mike followed, imitating her bent-over run. The dogs ran alongside them, just happy to be moving again and completely unaware of the reason.

"Why are we crouching? No one's shooting at us! We're not doing anything wrong!" whispered Mike. "And again, why am I whispering?"

Laura giggled. Tori flashed an annoyed glance at her. This was no time to act stupid just because a boy was with them. She scanned the dark wet earth around them, where van-man had just walked. "Laura, those bootprints." She pointed. "Do they match the ones in the photos?"

Laura nodded in understanding and pulled her phone out of her pocket. She tapped and swiped at the screen, then kneeled and held the phone near the bootprint. She placed her pencil alongside it. Her eyes met Tori's. "Yeah, I think so."

"It's him. It's the thief," said Tori. She felt her heartbeat accelerate.

Mike looked back at the van. "Uhhh . . . Tori . . . Laura . . . we have company."

The man had returned to his van from the west side of the building and spotted them. "Hi, kids. Everything OK?" His moustache bounced up and down as he talked.

"Yes." Tori called. She hoped van-man couldn't hear her pounding heart. She got to her feet. "We're just . . . just walking our dogs." Mike and Laura got up too and stood awkwardly. Laura held her phone behind her back.

Van-man smiled, nodded, and opened the rear door of the van. He pulled out a ladder.

Laura pointed at her phone, then at the ladder. Tori got the message. This was the guy.

The man reached into the van and picked up an electric drill. With the ladder in one hand and the drill in the other, he walked back toward the west side of the building.

"This is getting weird. You need to tell me what's going on," said Mike.

"OK. Let's walk our dogs, slowly, around to the back of the building," said Tori. She headed down the east side of the building and the others fell into step with her. As they walked, she and Laura quietly told Mike about the missing shelter dogs, the broken window, and the clues they had discovered. They turned left to walk along the back side of the building, keeping about fifty feet away from the perimeter fence.

Mike listened quietly, but when Tori and Laura finished their explanation, he shook his head and said, "Are you sure you know what you're doing? I mean, I really hope someone finds whoever is stealing dogs around here, but maybe you guys should let the *professional* detectives investigate. The police."

A small part of Tori wondered whether Mike wanted them to stop investigating because he had something to do with the stolen dogs. But then why would he suggest the police? She almost said, "Maybe you need to have a shelter dog, like Nick or Onyx, to understand why we're doing this." But maybe that was a mean thing to say. She didn't know much about Mike and Chase. Maybe he *would* understand.

Then, through the dense blackberry bushes, they spotted van-man standing on his ladder, working at the broken window with his tools.

"Looks like he's fixing the window, not breaking in," said Mike.

Another person rounded the far corner of the building and walked toward van-man. The spiky bleached-blond hair was unmistakable. Jordan!

Their voices were distant, but clear. "Hi, Juan. Thanks so much for coming out yesterday and today. We just discovered that broken window and wanted to get it fixed right away."

"No problem, Jordan. Let me know what else I can do around here. I can use the extra work."

"Well, we're fixing only the most important things. We hope to move to a new building soon."

The tension and excitement evaporated from Tori's body. "It's not him. The bootprints we found are from yesterday, when van-man was just looking at the window. And Jordan is here just 'cause he's working. Boy, I feel dumb."

"Well, we had good reason to suspect him, I think. We had good evidence," said Laura. "But yeah, I feel dumb too."

Mike rolled his eyes. "All right, well, this was fun," he said sarcastically. "But I gotta go. See you around. Maybe. C'mon Chase."

With long, sure strides, he walked away through the field where the girls had first seen him. Soon the vegetation swallowed Chase, so that all the girls could see of him was the white tip of his tail, waggling back and forth above the long, wet grass.

"Well, van-man is cleared. He's the shelter handyman," Laura said.

Tori watched Mike get smaller and smaller as he walked across the field. "Yeah, but now I'm wondering a little bit about Mike," Tori said slowly.

She and Laura looked at each other, then at Mike's shrinking figure.

"No. It's not him," Laura said firmly.

Tori pictured Chase's face as he gazed at Mike. "Yeah, you're probably right." The girls and dogs made their way through the grass and weeds to the front of the building. They couldn't do much more investigating today. "See you at the fun match tomorrow?" Tori asked.

"Yes," Laura replied. "See you at the fun match."

CHAPTER 28

Tori and Laura unrolled the huge canvas sign and spread it between two big oak trees at the park entrance. They attached it to the trees as high as they could. "MAPLE VALLEY DOG FESTIVAL!" it read.

"Thanks, girls! Take a break. You've been working hard," Jordan called to them from where he was unloading supplies from his pickup truck.

Tori and Laura smiled and waved at Jordan. *No, Jordan couldn't be the dog thief, could he?* thought Tori. Then she put the mystery of the missing dogs into a far back corner of her mind. There were too many other things to think about today.

The girls began to walk around the festival area. Big white shade canopies sprouted from the neatly cut lawn. The DSC was promoting dog training and hosting the agility fun match. Volunteers from the Franklin County Animal Shelter staffed an information booth and hoped to get contributions for the new building. They had brought some dogs and cats that were available for adoption. The Maple Valley Police Department K-9 Unit would be presenting a police dog demonstration. The local pet supply stores were setting up promotional booths with stacks of free product samples. A few independent dog trainers and veterinarians also had booths. Delicious aromas from a food truck floated through the air.

"My dad should be here by now with Nick. The fun match starts at ten. I better get over to the agility ring," said Tori.

"OK. I still need to help the DSC volunteers set up their booth, but I'll be sure to watch your run." Laura waved and headed toward a booth where a banner read "Maple Valley Dog Sports Center." Tori watched Laura, her springy dancer's walk making her long curly hair bounce on her shoulders. Tori tightened her skinny ponytail and sighed. She turned and walked toward the agility ring.

To create a temporary course in the park, Min and her volunteers had set up orange plastic fencing around the perimeter of an 80- by 100-foot area of relatively level lawn. They brought the jumps, tunnels, A-frame, dogwalk, see-saw, and other equipment from the DSC in trailers pulled by big pickup trucks.

It was easy to spot Min with her short black-and-pink hair. She stood near the agility ring, in front of a whiteboard that sat on a tall easel, and sorted through a stack of paper.

"Hi, Min." Tori peeked over Min's shoulder to see what she was doing.

"Tori! Can you help me post the gate sheets?" Min handed Tori the papers that listed the dog-and-owner teams who had entered the fun match, and Tori held them on the whiteboard as Min placed magnets on them. "You can check the gate sheet to see when you run," explained Min. She pointed out Tori's name on the list. "See? For the first run, you're after Harry. So plan to be near the ring and ready to run a few minutes before Harry and Gunnar go into the ring."

Tori nodded. The fun match started to seem real. And complicated. "Have you seen my dad?" she asked Min.

"Yes, he's over there." Min pointed to the minivan, parked under a large spreading oak tree about a hundred feet away, and Tori headed that way. "The walkthrough starts in about 15 minutes. Don't be late!" Min called after her.

Helping to set up the festival had been fun. Tori hadn't had time to get nervous. But now she felt a sharpness in her lungs and a slight churning in her stomach. Tori walked past her father, sitting in the minivan, on her way to the car's tailgate. "Hi, Dad."

"Oh, hi. Just finishing up a little work here." Dad sat in the passenger seat and kept his eyes on the computer in his lap. "Everything OK?"

"Yup. Just need to walk Nick."

Tori opened the tailgate. Nick's new crate faced the back of the car, and Tori smiled as she watched Nick through the metal grid of the crate door. His feet and nose twitched and his eyes fluttered underneath his eyelids as he napped. A cascade of tiny yips escaped from his mouth. *I'm so lucky to have him, the best dog in the whole world,* she thought.

"Sorry to wake you, boy. But we need to check the potty situation." Nick raised his head and his sleepy eyes found Tori. He watched her pull out the ramp Dad had made, a five-foot long wooden plank with a nonslip coating, and lean it against the car. It created a safe walkway from the car down to the ground.

Tori opened the crate door. Nick stood, put his front feet out the door and leaned back, elbows down, stretching the front part of his body. Then he stood tall on his front feet, head high, and stretched out his rear legs. Next, he shook his whole body, yawned, and licked Tori's face, including her glasses.

"Thanks for that, Nick." She took off her glasses and scrubbed off the dog drool with the hem of her t-shirt. "*You* don't look nervous at all."

Tori held out a hand and watched it tremble. Then she shook both arms, from her hands to her shoulders, took a deep breath, and let it go. "Wheeeew." She clipped the leash onto Nick's collar, and Nick walked carefully down the ramp.

Tori led Nick around the grassy area between the car and the agility ring and waited for him to do his business. Nick took his time, sniffing every blade of grass. Tori couldn't help glancing toward the agility ring every few seconds. She didn't want to miss the walkthrough.

Finally, Nick found just the right spot. "Good job, Nick," said Tori, and pulled a plastic bag from her pocket, picked up his poop, and deposited it into a trash can.

"Sorry, you've got to wait in the car for a little while. The sun's starting to heat things up, but the car will stay nice and cool under this big tree. I'll be back and then we'll run a course." Nick climbed up the ramp and into the car, ducked into his crate, and circled and scratched at his blanket before settling down. He licked his paws lazily. "See ya later. I love you." Tori couldn't help but take an extra few seconds just to admire him before closing the tailgate and heading toward the agility ring.

She passed her father again. "Gotta do the walkthrough," she said.

"OK. Hey, wait up." Dad closed the computer, set it on the floor, and opened the car door. He stepped out and stretched his body forward and back. "Oooof, I'm getting old," he said, mostly to himself. Tori smiled. His movements reminded her of how Nick stretched.

"How can I help?" asked Dad. "Do you need anything?"

"You can come and watch. The walkthrough won't be very exciting though."

Tori waited, shifting from one jittery leg to the other, while Dad locked the car. They walked toward the ring where several people worked at adjusting obstacles and placing cross bars on jumps. "Hey, who set up all the equipment?" asked Dad.

"Min organized the match. Volunteers do all the setting up and work in the ring. I think they're mostly students and their families and friends. I helped set up, earlier today."

Dad stopped at the edge of the group of people gathered near the ring. "I'll just hang out here," he said. That was OK with Tori. She wasn't used to important events like this, much less having her dad there watching her.

Nick—or Tori, for that matter—had never played agility outside of the DSC barn or Tori's backyard. So even though they both knew what to do for each obstacle, it seemed like an entirely different sport here in the park, with all the activity, noise, and people. And smells. Soooo many smells. On top of that, no treats were allowed in the ring. Nick had to wait until they finished the course and exited before he got his reward.

Tori joined the dog owners who gathered near the in-gate. She greeted those she knew from class at the DSC, but others were strangers. There were even a few other girls and boys her age. She hoped she looked athletic in her new blue running shoes and black pants with white stripes on the sides. Dad had let her use his credit card to order them. She wore a blue DSC t-shirt that Min had given her.

"Hey Tori, did you get a map?" Harry, from her agility class, handed her a small piece of paper.

"Thanks, Harry." The map showed the course as it would look from above, if you flew a drone over it. With her finger, she traced the path that Nick was supposed to follow, from jump 1 through jump 20. Twenty obstacles! In class, they practiced only a few obstacles at a time. Tori had never tried to run 20 obstacles without stopping. Between jumps 1 and 20, she would need to direct Nick through two tunnels, across the A-frame and dogwalk, over more jumps, through a set of 12 weave poles, and across a see-saw. All in the correct order. Yikes! Every skill that she and Nick had learned over the past few months would be tested in this one course.

Tori raised her eyes from the map and noticed, as though for the first time, all the people milling about, either waiting to run the course or to watch others run it. Lots of people. And they would be watching her and Nick. She fought the wave of panic that coursed through her body.

She remembered Min's advice: Think positive. *We can do it,* Tori told herself, even as her stomach tightened and her throat went dry. *Nick and I are a team. We can do it.*

"Handlers, the course is open for walkthrough!" announced Min. Tori was surprised to be called a dog *handler* along with all the adults. It seemed like a very grown-up thing to be. She followed the group into the ring.

Because this was just a fun match, no one was keeping score and there would be no winner or second place or third place. Some handlers wouldn't even run the numbered course laid out for them, but instead would train a particular skill or make up a course of their own. Min had suggested that Tori try running the numbered course—it would be good practice, she said. That's what a fun match was for. "OK. What could possibly go wrong?" Tori had joked, making her and Min laugh.

But now, faced with reality, Tori considered making up her own course—the easiest path she could think of. To heck with challenging herself. But . . . she thought about her dad, watching her run at a match for the first time, and she wanted to be the best team to run the course. Or at least *try* to be the best team. She decided to follow the numbered course.

CHAPTER 29

Tori tried to remember Min's advice on how to walk a course. *First time around, focus on memorizing the order of the obstacles and the patterns they make.* As she walked the course, Tori checked all the numbers and figured out that obstacles 1 through 9 were in the shape of a big circle. Ten through 14 made a smaller, oval-shaped circle in the middle of the course. Then 15 through 20 formed a medium-size semi-circle. She checked the map to make sure she hadn't missed anything.

The second time Tori walked the course, she thought about strategy. The first four jumps led more or less directly toward the dogwalk. But it was almost 100 feet between jump 1 and the dogwalk. Tori knew she wouldn't be able to run alongside Nick for that distance. He was too fast and she was too slow.

She decided to try a leadout. She would ask Nick to sit in front of the first jump and wait while she walked up to jump 3. Then she would call "break" to release him, and both of them would run. That way, they would arrive at the dogwalk at about the same time. She told herself to remember to cue Nick to stop at the end of the dogwalk contact zone.

Jumps 6 and 7, the tunnel, and jump 9 made a long line back toward the beginning of the course. Tori watched a few other handlers walk it. She noticed that they planned to send their dogs away from them, toward jumps 6 and 7, while the handlers took a shortcut and ran directly from the dogwalk to the tunnel. Tori thought about whether that strategy would work with Nick. She had practiced similar sequences, so she decided it was worth a try.

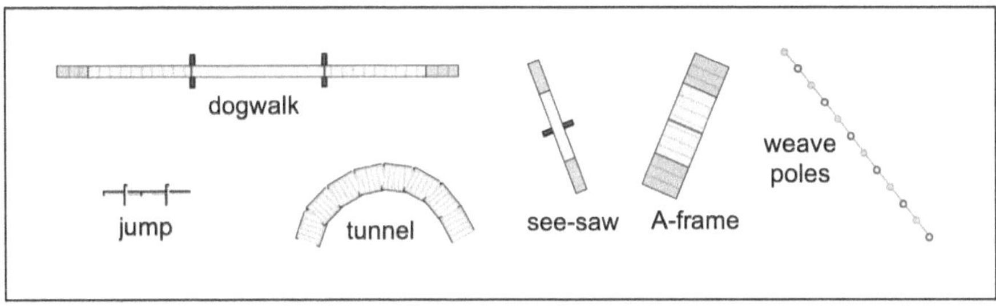

Key to Map

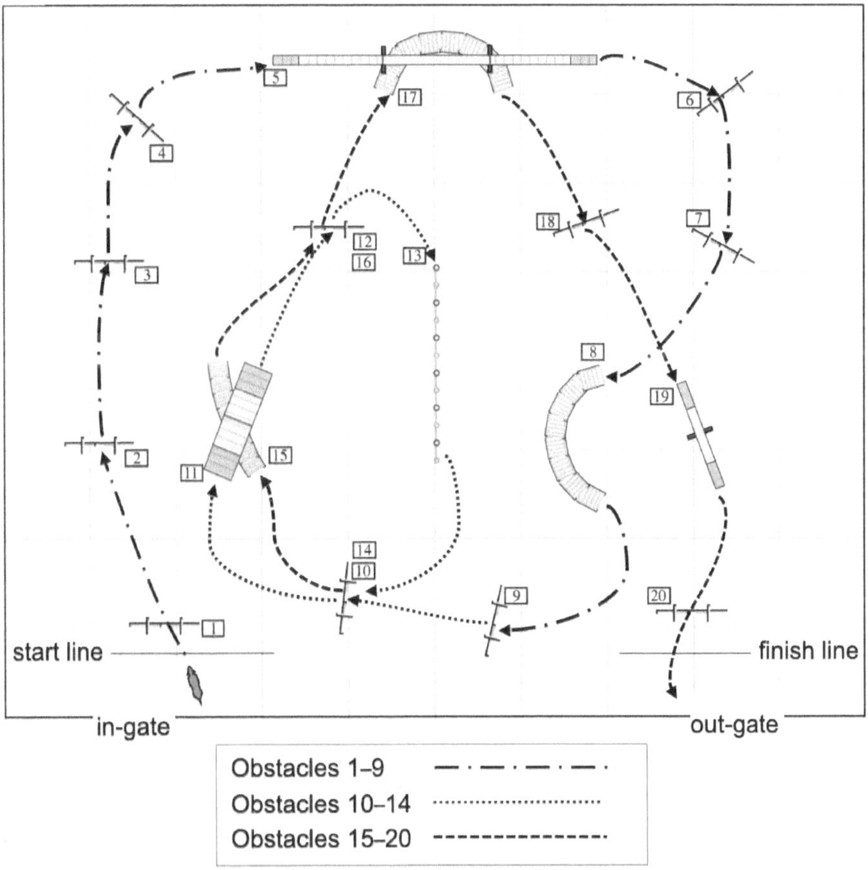

Map of First Course at Fun Match: Nick's Path

To stay on the inside curve of the line that obstacles 6 through 9 made, the 8 tunnel should be on her left. That seemed odd because the tunnel curved away from her. She wasn't used to that. But it would give her the shortest route to jump 9. She planned to check with Min about that idea later.

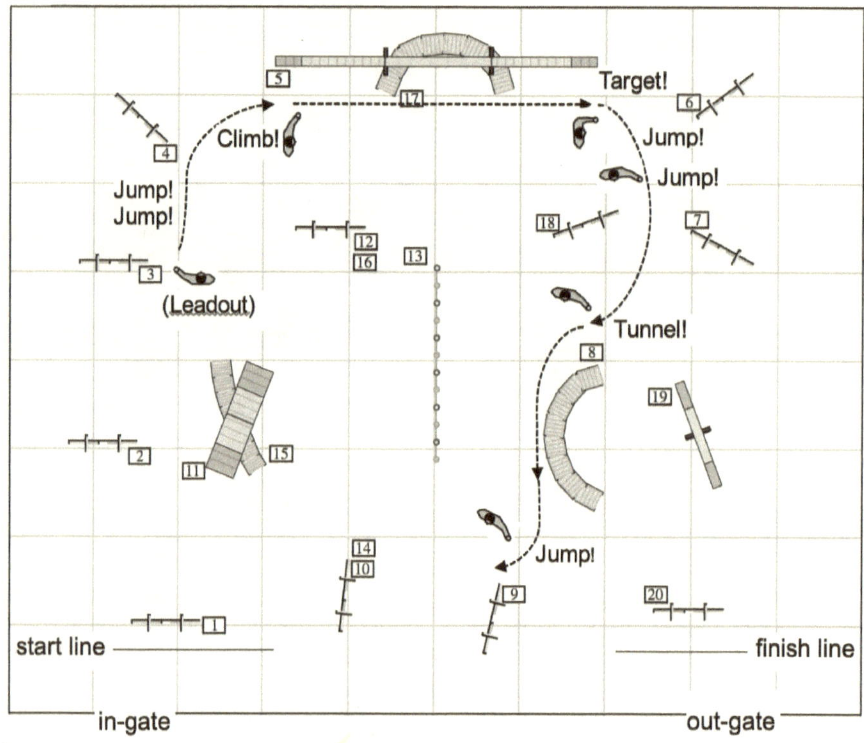

Tori's Path: Obstacles 1–9
First Course at Fun Match

The next tricky spot was the A-frame. The off-course tunnel entrance was right next to it. Tori had learned in class that a situation like this was called a *discrimination.* It was her job to clearly tell her dog which obstacle to do. Dogs tend to take the most obvious obstacle, especially when their handlers are slow! Tori told herself to run like heck toward the A-frame and say

Nick's A-frame cue early so he wouldn't take the tunnel. Nick loved tunnels. Then she had to remember to say Nick's running contact cue—*run, run, run!*—for the A-frame.

After jump 12, Nick needed to turn right toward the weaves, so Tori planned to call "jump right." She would trust him to enter the weaves correctly, with the first pole to his left, and keep going through all the poles.

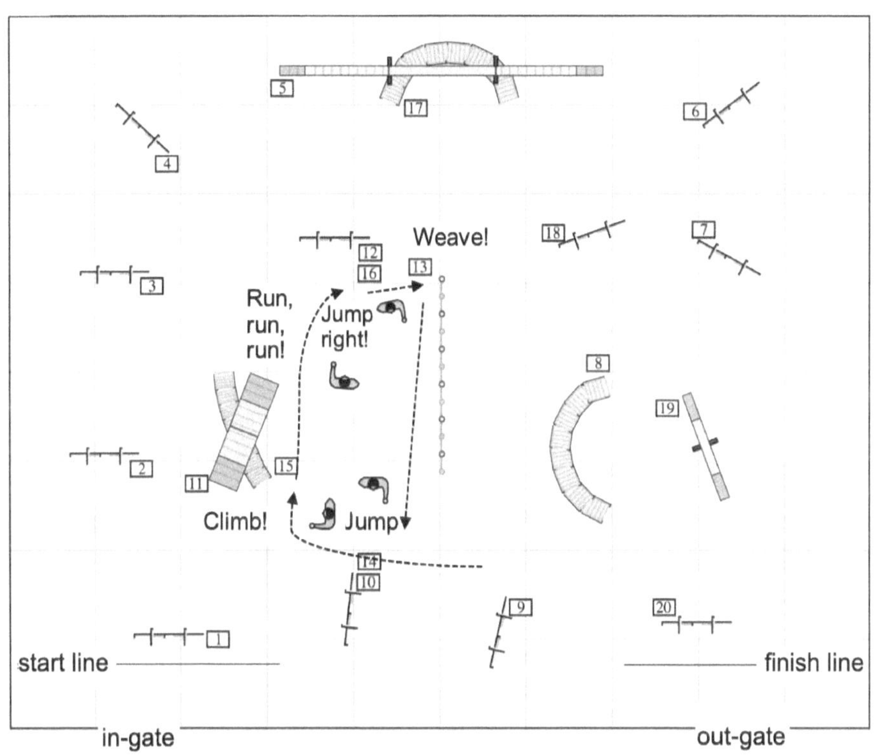

Tori's Path: Obstacles 10–14
First Course at Fun Match

After the weaves, obstacles 14 through 20 formed a big semi-circle. That would be a lot of running unless she could send Nick away from her to the 17 tunnel. That way, she wouldn't have to run all the way up to the tunnel entrance.

Nick knew to always stop at the end of the see-saw, so that should be no problem. Then there was just one last jump. *We got this,* Tori told herself. It was easy to say those words, but it was hard to believe them.

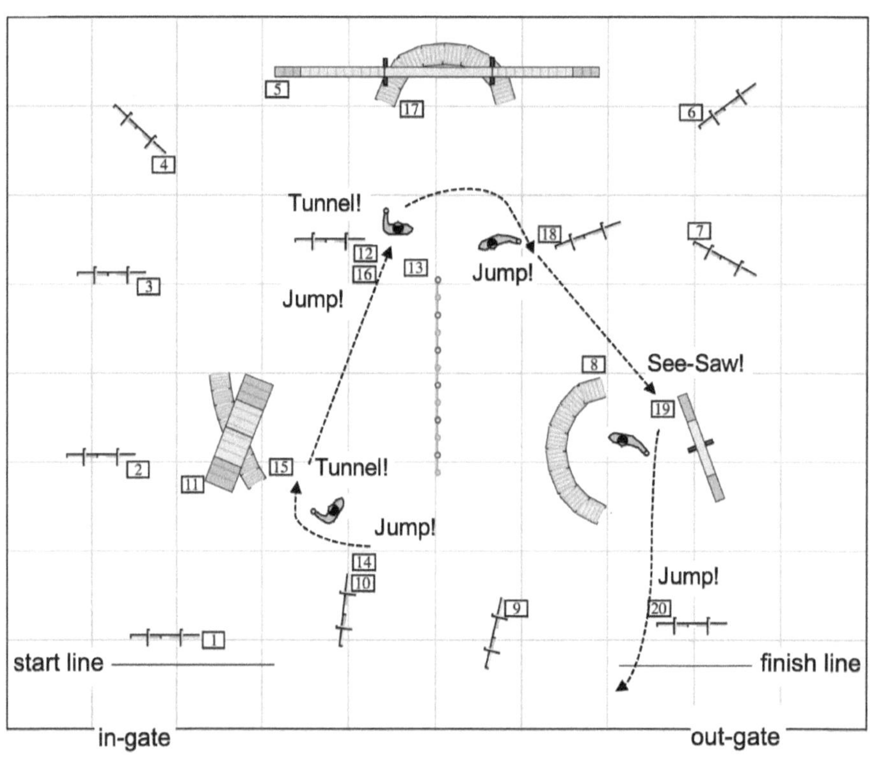

Tori's Path: Obstacles 15–20
First Course at Fun Match

"Time's up!" called Min from outside the ring. "Let's get ready to run, folks!" Everyone started toward the gates, taking last looks over their shoulders at the trickier parts of the course.

What? Walkthrough is over already? Tori walked backward toward the out-gate. She muttered her cues as her eyes followed the course . . . *jump, climb . . . run, run, run . . . jump right, weave* . . . She was the last handler out of the ring.

In the waiting area, Tori found Min and told her how she planned to run the course. "Sounds good," said Min. "We've covered all those skills in class, so this is your chance to combine them into one big course. I know it's hard to do in a strange place with an audience, but if you want to compete you need to get used to it. And to get used to it, you just have to do it, right? Just try. Do your best. You don't have to be perfect!"

Tori nodded. Her stomach turned somersaults. *We got this*, she told herself again.

The first handler arrived at the in-gate with his dog. Min's job as gatekeeper was to make sure everyone lined up and was ready to enter the ring on time. Tori studied the list of handler and dog teams. She had a few minutes to watch others run the course before she needed to get Nick. She found an out-of-the-way spot with a good view of the course. Her dad materialized from the crowd of handlers and dogs and stood tall at her side, hands in pockets. Even though they didn't touch one another, she sensed his warm strength. She sidled closer to him, hoping that some of his calm energy would seep into her.

First to run was a tiny Chihuahua with her rather large handler. The contrast made a few in the crowd chuckle. But, as the little dog raced through the huge course, the laughs turned to oohs and aahs. A perfect, fast run, and both dog and handler clearly had a blast.

A few handlers chose to use their time to train. One asked his dog to run over the dogwalk and A-frame a few times and rewarded the dog by throwing a favorite toy. Another focused on the weave poles.

A small terrier completely ignored his handler and zoomed around the ring, avoiding all the obstacles. He even ran up to a volunteer who sat on a chair in the ring, jumped into her lap, and tried to lick her face. Finally he ran back to his handler, who managed to get the little dog to go over the last jump and exit the ring.

Several more handlers did what Tori planned—try to get through the whole course as numbered. Tori noticed that if their dogs did make a mistake, they usually didn't make a big deal about it. They let the dogs believe that everything they did was correct! Even if they repeated a particular obstacle or sequence of obstacles for practice, they kept their words and actions positive. Min had talked about those ideas in her lessons, and now Tori recognized them in real life. She tucked away the images in her mind. That's the kind of handler she wanted to be.

"Hi!" Laura appeared at her side, breathing hard. "I didn't miss your run, did I?"

Tori, lost in her thoughts, gave an involuntary surprised yelp. "Aack!" She had lots to do before she and Nick entered the ring. "Hi Laura! I've got to warm up Nick. You'll video us, right?" She was already jogging to the car before Laura could answer.

Tori opened the tailgate and set up Nick's ramp. "Hey, Nick, time to warm up." Nick stretched forward and backward, shook his whole body from side to side, and lazily walked down the ramp. He sniffed the grass while Tori got her treat bag and closed the car.

Tori clipped her treat bag to her waist, prompting Nick to give her his full attention. He loved his treats. They walked and trotted in big circles, then she guided him through the warmup routine she had learned from Min. Tori delivered treats to Nick as she asked him to walk backwards, sideways like a crab, move from a sit to a stand several times, then from a down to a stand, and then gently bend his body left and right. She forced herself not to rush him through the exercises, even though her racing heart told her otherwise.

"Are you ready to run, big guy?" Tori exhaled. "Wheeew. Not sure I am." They walked to the in-gate, where Laura and Dad waited. She gave her father a quick nervous smile. Sweat began to ooze from every pore in her body. Her glasses slid down her slippery nose and she prodded them back into place.

"Harry and Gunnar are on course now. You're next!" said Min.

"Video ready," said Laura. She held up her phone to show Tori.

Tori nodded and handed Laura her treat bag—no treats were allowed in the ring. She tried to think about the course, but her mind was cluttered with mental videos of other teams running the course differently from her plan. Maybe watching others run before her turn wasn't such a good idea.

Harry and Gunnar completed the last jump and headed to the out-gate.

Min's voice sliced through Tori's thoughts. "Tori and Nick, you're up!"

CHAPTER 30

"Good luck, Tori!" called Dad.

"You got this," said Laura. She aimed her phone at Nick and stared at the screen.

Tori and Nick entered the ring. The sunshine felt so good earlier in the day, but now it seared her skin and stabbed her eyes. Nick sniffed at the grass and tried to pull Tori in every direction except toward the start line. "Nick, c'mon!" she whispered urgently and tugged at his leash.

They reached the start. "Sit," Tori said. She unclipped his collar and tossed it and the leash behind her.

Nick sat at her left side, but his head swiveled back and forth and up and down as he took in all the sights and smells—the fresh grass, churned up from the dogs that had already run, the food carts, the people and dogs, and a million other things that Tori couldn't even imagine.

Tori walked forward, following the line of jumps on her left. She reached jump 3 and looked over her shoulder.

It is SO quiet out here. Where Tori stood, far from the chatter of the other competitors and onlookers, an eerie silence blanketed the course. In the unexpected solitude, an inner voice, the voice that said *I have no idea what I'm doing*, rose and swelled, threatening to ruin everything. Tori shoved it down and focused on the dog waiting—far, far away, it seemed—at the start line.

"Break!" she called. Nick stood, then turned and trotted back toward the gate, nose to the ground. *Oh, no! My fault. If only I hadn't hesitated . . .* "Nick! Nick! Jump!"

At Tori's call, Nick raised his head and turned it toward her. He seemed to consider his options: sniff or run? Then he took one last quick sniff, turned, leaped over jump 1, and raced toward Tori. *He chose ME!* thought Tori.

She took off.

Tori felt her new shoes dig into the soft earth as she ran up the line toward the dogwalk. "Jump! Jump!" Nick flew over jumps 2 and 3 . "Climb!" Tori heard him, a few steps behind her, as he navigated the dogwalk—*thump, thump, thump* across the narrow wooden planks.

Nick stopped at the end of the dogwalk, front paws on the grass, rear paws on the yellow end of the board, and touched his nose to the ground. He fixed his golden eyes on Tori. *Look at me! I know exactly what you want me to do here!* his eyes told her.

"Good boy!" Tori wanted to celebrate, to raise her arms or dance a silly dance. But she made her mind work. While Nick waited for his cue, she looked ahead to the next line of obstacles. *Send Nick away to the jumps. I head to the tunnel,* she reminded herself.

"Break! Jump!" Tori motioned Nick toward jump 6 and began to run toward the tunnel. She glanced to her left. Uh-oh. Instead of continuing toward the jump, Nick had decided to follow her! Tori turned around and tried to redirect Nick over jumps 6 and 7.

But Nick put his nose to the ground. *Hmmm . . . there's a really delicious smell way over there . . . just give me a minute . . .* He followed the scent trail of who-knows-what all the way out to the fence.

"Nick, c'mon! Let's go!" Tori begged. Her hopes for a great run, or even a run that wasn't embarrassing, started to evaporate.

Finally, Nick lifted his head. *Where am I?* He looked around as though surprised to discover that he was in the middle of an agility course.

Well, jump 6 is a lost cause, thought Tori. *On to jump 7.* "Jump! Tunnel!"

Nick sailed over the jump, then saw the tunnel entrance ahead. *Oh boy, a tunnel!* He picked up speed, and Tori forced her legs to move faster.

Nick charged into the tunnel. It wobbled from side to side as he galloped through. Tori wanted to be at the tunnel exit in time to call him to jump 9. She pumped her arms as she sprinted past the shaking tunnel. "Nick! Right! Right! Jump!"

Nick glanced at her and followed her motion toward jump 9. His glistening eyes and open-mouth grin said, *Just tell me what to do, and I'll do it the best I can!*

Tori relaxed. *Whew. That worked. All is not lost.* Then she remembered the A-frame and tunnel discrimination coming up. "Climb! Climb!" She accelerated toward the A-frame.

Nick ignored the off-course tunnel and headed straight to the A-frame, just as he was supposed to! His paws hit the wooden plank. *Thumpity, thumpity, thumpity.* He was a black and tan rocket soaring over the peak. Tori practically heard him thinking *Whooooo! This is fun!* and her heart soared with him.

"Run, run, run!" she called. Nick's front paws, then his rear paws, hit the yellow contact zone and he raced to jump 12.

Tori reveled in Nick's perfect A-frame contact for a split second too long. Too late, she remembered that after jump 12, Nick needed to turn right. He was already over the jump and sprinting toward tunnel 17 before "jump right" came of her mouth. His paws on the thick sides of the tunnel sounded like thunder.

Tori froze, for just a moment. *What should I do? Uhhhh . . . we can still get to the weaves.* Then she ran to her right, positioned herself near the first weave pole, and turned so that her feet pointed down the row of poles. Nick's shining eyes searched for her as he exploded out of the tunnel. "Nick, here! Weave! Weave!"

Tori extended her arm toward the first pole, but Nick had gained so much speed in the tunnel that he couldn't collect himself in time to weave around it. Instead, he entered the row of weave poles between the third and fourth poles. Tori didn't have the energy to stop him and start over, so she let Nick continue weaving. *OMG. This is a train wreck. Now I just want to get out of this ring.*

"Jump! Tunnel! Jump! Tunnel! Jump!" Nick took obstacles 14 through 18 perfectly. But Tori was too far behind him to motion him toward the see-saw. She called, "SeeeeSaaaw!" But Nick saw the tunnel entrance and darted into it instead. *Another off-course. Just head for the finish and get the heck out of here.* "Go on! Go on! Jump!" She cued Nick for the last jump and sprinted, arms pumping, to catch up.

Nick leaped over jump 20, then turned and trotted to Tori, his eyes sparkling, his mouth open in a goofy grin. *That was fun!* his eyes said. *Do I get treats now?*

"Good boy." Tori bent over, put her hands on her knees, and gulped the warm air. A volunteer worker handed Nick's collar and leash to her, and she clipped the collar around Nick's neck and gave him a pat. Nick panted and pranced beside her, head up and eyes fixed on Tori's face, as they walked to the out-gate. Tori stared at her feet as they took her out of the ring. She heard a smattering of applause, as though from far, far away.

Tori heard Min call to her from the in-gate. "Nice run, Tori!"

"Woo-hoo! Beautiful!" Laura chimed in.

Her dad, waiting near the out-gate, gave her a clumsy pat on the shoulder. "Great job, Tori!"

Tori fought her tears. She had wanted Dad to see Nick and her play agility at a trial, but not like this. She had embarrassed herself and her dad. Maybe she just wasn't cut out to be an agility handler. "What do you mean?" she grumbled. "That was awful. I mean *I* was awful. *Nick* did his best."

"I thought you did great. Everybody makes mistakes. I've made lots of them," Dad replied. "Think about all the *good* things you and Nick just did."

"You're my dad. You have to say that." Tori muttered. Then she remembered Nick's perfect dogwalk and A-frame contacts and the joy on his face as he raced through the course. "I'm sorry. Yeah. You're right." She tried to smile. Dad was doing his best, just like Nick.

She kneeled in front of Nick and placed her forehead against his. Nick whined, and he reached toward Tori's cheeks to lick her sweat and tears. His fluffy tail wagged softly, the golden feathers waving in the light breeze. Tori straightened and searched Nick's eyes. Nick grinned and licked her nose. *I had so much fun with you!* he seemed to say.

Nick's magic began to work on her. She felt her mouth stretch into a small smile. "I better give Nick his reward and cool him down," Tori told her father. "Thanks for being here, Dad."

"There's nowhere else I would rather be today," replied Dad. "Go ahead, take care of your teammate."

Laura hovered nearby. Tori figured she was giving her some alone time with Dad. And with Nick. They had talked about how important it was to praise and reward your dog after training or competing. Laura gave her a small wave. Tori mouthed "thanks" to her friend and led Nick to the car.

She opened the car door and pulled out Nick's special end-of-run treat—a small container of roast chicken—and found a shady spot under the oak tree. She handed him bits of the meat. "Here ya go. You did good, buddy." As far as Nick knew, they had run perfectly. Tori's trembling hands and legs and her aching lungs started to work properly.

"You jumped great, and your contacts were perfect. You took the A-frame instead of the tunnel, just like you were supposed to. You didn't go to the jump after the dogwalk because I turned too quickly, right? Thanks for the feedback. I'll do better next time."

She held the empty container low so Nick could lick it clean. "Wish Dad would let you lick our dishes at home. That would save a lot of work." Tori began to walk Nick in big slow circles to cool him, and herself, down.

Tori saw Laura and waved her over. Laura joined her under the spreading branches of the big oak tree. "Do you want to see the video?" asked Laura.

Tori managed a weak smile. "Sure. How bad can it be?"

Laura held her phone so both she and Tori could see the screen, and pressed play. Tori watched silently. When it ended, she said, "Ya know, it's not as bad as I thought. Nick looked really good most of the time."

Laura nodded. "Yeah. *Both* of you were good. It was your first run at a match! You did better than a lot of the adults."

Tori smiled—a genuine smile this time. "Thanks." She bent over and patted Nick's side.

Laura slid her phone into a pocket. "I've got to tell you something," she said. "Remember Mac'n'Cheese, that scary guy we saw while we were walking Francois?"

Tori straightened and stiffened, and she met Laura's eyes.

"Tori, he's here."

CHAPTER 31

"I saw him when I was helping at the DSC booth." Laura told Tori. "He was kind of far away, but I could see that he was acting weird. He was staring at some dogs, but from a distance, like he doesn't want anyone to notice him. And he's carrying a big plastic bag."

"Really? He had dog crates in his car, that time we saw him. Maybe . . . maybe he's the dog thief. Maybe he's going to steal a dog today, from the festival." Tori thought for a moment. "What kind of shoes was he wearing?"

"Shoes? Oh, the prints under the window. Yes, there were a couple different sizes, weren't there? Juan's and someone else's," Laura said. She paused. "Hmmm . . . I'm not sure what Mac'n'Cheese is wearing. Come on, let's find him."

Tori put Nick into his crate in the back of the minivan. Nick seemed glad to settle into the cool car and rest. She locked it and scanned the area for her dad.

Dad wasn't hard to spot in the crowd around the agility ring. He towered over almost everyone else. Tori and Laura walked to the ring and found him deep in conversation with Harry, Gunnar's owner.

"Dad, Laura and I are going to walk around the festival during the break, OK? Nick's in the car and it's locked."

"OK, have fun," Dad said. "I'll be here. Maybe I can help Min somehow. Call me if you need anything. You've got your phone, right?"

Tori blinked. *Dad's volunteering to help with the fun match?* She hadn't expected him to get so involved.

"Yeah, got it." Tori waved her phone at her dad as she and Laura headed away from the agility ring toward the festival information and vendor booths.

Tori couldn't help glancing over her shoulder. *Am I hallucinating?* Nope. In his carpenter's pants, plaid shirt, and work boots, her father looked out of place among the dog handlers in their athletic gear. But he was there. She smiled to herself.

Tori and Laura walked quickly, scanning the shade canopies and booths for Mac'n'Cheese. "Tori?" said a voice. Tori turned.

Marion, the older woman the girls had met while walking Francois, approached them. She wore the same old, baggy clothes. Tori wanted to be polite, but she also wanted to find the skinny guy. She and Laura stopped. "Oh hi, Marion," said Tori.

"Hi, Marion," said Laura. "Are you volunteering at the animal shelter booth?"

"The shelter? No, I don't have anything to do with . . ." Marion glanced toward the animal shelter information booth. "No. I just wanted to watch the agility." Marion turned to Tori. "I saw you run with your dog. He's beautiful. German shepherd, right?" Marion stood in front of the girls, blocking their path. She smiled, and Tori noticed for the first time that she was missing one of her front teeth.

"Well, yeah, sort of." Tori tried not to look at the blank spot in Marion's smile. She let her eyes scan the festival grounds behind Marion.

"Shelter dogs are the best, aren't they? I used to have a dog." Maron's smile broadened, and behind her thick glasses her eyes blinked and crinkled.

"Oh, that's nice," Tori replied. It was getting harder to ignore Marion's missing tooth. "Would you excuse us though? We're looking for someone." Marion nodded, and the girls stepped around her and continued walking.

Laura leaned over to Tori. "Something's off about Marion, did you notice? I wonder whether . . ."

Then Laura ran—literally—into Abby and Gisele from school. They were staring down at their phones as they walked, and they bumped right into her and Tori.

"Hey, watch where you're . . . oh hi, Laura," said Abby. She re-wrapped her red silk scarf around her neck and tossed her black hair. Her eyes scanned Tori from her ponytail down to her new running shoes and back to her DSC t-shirt. She sneered, "Hi, *To-ri*. What are *you* doing here?"

Laura jumped in. "I'm just looking around. But Tori is running her dog in the dog agility match." Laura pulled in a sharp breath and looked at Tori. She mouthed "sorry."

Tori frowned at Abby. She didn't want to hear Abby's sarcasm today, of all days.

"Wow, really?" squeaked Gisele. "Can we watch?"

"Uhhh . . . yeah, sure, I guess so." Tori focused on Gisele and ignored Abby. She checked the time on her phone. "They're starting again in about 15 minutes." The last thing Tori wanted was more people watching her. The disappointment and embarrassment of her first run still hurt, even though everyone had reminded her of the good parts of their performance. Being polite could be very inconvenient, she thought. And time consuming.

Gisele looked right at Tori. "I'm trying to convince my parents to get a dog," she said quietly. "You're so lucky!"

"Yeah." Tori smiled at Gisele. She remembered being envious of everyone with a dog, not so long ago. "I've got to walk the course and warm up Nick, so I better get back to the ring."

"OK. Good luck! See ya," Gisele said with a smile.

"Yeah. Good luck with your dog, To-ri," said Abby.

Gisele grabbed Abby's arm and pulled her away. She gave Tori a small wave. Then she spoke to her cousin. "Abby, what . . ."

Tori turned toward Laura and rolled her eyes, but Laura was focused on a booth about thirty feet away. "There's Mike," Laura said in a low voice, and pointed with her chin.

Tori's eyes found Mike. "Oh, my gosh. We're never going to find Mac'n'Cheese if we keep having to talk to people. Ignore him."

They headed in the other direction, toward the agility ring. "Isn't it kind of funny that he showed up at the shelter the other day, and now here, where there are lots of dogs? Some valuable dogs too," said Laura. "And he's stolen before. Although we don't know what."

"It's scary to think it could be almost anyone," said Tori. Worry, like a blackberry vine, snaked its way into her brain. She craned her head to see over and around the crowd and toward the agility ring and the minivan parked nearby. Her father was nowhere in sight. She broke into a run.

Tori pressed her nose against the car window, searching for any sign of her dog. There was no movement in the crate. She pulled the car key out of her pocket and opened the tailgate. And sighed with relief.

Nick raised his head, his half-closed eyes found Tori, and his tail thumped against the crate floor. "Nick! I guess I didn't have to worry about you after all." Tori dropped a few small pieces of hot dog through the crate door. Nick scooped them up. "I'll be back for you after the walkthrough, buddy." She closed the door, locked it, and the girls headed toward the agility ring.

"Hi, girls. Did you have fun?" her father asked. He, Min, and Harry stood near the whiteboard at the in-gate.

Fun? The heat began in Tori's stomach, rose through her throat, and reached her face, flushing her cheeks red. She hadn't told Dad about her and Laura's investigations. But they weren't in any *real* danger, she told herself. They were just looking around. If they discovered anything definite, she would tell Dad.

CHAPTER 32

Tori picked up a map from the table and studied it. The obstacles were in about the same positions as they were for the first run, but the numbers had been changed. She checked the gate sheet and found her name among the first group of teams. No time to watch others run this course. Just as well—watching other teams had just confused her last time!

"Hey, Tori! What's your plan for this run? Need any help?" Min's cheery voice interrupted Tori's thoughts.

"Oh hi, Min. Wellll . . ." Tori remembered Min's lessons about learning courses. "This time, I'm going to walk around the course at least four times and focus on something different each time."

"Good idea."

"Annnnd . . . I'm going to try to forget about the dumb things I did during the first run!"

"Hey, don't be too hard on yourself! Your first run was fine! But starting with a clean slate is a good idea too. Obsessing about past mistakes won't help. *Learning* from them will. At your next lesson, we'll talk about what you learned today, OK?"

When the handlers entered the agility ring for the walkthrough, Tori was at the front of the pack. If she wanted to walk through the course at least four times, she needed a head start.

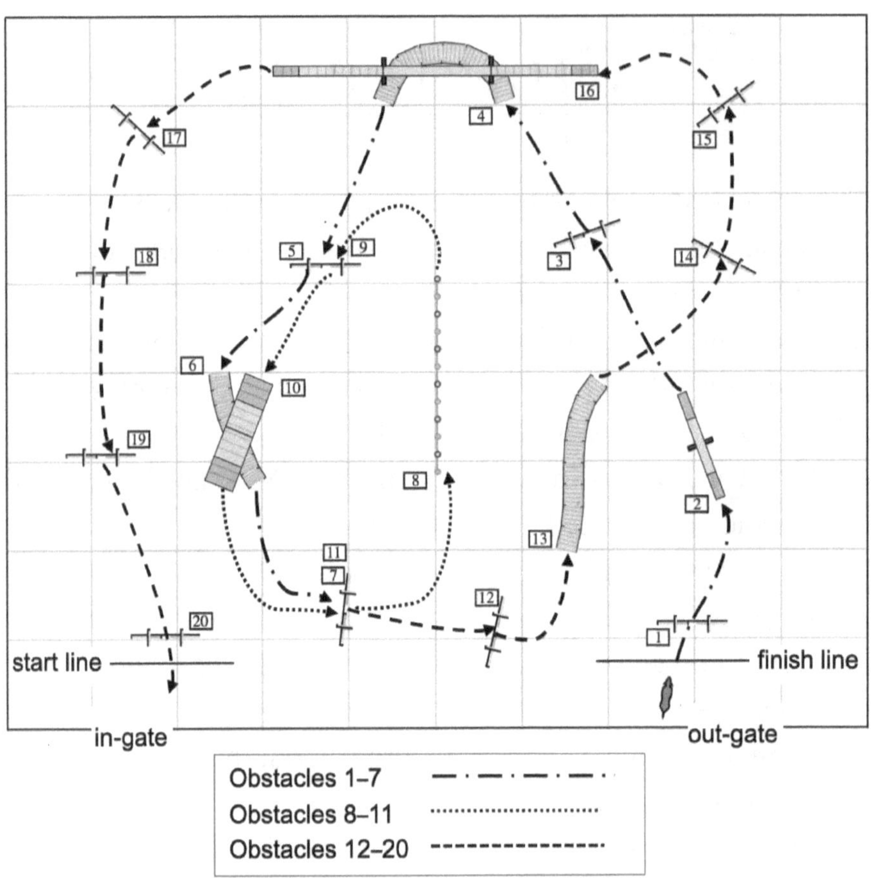

Map of Second Course at Fun Match: Nick's Path

During her first walk around the course, Tori focused on learning the numbered path and the patterns the obstacles made. During the next, she thought about her own path and where she should run so that she had the best chance of cuing Nick correctly. The third time around, she thought about the more difficult places and the best way to tell Nick what to do there.

The long line from jump 12 all the way to the 16 dogwalk was going to be hard. She practiced running as fast as she could up that line. Nick might get confused if she fell too far behind.

Another spot was the weaves to jump 9 to the A-frame. She had to be sure to cue the left turn after the weaves, because Nick would see the 4 tunnel and want to go straight into it. Tori practiced running toward jump 9 and turning her shoulders to her left. That should help Nick understand that he should follow her.

Then there was a pesky discrimination to worry about—the 6 tunnel and the 10 A-frame were close together. She had to remember not to stick out her arm and accidentally point toward the tunnel when Nick was supposed to take the A-frame.

Tori glanced at the countdown clock. One more minute of walkthrough time remaining. On her fourth walk, she ran through the course in order and said all her cues, while imagining that Nick was running too.

The buzzer sounded. Walkthrough was over. As she left the ring, Tori felt satisfied that she had finally done something right, for the first time that day.

Tori got Nick from the car and led him through his warmup routine, staying close to the in-gate. Laura stood nearby in case Tori needed help with anything, and Dad watched the ring so he could call Tori when it was time. There were only four teams running ahead of her.

A sixth sense made Tori glance behind her. She froze. Walking past her, just a few feet away, was Mac'n'Cheese. The skinny guy. The *scary* skinny guy with the zig-zag nose who might be stealing dogs. And he had been watching Nick and Tori.

"Laura!" she half whispered, half shouted. Laura's eyes met Tori's. She had seen Mac'n'Cheese too.

"Tori!" Dad's voice startled the girls. "Tori, you're up!" In the past few moments, Tori had almost forgotten about her agility run.

"C'mon, Nick." Tori jogged to the in-gate. Nick trotted at her side. A few feet inside the ring, Tori came to a halt. She couldn't even remember where the course began. She looked right and left and forced her mind to work. *Oh, yeah, the start jump is right here.*

Nick started well, did a great see-saw contact and ran through the obstacles to jump 5, but then Tori had to stop to think about where to go next. That confused Nick and he started to sniff the ground, and Tori had trouble getting his attention when she finally remembered the course. Nick started up the off-course A-frame, and she had to call him back and motion him to the 6 tunnel. He ran through the weaves and over to jump 9 perfectly, but Tori accidentally motioned him toward the off-course tunnel rather than the A-frame, so Nick went into the tunnel. Then she was too slow to keep up with him from jump 12 to the dogwalk and over all the jumps to the finish, so Nick ran slowly and turned several times to see where she was.

Tori was even more disappointed in herself than she had been after the first run. Head hanging, she led Nick through the out-gate.

Laura, Min, and her father waited for her. Dad gave her a quick, awkward hug.

Tori kneeled beside Nick, wrapped her arms around his shoulders, and buried her face in his sleek fur. Nick curled his body into hers, knocking her over, and she ended up sitting on the ground with Nick on her lap. He made happy gurgly noises and licked Tori's face. Then, with gleaming eyes, Nick searched the faces of his friends and family. *Hey, did you see me? I had fun! Who's got the treats?*

"Don't be too upset, Tori," Min said. "You did a lot of things right, too! Everybody makes mistakes, especially at their first trials. We'll review the focus and memorization techniques again at your next lesson." She smiled at Tori. "Take some deep breaths. Reward your dog. Be positive for your dog. He's teaching you so much."

Tori nodded and stroked the soft fur under Nick's ear. Nick's warm tongue reached for Tori's cheeks. He licked, then nuzzled her face. "Thanks, Nick," Tori whispered. She sensed her dad watching them, and she glanced up at him.

Tori's father kneeled beside her and ran his rough carpenter's hands down Nick's side. "It's amazing what you and Nick have accomplished," he said quietly. "You've worked really hard. I'm proud of you, Tori. Your mom would be proud of you too."

Proud of you. Tori hadn't realized how much she had wanted to hear those words until she did. "Thanks, Dad." That was all she could say without blubbering like a baby in front of her teacher and friends.

Dad put a hand on her shoulder and squeezed. "You better go cool down your dog," he said with a smile.

Laura handed Nick's treats to Tori and the three of them found an open area near the minivan. Laura waited while Tori walked Nick in big circles to cool him down and gave him his special reward—roast beef. Her dad's words of praise bounced around inside her like party balloons. They grabbed hold of her bad mood and lifted it away.

"You did so good, buddy. I'm so proud of you." Tori wondered whether Nick liked getting her praise as much as she liked getting Dad's praise. Nick smacked his lips and smiled up at her.

"The dogwalk was perfect, again. The weaves were beautiful." She remembered the amazing feeling of running as a team with her best friend. She took a deep shaky breath and exhaled. Her muscles softened and relaxed.

Then another image formed in her mind. What had distracted her at the beginning of their run? She turned to Laura. "Where did Mac'n'Cheese go?"

Laura pointed toward the police dog demonstration area. Tori glanced over at the agility ring. Dad was busy helping Min adjust some equipment. "Let's go," said Tori.

CHAPTER 33

Laura led the way toward the police dog demonstration area, clearing a path for Tori and Nick through the gathering crowd. Laura stopped abruptly and Tori, who was looking down at Nick to make sure he was safe, just about ran over her. Laura pointed away from the crowd toward a shade canopy that housed two dog crates marked in huge letters: POLICE – DO NOT APPROACH.

There, kneeling by one of the crates, was Mac'n'Cheese. And beside him, of all people, was Mike.

Tori and Laura looked at each other, brows wrinkled. "What should we do?" asked Laura.

Tori thought for a moment. "Well, we can at least make sure they don't steal the police dogs, right? If we go over there, they'll know someone is watching and they won't dare take the dogs."

Laura nodded. They walked toward the police canopy. A waist-high yellow tape marked DO NOT ENTER ran around the perimeter. "Hi, Mike," called Laura.

Both Mike and Mac'n'Cheese wore navy blue polo shirts and slacks. Mike looked grownup in the unusual clothes. He saw the girls, said something to Mac'n'Cheese, then stepped toward them.

"Hi, Laura. Hi, Tori," he said evenly. Nick wandered under the tape as he sniffed the grass. "Hi, Nick! How are ya, buddy?" Mike cooed. Tori pulled her dog back.

Mike's attention shifted back to the girls. "Are you going to watch the police dog demonstration?"

He's acting like he's not doing anything wrong, thought Tori. *But there he is, behind the "Do Not Enter" tape.* To heck with being polite. "What are you doing in there?" Tori said.

Mike froze and stared at them. Laura nudged Tori, then said, "What Tori means is, 'what's up?'" She tilted her head, smiled, and giggled.

Her ruse worked. Mike relaxed and smiled back. "Well, I'm not sneaking around, spying on people. How 'bout you?"

Behind Mike, Mac'n'Cheese opened a crate and attached a leash to the collar of a powerful-looking German shepherd. Nick seemed tiny compared to the massive police dog. The young man said "Frei, hier," and the dog exited the crate and stood calmly by his side. He began to put a sturdy harness on the dog. Tori noticed that Mac'n'Cheese wore sneakers, not work boots.

Looks like the dog knows the guy, thought Tori. "Sorry. Really, I was just wondering what you're doing with the police dogs. The tape says, 'do not enter.'"

Mike's smile faded, but his dark eyes twinkled. He glanced to his right and left, leaned toward the girls, and whispered dramatically, "We're stealing them. Don't tell anyone." He raised an index finger to his lips and winked.

The girls' eyes went wide and they both took a giant step back. Mike stood up straight and laughed. "Had ya goin' there, didn't I?"

Tori's face flushed. Laura ran a hand through her curly hair. They fake-laughed along with Mike. But they were still uncertain whether Mike was a good guy or a bad guy.

Mike folded his arms across his chest. "My dad's a cop. He's a dog handler. Cole . . ." Mike nodded toward Mac'n'Cheese ". . . works at the police kennel and he's helping out today. He's good with dogs. He used to work at the shelter." Mike reached down and patted Nick, who continued to sniff the grass around the girls' feet. "You should watch the demo. It starts after the agility match."

Both Tori and Laura exhaled, releasing the tension of the last few minutes. Mike and Mac'n'Cheese were good guys.

"Yes, maybe. We have to help pack up the agility equipment though," said Laura. Then she called to Mac'n'Cheese, "Hey, Cole. We met once. On Hemlock Street. Do you remember?"

Cole glanced over at the girls. "Yup." He went back to preparing the German shepherd.

"Cole isn't very talkative," explained Mike.

A tall, broad-shouldered police officer ducked under the shade canopy. He wore a sturdy belt that held a serious-looking gun, as well as a dog muzzle, leash, and a bag that looked a lot like Tori's dog treat bag. He put a friendly hand on Mike's shoulder. "Michelangelo! How are you guys doing? Need any help?"

Michelangelo? Tori and Laura shot each other surprised looks and mouthed the name.

"We're good," said Cole.

"Yeah, everything's fine," said Mike. His eyes flitted toward the girls for a moment.

The officer noticed Mike's glance. He smiled at the girls. "Who are your friends?"

"Oh . . . uhhhh . . . Laura, Tori, Nick." Mike motioned toward each of them. "This is my dad, Malik."

Tori couldn't imagine calling a police officer by his first name. She squinted at the name tag pinned to his crisp blue uniform. "Nice to meet you, Sergeant Armstrong," she said.

"Nice to meet you, Malik," said Laura.

"Hi girls. Enjoying the festival?"

Tori and Laura nodded. *Don't be nervous,* Tori told herself. *You haven't broken any laws. Today. Yet.*

"Good, good." Malik turned back to Mike and Cole.

"We better let you get ready. See ya later." Tori spoke a little higher and faster than she meant to.

"See you later, Michelangelo," said Laura. Mike glared at them, then turned back to continue working with his dad and Cole. The girls headed toward the agility ring.

They walked about 30 feet, then they both whispered *Michelangelo!* and giggled.

When Tori had gained control of herself, she said, "Well, I guess they really are with the police. Boy, I feel dumb. No wonder Mike told us, yesterday at the shelter, that we should leave the investigating to the police."

"The thief could still be Mac'n'Cheese. I mean Cole," said Laura. "Mike kids around so much, it's hard to know whether to believe him or not."

"Yeah, and Mac'n'Cheese still seems pretty weird."

"I agree. Let's just watch some more agility. I'm ready to take a break from detective work."

The last few teams were running the agility course. Tori and Laura got to the ring just as Harry and his Lab Gunnar started their run. The girls found seats on the bleachers and tried to relax. Nick sat beside them and watched Gunnar intently.

Harry and Gunnar started their run well. But Harry forgot to signal the turn to the weaves, so Gunnar powered to the off-course jump and then to the irresistible tunnel. Harry, who was more of a trotter than a runner because of his size, stopped, put his hands on his knees, and caught his breath while Gunnar galloped through the tunnel—and then realized his handler was nowhere in sight. The yellow Lab turned his head back and forth, searching for Harry.

"Gunnar! Let's go! Weave! Weave!" Gunnar hopped and bounced enthusiastically back to Harry and entered the weaves— but he began in the middle of the row of poles, not at the end. Harry asked him to start again. Gunnar wound his stocky body around all twelve poles. On to the jump and A-frame.

Tori couldn't believe what happened next. Gunnar started up the A-frame at a good clip, but then slowed to a trot, then a walk. He perched at the very top of the obstacle and arched his back, as dogs do when they are about to . . . poop.

With a goofy smile on his face, Gunnar gazed at the audience as the first glistening brown nugget rolled down the A-frame and landed with a bounce on the grass. The crowd began to laugh and point. All Harry could do was watch his dog finish his business.

A second nugget made its way down the wide wooden plank. The laughter got louder. Harry's face got redder. Then a third. It landed crossways on the first and formed a soft, brown arch.

His business finished, Gunnar galloped down the A-frame with a broad grin, his tongue flying out to the side of his face. He stopped to shake his whole body from front to back, then hopped and skipped to his handler. Harry shook his head and chuckled as he escorted his happy Lab, who seemed completely unaware that people considered his behavior inappropriate, to the out-gate.

Tori and Laura cracked up. Tori snorted. They laughed even harder. Nick, his forehead wrinkled in confusion, put his front paws in Tori's lap and stretched his head up to lick her face. *What's so funny about poop?* he seemed to ask Tori.

"Oh. My. Gosh," Tori could barely speak through her giggling. She rubbed Nick's shoulders. "Well, at least *that* didn't happen when Nick and I ran!"

🐕 🐕 🐕 🐕 🐕

Tori balanced on her toes, leaned forward, and shifted all her weight onto the side of the heavy plastic trunk of agility equipment. It slid, reluctantly, into the trailer. She stepped back and brushed her dirty hands on her new athletic pants, which hardly looked new anymore, as Dad and Laura swung the trailer doors closed and latched them.

"Are you still staying the night at our house?" Dad asked Laura.

Laura's parents were out of town. "Yes, thanks for having me," she said.

"No problem. We'll stop at your house and pick up Onyx, then go to ours."

Min walked slowly toward them, Zen at her side. The usual spring in her step was missing, and her black-and-pink hair clung to her sweaty forehead. Even her eyebrow piercing looked, somehow, tired. Tori realized for the first time how much work it must have been to organize the fun match.

"Hi, Min. Thanks for everything today." Tori said. Laura and Dad added their thanks.

"You're welcome. Thanks for your help, *all* of you," said Min. "Tori, I hope you're not discouraged. You did fine, especially for your first match. Better than a lot of the adults!"

"Thanks. Well, I got discouraged, earlier today," answered Tori. "But I'm going to keep trying. For Nick. He loves it."

Min smiled. "Working with dogs can sometimes be like a roller coaster ride. One day your dog is brilliant, the next day it's like he's forgotten everything! Up and down. Two steps forward, one step back."

She opened the door of her pickup truck, and Zen jumped in and dove into his crate. "See you at your next lesson. And thanks for helping set up and take down all the equipment!" She waved and slid into the driver's seat. The truck roared to life and rolled slowly down the park road, the big trailer full of agility equipment rattling along behind it.

Journal Entry, June 14

The fun match wasn't always FUN. ~~Exawsting~~ Tiring, yes. Frustrating, yes. But Nick had a great time, and I learned a lot. I feel like Nick and I have passed a big milestone in our dog agility career. We ran two full agility courses, in public. Six months ago I couldn't have imagined such a thing. Thanks, Nick. I love you.

Nick at fun match zooming through a tunnel

P.S. Dad said he was proud of me and that Mom would be proud of me. WOW.

CHAPTER 34

That evening, Tori and Laura lay awake on the twin beds in Tori's room. Moonlight and the cool night air streamed in through an open window. Nick sprawled next to Tori, forcing her to the edge of her bed. Onyx lay next to Laura, curled into a neat ball, her nose tucked between her petite front paws.

The girls had waited to talk about their secret—waited until after the drive to Laura's house to get Onyx and then to Tori's house, a pizza dinner, reviewing the fun match videos, and walking and playing with their dogs in the backyard. Now, in the dark bedroom, they could talk privately about their search for the dog thief.

"Did you get the feeling that someone followed us here?" asked Tori.

"Yes," Laura replied. "I could swear I saw a van behind us on Oak Street. A blue van, like Juan's. But maybe I'm just being paranoid. There were other cars behind us too."

"No. I think you're right." Tori realized that Nick's smelly feet lay uncomfortably near her face. She shoved him, gently, further down the bed.

"Let's think about suspects," said Laura. "Who's connected somehow to the shelter?" Tori noticed that Laura liked to use words like suspect and evidence, as though the girls were real detectives. Laura continued. "Juan. The van guy. He knows about the broken window and he has a ladder. He has means and opportunity. And if he did follow us home, maybe it's because he wants to stop us investigating."

"Then there's Jordan," said Tori. "We know he has some kind of money problem. But I can't imagine he would take dogs from the shelter where he works."

"It's a little suspicious that the shelter isn't publicizing the missing dogs, though." Laura reached behind her head and adjusted her pillow. "Maybe Jordan took the dogs and faked their adoptions, so the other staff don't even realize they are missing."

"But then why would he tell Min?" Tori clearly remembered the conversation she had overheard between Min and Jordan. "That doesn't make sense. Unless he lied to her for some reason."

"Hmmm . . ." Laura ran a hand through Onyx's short curly fur. "It could be someone like Marion. Someone who just likes dogs and wants one. But why break the law by stealing?"

"It has to be someone who can get in and out of that broken window carrying two small dogs."

"Marion said she volunteers at the shelter," said Laura thoughtfully. "But maybe that's not true. When we saw her at the match today, she seemed uncomfortable when we asked about the shelter. Although she seems too old to be able to break in through the window and carry out dogs, even small dogs." Onyx raised her nose, sniffed the cool air drifting in through the window, then curled herself into an even tighter ball and sighed.

"What about Mac'n'Cheese? Cole, I mean." Tori mused. "Mike said Cole used to work at the shelter. So he would know his way around the building. Maybe he was fired, and he wants to get revenge. That's motive, right?" She turned her head toward Laura and saw that Nick's feet, along with the rest of him, had crept up the bed and were next to her face again.

"Yes. Right. And he was acting suspiciously at the festival, staring at all the dogs. We saw dog crates in his car."

"But now he works for the police, so how . . . why . . ." Tori sat up and rolled Nick over so that his feet pointed away from her, then realized that the sheet and quilt had bunched up under him. She yanked them out, lay on her back, and arranged them over herself.

"Sometimes people close to the police feel like they can get away with crimes." Laura said. "That happens in books and TV mysteries, anyway."

"What about Mike? His dad's a police officer. And he has a record of stealing." Both girls fell silent. Thinking.

"No," said Laura.

"I agree. Not Mike." Tori stretched out her arms, then put her hands on her forehead. "Ooof, my brain's tired. Let's talk about something else."

In unison, the girls sighed, then laughed at themselves for sighing, then giggled at themselves for laughing. They snuggled under their covers, taking care not to disturb the sleeping dogs.

"Hey, Tori? Can I ask you something personal?"

No one had ever asked Tori that question. "S—sure. I guess so."

"Where's your mother?"

"Uhhhh . . . she died. When I was nine. Cancer." Tori spoke matter-of-factly.

"Oh, I'm sorry!" Laura's sheets rustled as she shifted onto her side to face Tori. "Is that her in the photo in your living room? I noticed it earlier."

"Yes."

"Is that her border collie sitting next to her? Did they compete in agility?"

"Yes. And yes. I just found out a few months ago that she and Kahu played agility." Tori's voice became raspy. "I never thought to ask her when she was alive. That's a really old photo from before I was born. I barely remember a time when she wasn't sick."

"You don't have to talk about her if you don't want to."

"It's OK. It's getting harder to picture her face in my mind. I don't want to forget . . ." Tori cleared her throat. "My dad . . . he's still really sad about her. When he plays his guitar, I know he's thinking about her."

For a few moments, Tori studied the moonlit ceiling. "I feel . . . I feel like she was stolen from me. Way before it was her time to die. And maybe that's why I'm so afraid of losing Nick, of having *him* stolen from me too." Tori stroked the soft fur on Nick's back. Nick stretched and sighed.

Tori's words floated above the girls and dogs, circled the room, and escaped out the window and into the universe. *That was the first time I've said those words aloud to someone,* thought Tori. *It's nice to have a friend I can trust, someone who's on the same wavelength.*

Laura's hand found Onyx's velvety ear and she rubbed it gently. Finally, she said, "We'll discover who's been taking the dogs. You are the most determined person I've ever known."

"Yeah, we will. Heck yeah, we will." Tori smiled at the ceiling. "Your turn, Laura. Tell me something you've never told anyone else."

Tori could almost hear Laura's brain-gears spinning.

Laura took a deep breath and unleashed her words. "I hate how people assume I'm a spoiled brat. Just because of my looks and because my parents have money. Yeah, they have money, but they work hard for it. I know I'm lucky to be able to have things that other kids can't afford. I still do chores at home, and I have to work hard for good grades."

"You are the opposite of a spoiled brat!" Tori blurted. "And I know how hard you work on freestyle with Onyx. You're an amazing dog trainer. That's has nothing to do with money. Or looks."

"Thank you," replied Laura seriously. Then, with humor in her voice, she said, "Yer not so bad yerself!"

The girls giggled, then became quiet, lost in their own thoughts. "Well, good night," said Laura.

"'Night," answered Tori.

Onyx yipped and moved her legs, as though dancing in her dreams. Nick snored softly, lulling everyone else to sleep.

CHAPTER 35

Tori stood at the sink washing the breakfast dishes. Laura's parents had picked up her and Onyx, and the house seemed empty and quiet. Without them to distract her, Tori's thoughts drifted back to yesterday's fun match and her disappointing performance. She tried to think instead of Nick flying over the A-frame, zipping around the weave poles, thundering through the tunnels, and, most of all, the amazing connection growing between them.

Nick ambled to the back door. He glanced back and forth between the door and Tori. *Who says dogs can't talk?* she thought.

She opened the door and Nick trotted down the steps and into the fenced yard. She peered toward the chain-link gate. It was closed tight, lock in place. Her hand felt for the key that hung inside the kitchen, next to the door. Still there. "You must be tired after yesterday, Nick. I know I am. Have a good sniff."

She heard Dad open the closet near the front door and pull out his jacket. "Tori?" he called. "I have to go to the hardware store for a while and then do some errands, OK?"

"Sure," Tori answered. "I might take Nick for a walk."

"OK, see ya!" She heard the front door close and the minivan back out of the driveway. The hardware store was one of Dad's favorite places. He would be gone for a while.

Dishes done, Tori relaxed on the couch. *For just a minute,* she thought. *I'm so tired . . .*

She woke with a start. A vivid dream—something about a dragon on an agility course—streamed through her head, then faded.

Tori craned her neck to check the wall clock above the couch. She had slept for more than an hour! She swung her legs off the couch, stood up and stretched, and looked around for Nick. He usually got up whenever she did. *Oh! He's still in the backyard.*

A tightness grew in her stomach as she walked to the back door, each step quicker than the last. She opened the door. "Nick!" Tori called. Nothing. No black-and-tan dog bounded toward her. She trotted down the steps and called again. "Nick! Where are you, boy?"

Tori's eyes scanned every corner of the yard. Panic rose in her gut. She jogged around the yard, peering behind the bushes and the homemade agility equipment. Around Dad's workshop. No Nick. She came to the side gate. The padlock hung open, the thick metal cleanly cut, the gate unlatched. She stared at it, paralyzed by disbelief.

Like ice water, it hit her. Nick was gone.

Hot emotion washed over Tori. She couldn't think. Couldn't move. Couldn't breathe.

Then Tori turned and ran, flew up the steps two at a time, and burst into the house. She found her phone on the coffee table in the living room, opened the contact list, and hit her dad's phone number.

A familiar jazzy ringtone came from her dad's office. Unbelievable. Dad had forgotten his phone. She ended the call.

Now what?

She crossed her arms and held herself tight, as though that would contain her fear and concern for Nick. Her eyes roamed around the living room. Nick's fleece tug toy and favorite ball lay on the floor. A bag of turkey dog treats sat on top of the TV. A soft dog bed nestled beside Dad's chair. The silence rang in her ears.

It was torture not to be able to DO anything. She had never felt so alone. Her eyes found the photo of her mother that hung above the chair. "If Kahu went missing, I don't think you would sit around and wait," she said to the photo. "Neither can I."

CHAPTER 36

Tori pedaled her bike hard and fast, her legs like pistons, powered by panic and fear and worry. Blood roared in her ears. Her eyes burned from the wind, burned from the shame of losing Nick.

Nick trusted me to keep him safe, and I failed. The thought ricocheted endlessly inside Tori's brain.

Out of habit, she found herself heading to the DSC. She turned into the driveway, leaning into the curve. There, in the parking lot, sat the blue van. Juan stood beside it.

For a second, Tori froze in surprise and let the bicycle carry her forward. Then she stood on the pedals and put all her weight into each turn of the crank. When she reached the van, she squeezed the brakes hard. The bike skidded noisily on the gravel. Juan started and turned toward her.

Tori placed both feet solidly on the ground. "Where's Nick?" she demanded.

Juan stared at her. "What?"

"Where's my dog? You followed us home last night. You took my dog this morning." Tori's words were razor sharp.

"I'm sorry, I don't understand. I didn't take anyone's dog." Juan took a step toward Tori.

The heavy barn door creaked open and Min stepped outside. "Tori! What's the matter?"

Words tumbled out of Tori's mouth. "Nick is missing. Stolen. Someone broke the lock on our backyard gate. And yesterday after the festival, a blue van like this one followed us home. I think this man took . . . Nick." Her voice faltered as she said her dog's name.

"I did follow an old gray minivan yesterday afternoon. I thought it belonged to someone else." Juan's voice carried genuine concern for Tori.

Min walked quickly to Tori. "I'm so sorry Nick is missing," she said. "What happened?"

Tori took two shallow, shaky breaths. With a husky voice, she told Min the events of the morning.

Min and Juan glanced at each other. "Juan has been helping Jordan and me with a . . . a special project. I'm sure he wouldn't take Nick," said Min.

"I know about the stolen shelter dogs," said Tori. "The person who stole them might have taken Nick too."

"Ohhh." Min and Juan exchanged long looks. "Jordan asked us to watch for a gray minivan with a big dent in the passenger door," said Min. "He noticed it at the shelter a couple times after hours. But he never got a really good look at the car or the driver."

Juan nodded. "Yes, I followed your minivan for a while because I thought it was the one Jordan saw, but eventually I realized yours wasn't the right one. Yours isn't dented."

"Oh." Tori gave a heavy sigh. If Min trusted Juan, Tori couldn't believe that he had anything to do with Nick's disappearance.

"I'm sorry," Tori apologized to Juan. She put her feet back on the bike pedals, raised up on shaky legs, and turned to ride back down the driveway. Min called to her, but Tori ignored her. Her heart felt like the gravel that crunched beneath her tires.

She rode aimlessly. Pictures of what might have happened to Nick flashed through her imagination. Where was he? Was he hurt?

Who took him? Then she stopped and pulled out her phone. She texted Laura:

Nick stolen from backyard. I'm searching for him.

A minute later, her phone beeped. It was Laura:

OMG. How can I help?

Tori wrote back:

Meet me at my house. 20 minutes.

Tori stuffed her phone back in her pocket and started pedaling again. Up and down almost every street between the DSC and home. She rode more slowly now, her damp eyes searching every yard.

Her own house came into view. Four familiar figures—two human, two canine—stood in the front yard. Tori leaned forward and forced the pedals to spin faster and faster.

CHAPTER 37

Tori swung off her bike and laid it on the lawn. "Hi," was all she could manage to say. Laura gave her a quick hug. Then Tori focused on the boy. "Mike, how . . . why . . . thanks for coming."

"Sure," Mike said, staring at the ground.

"I called his dad at work and said I wanted to ask Mike where he learned about tracking," said Laura. "So his dad gave me his phone number. But of course I really wanted to tell him about Nick. And ask him to help."

"Yeah," Mike continued. He raised his head and looked right into Tori's eyes. "Maybe Chase can help somehow. Cause he's, ya know, a trailing dog."

Tori held his gaze for a few seconds. Then she lowered her eyes to the beagle sitting calmly at Mike's feet. She kneeled on one knee and petted the dog's chest gently. Chase lifted his nose and sniffed Tori's tear-streaked face. "Chase." She looked up at her friends. A smile played at her lips. "It's worth a try, right?"

Mike cleared his throat and looked at Tori. "To be clear, Chase is trained to follow human scents. If I ask him to follow a dog's scent, he'll get confused."

"Oh," Tori said flatly. "I didn't know that."

"But . . . show me the gate. Maybe I can think of something."

Tori led the way to the open gate. *Creeeak.* It swung lazily back and forth. "Stay back," Mike told the girls. "Don't disturb the scent trail. If there is one." He studied the gate and the ground around it. "Someone on a ladder, even a small step ladder, could probably reach over this gate and cut the lock with a bolt cutter. I've seen my dad use one." Mike pointed to a bit of yellow cloth stuck to the gate latch. "Is that yours?" he asked Tori.

"No. Don't know where that came from."

"Then we might be in luck."

Mike fished a small plastic bag out of his pocket and turned it inside out. He carefully picked up the cloth, touching it only with the plastic, and turned the bag so that the cloth was inside. Then he kneeled beside Chase and let the beagle stick his nose into the bag.

Chase's nostrils flared as he soaked up the scent. Several long seconds ticked by.

"Find," said Mike.

Chase put his nose to the ground, snuffled around the gate, then followed his nose down the brick walkway to the sidewalk. He stepped off the curb into the street and sniffed the asphalt. Then he lifted his head, sniffed the air, turned right and trotted down the street, moving right, left, and forward, according to where the invisible trail in the air led him. Mike followed at the end of the long leash, allowing his dog to make the decisions. Tori and Laura, with Onyx on leash, brought up the rear.

But half a block from Tori's house, the beagle slowed and stopped. He whined and gave Mike a confused look. "Good boy! It's OK, Chase. You did good!" Mike praised and petted Chase. Then he looked at Tori.

"The trail seems to end here," Mike said. "That cloth looks like torn clothing. If it's from the person who took Nick—and I bet it is —I think they got into a car near your house and drove off. Chase can follow the trail of someone in a car for only a short distance, and only if the car window is open."

Tori's face fell. She was so hoping that Chase was the answer, that he would lead them straight to Nick. No such luck.

Thinking about Nick getting into a car reminded Tori of Juan and his van. She told Mike and Laura about meeting Juan at the DSC, learning that he too was looking for the dog thief, and that he had followed Dad's minivan yesterday because it was similar to the minivan Jordan had seen near the shelter after hours. "But that minivan had a big dent in the passenger door," Tori said.

"A dent? In the right front door? Laura's face brightened. "Mac'n'Cheese—errr . . . *Cole*—he has a gray minivan with a dent like that. Tori and I saw it that day we walked Mrs. Johnson's dog!"

"That's right! So he was at the shelter when he shouldn't have been."

"Wait a second, you two," Mike interrupted. "I know Cole. He's a good guy. Why would you suspect him of stealing dogs?"

"Well, he acts weird," said Laura. "That day we saw him on Hemlock Street, we said hi, but he didn't say a word."

Tori nodded. "At the festival, he was going around the park looking at all the dogs, carrying a big bag. He acted secretive. He's got two dog crates in his car. And maybe he's mad at the shelter, for firing him."

Mike's dark eyes narrowed. "OK, first of all, Cole stutters. Do you know what that is? He has trouble getting his words out, so he's self-conscious about speaking." Mike's words were crisp and biting, his voice deeper than usual.

"And at the festival, he was collecting cans and bottles so he could return them for the deposit. He needs the money, but he doesn't want people feeling sorry for him, so he tries to collect them on the sly. He was probably at the shelter collecting cans and bottles from the trash.

Mike deftly moved Chase's leash from one hand to the other as Chase circled him and sniffed the ground.

"He quit his shelter job to take an internship with the police K-9 Unit. He's good with dogs. He has a couple of his own. He even wants to start his own dog training business, so of course he has dog crates in his car."

The spark of hope in Tori sputtered and died. If Mike was right, Mac'n'Cheese didn't take Nick. "I'm sorry, Mike. We jumped to conclusions."

The anger in Mike's face faded. "That's OK. I guess I would be grasping at straws too, if Chase were missing." The three kids and two dogs began to walk aimlessly, silently, down the sidewalk. Finally Mike said, "Let's go talk to Cole. He knows a lot of dog owners in town. Maybe he'll have some ideas."

Tori looked down the block toward her house. The driveway was still empty. Dad hadn't returned yet. "I should tell my dad what's going on, but I can't reach him," said Tori. She looked at Laura, her face asking, *What do you think?*

"Talking to Cole is better than doing nothing," said Laura.

Tori nodded, then turned to Mike. "Sure, let's go."

Laura held Tori back until Mike was ahead of them, out of earshot. "Tori, I asked Mike about his . . . trouble," Laura whispered. "He shoplifted a baseball glove about three years ago. That's all. He got caught and paid for it. He wouldn't steal a dog. Any dog."

Tori nodded her head in relief and gave Laura a grim smile.

They hurried to catch up to Mike and Chase. After ten minutes of silent walking, each of them lost in their own private thoughts, the group reached Cole's small apartment building. The gray, dented minivan was in the driveway.

"I'll go tell Cole what's going on. You wait here. He'll be more comfortable talking with just me," Mike said. "Hold Chase for me, OK?" He handed the leash to Tori.

From the driveway, the girls saw Cole answer his door and Mike talk with him. Cole looked over at them and gave a small wave. Tori and Laura waved back. Cole closed the apartment door and Mike returned to the driveway.

"Like I thought, he was at the shelter at odd hours collecting bottles and cans." Mike said "That's why his minivan was there sometimes. He didn't even know that someone had stolen dogs from the shelter."

"Ohhhhh," Tori took a deep breath and exhaled a heavy sigh. Her shoulders slumped. She looked down at Onyx and Chase, who lay on the concrete, absorbing the warm afternoon sun. A poodle and a beagle. Poodle and beagle. A vague memory began to take shape in her mind. She had heard someone say those words before. It was Jordan—when he described the missing shelter dogs to Min. *And . . . someone else . . .*

Tori tried to focus her memory, as she had learned to do for memorizing agility courses. *Let everything else melt away, and just think about what's important,* she told herself. The answer began to take shape in her mind.

CHAPTER 38

All the memories from the last few days whirled around in Tori's brain as though in a blender. *Slow down*, she told herself. *One step at a time. You can do it.* She closed her eyes and tried to visualize a pattern.

Tori seemed to grow an inch taller as she organized her thoughts. Onyx and Chase lifted their noses and sniffed the air. Tori's eyelids slid upward and she stared blankly into the distance.

"I know who took the shelter dogs. And Nick, too, I think," Tori said at last. "Marion."

"What?" Laura and Mike spoke together.

"That old lady? I knew you were crazy," added Mike.

Put your thoughts in order, like an agility course, Tori told herself. What happened first, then next, and next. She faced her friends. "Listen. The first time I saw Marion, she was unloading a huge bag of dog food from her car. She lifted that bag easily."

"So what? That doesn't mean anything," said Mike.

"I'll get to that in a second," said Tori. "Then, when Laura and I talked to Marion a few days later, she said she knew about the stolen shelter dogs and—this is really important—she knew they were a *poodle* and a *beagle*! I thought at the time that Jordan must have told her, because she said she volunteered at the shelter. But I think she was lying. At the match yesterday, Marion implied she *didn't* volunteer at the shelter. If that's true, how would she know the dogs' breeds, unless she was the one who stole them!"

"Yeah." Laura nodded. "Jordan said that no one outside the shelter was supposed to know!"

"Right. And, if she can lift a big bag of dog food, she's strong enough to get a couple of dogs through that window and use a bolt cutter. She could have used a ladder to reach over the gate." Tori mimicked the motion of cutting the padlock. "She might be old, but she's just been *pretending* to be weak.

"And we didn't see ladder prints at your house because of the brick walkway," Laura added.

Tori nodded. "Another thing. When we met Marion at the dog festival, she said she *used to* have a dog. Meaning she doesn't have a dog now. Well, if that's true, then why did she even *have* a big bag of dog food?"

"Because she has dogs in the house," Mike said matter-of-factly. "I admit, that's decent evidence, for a crazy girl."

"Heck, yeah." Tori said. "One more thing. Laura, can you find those photos you took at the shelter?"

Laura dug her phone out of her pocket and handed it to Tori. Tori scrolled through the photos, tapped on one, and expanded it with her fingers. She held up the phone so everyone could see. "We were focusing on Juan's big bootprints before. But Laura took a photo of a smaller bootprint too. They were harder to see, because Juan tromped all over them. Marion wears work boots with a waffle sole just like that, I think. I noticed them when she was sitting on her porch, that day we walked Francois."

"I should call my dad," said Mike. "We're getting into serious stuff. He can help." He pulled out his phone.

"Your dad, the policeman?" Tori hadn't even thought about calling the police.

"Yeah, my dad the police *sergeant*." Mike jabbed his phone with his finger. "Tori, give me your dad's phone number. My dad can try calling him."

"OK, but Marion's house is nearby. It's that big old farmhouse just down the street. I don't know the number though. Let's go there. I can't stand around and wait, knowing that Nick—and the other dogs too—are probably there."

With Tori in the lead, Laura handling both Onyx and Chase, and Mike behind them talking on his phone, they headed toward Marion's house. And, if Tori was right, toward Nick.

The group had covered two blocks, then Laura spoke. "Mike? Chase is acting funny. Do you think he's found a trail again?"

Mike stuffed his phone in his back pocket and caught up to Laura. She handed him Chase's leash. He watched his dog closely for several seconds. "Yes. He smells *something*. Let's see where he goes," Mike said quietly. "Chase, find."

With his nose in the air, Chase trotted down the sidewalk. As Marion's ramshackle house came into view, he pulled on the leash and galloped toward it. The kids ran to keep up.

The odd shape of the farmhouse made it look as though rooms had been added several different times in the past, creating lots of random alcoves and extensions. The peeling paint, covered windows, sagging porch, and weed-choked yard made the old house look abandoned. But Marion's green hatchback sat in the driveway.

Chase investigated the car first. He sniffed all around it, then, with his nose to the ground, he made a beeline toward the porch, up the steps, and straight to Marion's front door. With no hesitation, he plunked his rear end down and turned his head toward Mike, who was just catching up to the dog and trying to gather the long leash without tripping on it. Chase's big chestnut eyes beamed with pride. He panted, his tongue lolling. *I found her!* he seemed to say. *See, I found her!*

Mike stumbled up the steps. "Good boy, Chase!" he whispered. "But let's get off this porch, OK? Come, Chase." He patted his leg and started down the steps, and Chase stood, gave one last glance at the door, then followed.

Tori peered through the back window of the green hatchback. "Laura, look! A step ladder!"

Laura joined Tori at the car. "Looks like it fits the ladder prints we saw under the window at the shelter. And the feet of this ladder are muddy."

Mike joined the girls. "Chase says the person who lost that piece of yellow cloth is here. And we think that person stole Nick. Therefore . . . "

Tori's jaw tightened. She continued Mike's thought. "The person who stole Nick is in that house. Marion."

"Yeah. When Chase sits like that, he's indicating that he's found something related to the article—the cloth, I mean—that he sniffed earlier." Mike pulled a small toy out of his pocket and began to play with Chase. "But we should wait for my dad to get here. We're trespassing if we go onto Marion's property."

Chase grabbed the toy and shook it back and forth. Then he dropped it, held it down with his front paws, and tore at it with his sharp teeth. Fluffy white stuffing started to pile up around him. Mike glanced at the car's license plate. He pulled out his phone and tapped the screen. "Dad? I've got an address and a license plate number . . . "

Mike paced up and down the sidewalk, immersed in his phone conversation. Chase walked beside him, carrying his toy. Bits of stuffing fell from it, creating a breadcrumb-like trail behind them.

Nervous energy coursed through Tori. She shifted her weight from one jittery leg to the other and folded and unfolded her arms. "Nick's here. I just know it," she whispered to Laura.

Mike ended his phone call and headed back toward the girls. "Oh, no. Here we go again with the whispering," he muttered.

Mike joined the girls standing behind Marion's car. "I can't wait," Tori said in a low, steady voice. "I'm getting Nick out of there. With or without you two." She started toward the house with a determined stride, leaving Laura and Mike behind before they could stop her. Seconds later, she heard Laura whisper-call, "Tori, wait! You can't go alone!"

Tori glanced back to see Laura rushing toward her with Onyx in her arms. "I can't believe I'm doing this," Laura murmured. A tiny smile flashed across Tori's face. She could always count on Laura. They reached the porch steps.

Then Tori heard a whispery shout from Mike. "Hey! What are you doing? Come back!" She saw him waving at her and Laura, his face scrunched in concern. Tori and Laura looked at each other, then at Mike. They shook their heads at him. No.

Mike frowned and tossed his hands, as if to say *I give up,* then he and Chase raced to the left side of the house and disappeared. A moment later, he peeked around the corner. Tori could see the doubt and worry on his face even from that distance. She wanted to apologize for involving him in her problems, but at the same time she was glad he was there to back them up.

Tori and Laura climbed the porch steps. And froze. A tool, like giant pliers, lay on the porch. *A bolt cutter.* The heavy metal tool gave Tori chills. The window next to the big solid door was covered inside, making the house seem even more forbidding. She raised her hand to the door, made a fist, and glanced at Laura. With a grim expression, Laura nodded in agreement.

Tori knocked. Silence answered. She knocked again, louder, stronger. The girls heard faint rustling from somewhere deep in the house, then footsteps approaching, and the metallic clicking of a turning lock. The door creaked and moved inward a few inches. A familiar face peered through the dark crack.

"Yes?" said Marion.

Chapter 39

"Oh hi, Marion! I'm Tori, remember? And this is Laura," Tori said in a high quavering voice. She noticed that one sleeve of Marion's yellow t-shirt was torn.

Behind her thick glasses, Marion's eyes were impossible to read. "Hi. Sure, I remember you. What do you want?" She spoke in a flat voice, neither friendly nor distant.

"Well, my dog Nick has gone missing. We're just wondering whether you've seen him. He's black and tan, like a German shepherd, about 50 pounds."

"No. No. Haven't seen any dogs like that." Marion glanced over her shoulder into the house. Then Onyx, nestled in Laura's arms, caught her attention. "I didn't know you had a poodle."

Onyx raised her delicate, coal black nose and sniffed at the dank air wafting through the doorway. Tori and Laura glanced at each other and, through their shared wavelength, silently communicated a plan. "This is Onyx." Laura said. "Would . . . would you like to come out and meet her?"

Marion pulled the door inward, creating a gap just large enough for her to slip through and onto the porch. She kept one hand on the outer doorknob. The other hand held a small flashlight. Marion stuffed it into her pocket, then reached toward Onyx. Laura kept to the right of Marion, luring her away from Tori. The old woman kept her attention on the poodle. Tori stepped to the left and toward the narrow crack in the doorway.

"Hello, Onyx . . .," Marion cooed.

Tori saw her opportunity. And took it.

She channeled all her worry and fear and determination into a single powerful kick at the door. The doorknob tore away from Marion's hand. Tori charged into the dark house and slammed the door behind her. Her shaky hands fumbled at the door, searching for the lock. She found the cold metal deadbolt, flipped it to the side, and heard the bar slide home.

Tori stood frozen at the door. *Now what do I do?* She heard Marion yell, "Hey!" Then someone—Marion, it had to be—shook the doorknob so violently that Tori thought it would disintegrate. But the deadbolt held the door firmly in place.

In the darkness of the old house, every sound hit Tori's ears clearly, intensely, fiercely. She heard Laura shriek, "No!" Then a thump like a body falling to the porch floor, light footsteps running down the stairs and fading away into the distance, and low moaning from a voice she recognized as Marion's.

Tori took a quick shallow breath. Stale air and the sour stench of urine and feces invaded her nose and lungs. She snapped out of her frozen trance. *Get moving,* Tori ordered herself. *Before Marion finds a way inside.*

"Nick! Nick!" Tori called blindly into the dark house.

"BARK! BARK! BARK!" Nick's voice, though muffled and distant, was unmistakable. Tori gasped in relief. She heard excitement and joy in Nick's bark as he realized she was close. She took an automatic step toward the sound, and stumbled. Light. She needed light.

Tori felt for a light switch on the wall, found one, and flicked it upward. Nothing. She tapped where the window should have been and heard a solid, wooden sound. Her dumb phone didn't have a flashlight app. She would have to figure this out in the dark.

She turned to face the room, and as her eyes adjusted, an assortment of old dusty furniture and random piles of junk gradually came into focus. More dog voices joined Nick's. The frenzied barking seemed to come from a hallway that began across the room and extended into the back of the house. The noise and smell reminded Tori of the animal shelter. *Nick must think I sent him to another shelter*, thought Tori. Her face sagged at the thought.

Tori navigated through the maze of clutter toward the sound. The barking got louder, the stink got stronger. Both sides of the hallway contained several doorways. Tori followed her ears toward Nick.

"Nick! I'm coming!"

CHAPTER 40

S tacks of junk lined the hallway, and the light was even dimmer than in the front room. She used her hands and feet to check her surroundings as she blindly shuffled toward the barking dogs. It would be so easy to trip or knock something over. She couldn't risk doing anything that might slow her down.

The barking got louder as she moved closer to the third door on the right. Her hands glided down the smooth wood door and found the doorknob. She turned it, pushed, then stood at the doorway and peered inside.

Her eardrums puffed and pounded from the noise. Her nostrils flared at the overpowering scent of dog waste. Wooden boards covered the single window and blocked the outside world, except for one thin blade of light that sliced the darkness and slashed the wall beside Tori. She could hardly fathom what she saw.

Dog crates, large and small, too many to count, were strewn across the floor. Some were empty, but in others small furry bodies bobbed and turned. She headed toward the sound of Nick's barking, stepping around and tripping over crates. "Nick! I'm here, buddy!"

Nick stood in a too-small wire crate, his back pressed against the top. Tori kneeled in front of him and stuck her fingers through the crate door. Nick whined and frantically licked Tori's trembling fingers. His whole body wagged back and forth as much as the small crate allowed.

"I'll get you out of here, boy, I promise." The words caught in her throat and her voice faltered. Her mind catapulted to Nick's adoption day at the shelter, when she had made the same promise to him. *We can do this,* she told herself as her hands searched frantically for the door latch.

She wrestled with the rusty, bent latch. Finally, it popped free and Nick bolted out, knocking Tori onto her back. Nick's front paws drove into Tori's chest and pinned her down. He scrubbed her face, then her ears, with quick warm licks.

Nick bobbed up and down on Tori as she half-laughed, half-coughed, until his weight made it impossible for her to breathe. She gently pushed him off to her side, allowing her lungs to work again, and inhaled some stale air. "Sorry, Nick, but I have to breathe," she croaked through her coughing. She struggled to her feet and rubbed Nick's shoulders and neck. "I'm SO happy to see you! But we've got to get out of here." Nick grumbled and danced around her feet, his eyes constantly searching for hers.

The barking faded, except for two small terriers who continued their high-pitched yapping as they hopped and bounced against each other in the crate they shared. The other dogs stared at Tori.

She saw a small light-colored poodle and a mostly white beagle. She couldn't make out the true colors in the dim light. *Must be the shelter dogs.* A German shepherd puppy crouched in a crate far too small for him. He turned his face away from Tori and glanced sideways at her, the whites of his eyes shining through the dim light. A scruffy grayish dog with matted fur watched Tori with hard, wary eyes. A fluffy white ball at the back of another crate turned out to be a dog too. The ball raised his head briefly, looked at Tori, then lowered it and closed his eyes. Tori wondered whether she had seen their pictures on the Lost Dogs website. She desperately wanted to save them all.

"Ohmygosh, Nick. I can't leave your friends behind." But how much time did she have before Marion caught up with her? She hoped Laura and Mike were OK.

The closest crate held the poodle. She slid the latch, swung open the door, and the poodle leaped out and into Tori's arms. His damp rough tongue scoured her cheeks, her nose, her forehead, everywhere the little dog could reach.

With her arms full of squirming, licking poodle and Nick at her side, Tori stepped over to the next crate. With one hand, she worked at the rusty latch until it slid open. The trembling small white dog stood and pressed his side against the back wall of the crate. Every rib and vertebrae of his arched spine were visible under a thin layer of skin. He stared at Tori, his wide black pupils ringed with white. "C'mon, little guy, let's go," she said as gently as she could.

The cheerful, incongruous tones of an incoming phone call made her jump. "What the . . .," she muttered. She pulled out her phone. Through crackly static she recognized Laura's voice. "Tori! Are you OK?" Laura sounded worried, verging on frantic. Tori had never heard her like that before.

Relief at hearing from Laura eased some of Tori's tension, and the poodle in her arms felt it and squirmed. "Yes, I'm OK! Are you OK? Where are you?"

Laura spoke quickly, urgently. "I'm fine. I tripped Marion and she fell, but I think she's still trying to get through the front door. Mike and I found a back door. You can probably escape here."

Tori adjusted her grip on the poodle. Nick danced around her feet and she kneeled to be closer to him. "OK. I found Nick and a bunch of other dogs. I'm trying to free them."

Mike's distant, muffled voice said, "Laura, the door's stuck. Help me push it." Then Tori heard thumping and grunting and grumbling and a great crash and finally the scrape of wood against concrete.

"Laura! Are you there? What happened?" Tori almost shouted with worry. The dogs in their crates started to bark. Someone coughed into the phone.

"The door's open." Laura's voice was hoarse. She coughed again and her voice cleared. "We have to move some junk that fell, but we think you can get out this way. Hurry . . ."

The call dropped and Tori became aware again of the dogs around her, the smell, the darkness, the barking . . .

SMASH. The unmistakable sound of shattering glass broke through Tori's thoughts. She whipped her head around toward the front of the house.

"TORI!" Marion shot her name down the hallway, into the dogs' room, and it pierced Tori's chest like a bullet. She gasped.

She would have to leave the other dogs behind. There was no time to pull or coax them out of their crates. "I'm sorry. I'll come back for you," Tori whispered into the dim room. Nick headed toward the door, ahead of her. Tori started to follow but tripped on a crate and landed heavily on one knee. "Owww," she moaned. She just managed to hang on to the poodle. Nick turned to her. Tori put one hand on his shoulders and struggled to her feet. "Weave, Nick! Show me the way out! Weave!" Nick led the way around the crates, left, right, left, right, forward. The barking surged as the remaining dogs saw their hope of rescue disappear through the hallway door.

The back door. Where . . .?

A flash of light, framed by a shadowy human silhouette, almost blinded her. Tori stopped short and yelped, "Aagh!" Adrenaline surged through her body. Nick gave a sharp bark.

"Follow me. Out the back." The silhouette turned, aimed the light down the hallway, and headed toward the back of the house.

Mike. Tori's heart started to beat again. She took a dusty breath, then went after him, with Nick close behind. The door to the big back room was only a few feet away. They went through.

A narrow shaft of sunlight from the back door lit the large room just enough for Tori to see piles and piles of newspapers, magazines, books, cardboard boxes, furniture, plastic containers . . . so much stuff that the floor was not even visible, except for a narrow winding path to the back door.

Mike aimed his phone flashlight down the trail through the piles of junk. Tori followed, holding the little poodle tight. When they were about halfway to the back door, Tori turned to make sure that Nick was right behind her.

Her elbow knocked a tower of cardboard boxes and loosely stacked magazines and newspapers. Time stood still as the paper began to slip and slide and drop to the floor one by one . . . then five . . . then twenty . . . then CRASH! The floor vibrated, right up Tori's feet to her legs and up her spine, making her teeth clatter from the thunderous sound. The entire pile collapsed into the path behind Mike and her, creating a five-foot wall of dirty, crumbling paper.

Nick was nowhere in sight.

CHAPTER 41

Tori stared with wide eyes at the avalanche of ancient paper. Dust and dirt floated through the stale air and filled her nostrils, her eyes, her throat. Her mind buzzed and went blank at the same time.

Nick. Where is Nick?

"TORI!" She heard the tinkling of window glass and something heavy thumping against wood. She imagined Marion at the front window, trying to break through the wooden covering.

"Mike! Hand me your phone!" Tori exchanged the trembling poodle for Mike's phone. She stood on tiptoe, craned her neck, and peered over the wall. The light found Nick, cowering at the hallway door, twenty feet away. His huge glowing eyes peered at her over a table that had fallen in the path. Ears pinned flat against his skull, he pawed at the darkness with one raised leg. *At least he's not hurt. I hope.* Tori's heart hammered at her chest, sending blood to beat against her eardrums.

"Let's move the paper," Mike said. The poodle squirmed and almost escaped his arms.

"No. It might fall and bury Nick. Or us. But maybe . . ." Tori raised herself on her toes again and peered over the wall.

I've got to try.

"Nick—push! Push!" The familiar cue jolted Nick out of his fear. He turned and pushed at the hallway door with his paw until it clicked shut. "Lock! Lock!" His nose found the small button lock on the doorknob and he pushed it. He found Tori's eyes again. *Tell me what to do. I trust you,* his eyes told her.

"Good boy! Perfect!" Tori hoped the locked door would slow Marion down. She allowed herself a moment of pride for Nick, but just a moment. They weren't out of trouble yet.

Now for the next problem—the fallen table that lay between Nick and the wall of paper. The three-foot tabletop formed a high, solid barrier across the path, junk piled high on both sides.

"TORI! DON'T TAKE MY DOGS!"

Tori heard the bangs and thuds of falling junk. Marion was inside. She must be having trouble moving through the dark house too.

"Jump, Nick. Jump!" Tori coughed and fought the dryness in her throat. "I know you can't see the other side," she croaked. "But trust me. You'll land OK."

Nick whined and paced from the door to the jump and back to the door. He trotted up to the table, raised up on his hind legs, and pawed the air. He lowered his legs, circled and approached the table, collected his body like a coiled spring—and shot up and over the three-foot jump. THUD. He landed, hard, on the concrete floor.

"Good boy!" Every muscle in Tori's body felt as though it too had coiled, jumped, and hit the floor. Her lungs demanded oxygen, and she inhaled the stale, dusty air.

Think. Next problem. The wall of paper. Maybe Nick could go around it, find a way through the smaller piles of junk on either side.

Still on tiptoe, her calves screaming, Tori cued Nick. "Nick, run right! Run right!" Nick turned to his right. His shoulders and paws prodded the stacks of old furniture and boxes, but he found no clear path through. He put his front paws on a desk, tried to jump on it, and slipped on the bare wood. His frustrated whining ripped Tori's heart.

"Nick, run left! Run left!"

Nick turned to the opposite side of the blocked path. He faced towers of crumpled cardboard boxes. He pawed at them and whined. He turned his head toward Tori. The soft skin of his muzzle crinkled and tensed, his brow wrinkled. "BARK! BARK!"

Tori's legs trembled and burned, blood pounded in her ears, her throat ached. *There's only one possible way out now.*

"TORI!" Marion yelled, louder. Closer.

"Back, Nick. Back. Back."

Nick backed away from the boxes until his rump touched the tabletop.

BAM. BAM. The hallway door puffed in and out as Marion's clenched fists slammed against it. BAM. BAM. "OPEN UP!"

"Climb! Climb! Come to me, Nick! Climb!"

Tori lowered her cramped feet. Ignoring the pain in her knee, she hopped up and down so Nick could see her above the wall. *This HAS to work.*

"BARK! BARK!" Nick paddled his feet. His eyes found Tori as she bobbed above the wall. Five long seconds ticked by. Then he approached the wall of junk that separated Tori and him. He placed one paw on the jumbled pile of paper. Then another. And another. And he began to climb.

"TORI! THOSE DOGS ARE MINE!" The doorknob rattled. BAM BAM BAM.

Though she couldn't see Nick, Tori felt their connection, their trust, pulling him over the wall to her. "You can do it, boy. That's it. Good job, buddy." A paw reached over the top. Then Nick's nose poked above the wall. "C'mon, Nick. Good boy." Then another paw. "You're almost there. Almost there." He perched atop the wall, his legs quivering, his body rocking from side to side.

"TORI!"

"Nick, run, run, run! Run, run, run!"

Nick shifted his weight back.

"Trust me, Nick." Tori summoned all her confidence and trust in her dog, wrapped it in a mind-message, and beamed it to him.

Nick's eyes found Tori and he gave a gurgly whine. He carefully moved one front paw down a few inches, then moved the other. His rear paws followed. Then front. Rear. Front.

"Good boy."

"THOSE ARE MY DOGS!" BAMBAMBAMBAMBAM. The door shook.

Nick moved his rear paws and they shoved the unstable top layer of paper. Tori heard something slide and hit the floor behind him. Thunk . . . Thunk Thunk Thunk. THUNKTHUNKTHUNKTHUNKTHUNK . . . The noise thickened as more and more ancient magazines and newspapers and cardboard boxes cascaded to the floor.

Nick drove his powerful hindquarters into the wall of paper and launched himself toward Tori. She dropped the phone, half caught him as he landed, and helped him into a wobbly stand. His shoulders, his back, his ribs felt so good in her hands, she took a moment to stroke him, to reassure him, to love him.

Behind her, the earsplitting sound of the thick wooden door smashing and splitting rang out. Tori's insides twisted and hardened. Nick's ears flattened and he shot Tori a terrified look.

Mike grabbed his phone from the floor. "GoGoGo!" He herded Nick and Tori ahead of him. A dusty sliver of sunshine pierced the doorway and promised escape.

Tori sent Nick through the narrow crack in the doorway. Laura corralled him. Then Tori and Mike, clinging to the poodle, sidestepped through.

For a few seconds, the bright sunlight blinded her. She gulped the clean air. Then Tori ran her hands down Nick's back. *He's really here. Safe.* Her shaking fingers found several spots where his fur had been scraped away. Nick licked her face and his trembling nose knocked her glasses to one side.

"YOU TOOK MY DOGS! YOU TOOK MY DOGS!" They could still hear Marion's voice from the house. She must be in the back room. But, with luck, still behind the collapsed pile of paper.

"No time for petting dogs. Let's go!" Laura yelled. She led the way through the unkempt yard. They ran past mysterious pyramid-like mounds covered with blue tarps and piles of rotting trash, dodging thistles and jumping over thorny blackberry vines that reached for their feet. Tori cued Nick to run at her side. "Me-me-me-me-me!" Around the house and into the front yard. Nick stuck to her like glue.

A police car and Dad's minivan sat on the street in front of the house. Tori's father and Sergeant Armstrong, in his police uniform, stood on the porch, knocking on the door and examining a broken window. They saw the kids and hurried down the steps.

Dad pulled Tori in for a long, tight hug. Tori's ear pressed against his chest, and his beating heart met the pounding pulse in her head. "I was so worried about you," Dad whispered.

"Oh, man, am I glad to see you," Mike said to his dad. He fought to control his breathing. "The old woman, Marion—she stole Nick and this poodle. Tori rescued them . . ."

Tori pulled away from her dad and interrupted. "There're more dogs inside. We've got to rescue them too!"

"OK, kids, slow down and tell me exactly what happened," said Malik.

"Well, Tori figured out that it was Marion who took Nick. We found some clues . . ."

"Chase led us to Marion's house . . ."

"Yeah, and Laura distracted Marion so Tori could go inside and look for Nick . . ."

"I found Nick and some other dogs. But I couldn't get all of them out of their crates. Just the poodle. Then I heard Marion coming. Nick and I got out the back door . . ."

It seemed like hours had gone by since they first arrived, thought Tori, but it had been only a few minutes.

BANG! The front door burst open. Marion charged out onto the porch. She saw the group in the front yard and skidded across the floor. She started to topple down the steps. One hand grabbed the stair railing just in time. The other hand gripped the bolt cutter.

Marion straightened and gaped at Malik, her mouth forming an O of surprise. She ran one hand through her tousled gray hair. Bits of yellowing, crumbling paper fell to the porch floor.

Chapter 42

Marion withered and crumpled. Her body folded and slumped onto a porch step and she bowed her head. Anger and frustration melted from her body. The bolt cutter fell from her hand, finger by finger, and landed with a thud on the wooden step.

Sergeant Armstrong stepped toward the porch and kicked the bolt cutter away from the old woman. He spoke in a calm, authoritative voice. "Marion Krazinski, I'm arresting you for possession of stolen property. And other charges, to be determined."

Marion raised her head and grabbed the handrail. All the muscles in her wiry arm popped and strained as she slowly pulled herself to a stand. She thumped down the steps, turned, and held her hands behind her back. Her face was blank as Sergeant Armstrong placed handcuffs on her wrists.

Seeing Marion powerless, the kids, almost as one, exhaled loud sighs of relief. Marion couldn't harm any more dogs. Tori turned to her dad. "The other dogs—they're so scared . . . I think one is sick . . ."

"The animal control officer is on the way," said Dad. "She'll take good care of the dogs." He turned to Laura. "Laura, I called your parents and they should be here soon. C'mon, everyone, let's get out of the way." He herded the kids and their dogs away from the house and onto the sidewalk beside the minivan.

"Dad, how did you know where to find us?" asked Tori.

"I got home after you left with Laura and Mike. I thought you had gone for a walk with Nick. I checked my voicemail, and Min had called. She was worried about you. Then Mike's dad called me." Dad put his arm around Tori's shoulders. "I'm so sorry you couldn't reach me. I tried calling you, but it went to voicemail."

"You must have called when I was . . . well, busy . . . inside." Tori studied the old house. She would never forget what happened there. She looked up at her dad's face. "I'm really glad you're here."

Nick carefully folded his quivering legs beneath him and lay on the sidewalk. He rested his chin on his front paws, groaned, and closed his eyes. Tori kneeled and examined the sores on his back. *Not too bad,* she thought. *But we're going to the vet. Today.* She sat next to Nick and petted him in long soothing strokes down his side. Nick lay his muzzle on her thigh. With each stroke, she felt his— and her—muscles relax and breathing slow.

Tori looked at her friends. Laura's long chestnut hair stuck out in all directions and her face and clothes were streaked with dirt. Tori had never seen her look so disheveled. Laura picked up Onyx, held her close, and whispered into her ear. Onyx wagged her tail and licked Laura's face.

Mike—sarcastic, stoic Mike—cradled and stroked the frightened poodle, while Chase sat calmly between his feet and gazed at Mike's face.

"Laura?" whispered Tori. Laura sat down beside Tori and Nick. "Did you really trip Marion?"

"Yes, but . . ."

"Hey, no more whispering," interrupted Mike, loudly. "I always get into trouble when you two start whispering."

The girls managed to smile. "Sorry, Mike. But thanks for helping us today. You and Chase were awesome," said Tori.

"Sure, no problem. But don't expect me to hang out with you girls. That only happens in stupid kids' books. We go our separate ways now."

"OK, OK, *Michelangelo*," Laura agreed. "But you are welcome anytime."

"That goes for me too," said Tori.

"And if you ever tell anyone that my name is . . . well, you know . . ."

"We shall never speak of it again," Tori and Laura said in unison, and laughed.

Tori nudged her grimy glasses into place. An unpleasant odor drifted to her nose. She sniffed Nick's fur. "Oh no, Nick. You really need a bath." She sniffed again. "And so do I."

CHAPTER 43

The animal control officer collected all the dogs and took them to a veterinarian. Several police officers and detectives had been in and out of the old house, collecting evidence and making sure that no more animals—or humans—were inside. Marion talked to the detectives, then was taken to police headquarters for more formal questioning. Tori, Laura, and Mike were told to go to the station the next day to give their statements.

Laura's parents arrived, looking not at all like a lawyer and a doctor. Tori was used to seeing them in business suits, but today they wore blue jeans and sneakers and worried-parent looks on their faces.

Malik told Tori and the others his part in the afternoon's events. "Mike gave me Marion's car license number, so we were able to search our database and get her name. We also discovered that she was arrested in Washington once for trying to sell stolen dogs, but there wasn't enough evidence to convict her. She is connected with a larger ring of criminals who steal dogs and sell them to labs and unethical breeders. The police department here wasn't aware that she was in town."

"But the dogs she stole aren't all purebreds. Except for the German shepherd. How . . . why . . ." Tori couldn't understand how anyone could even buy a stolen dog, much less steal a dog.

"If the dog looks almost like a purebred, that's close enough," Malik continued. "The thieves sell them for much less than a real purebred would cost. The dogs are used for things like breeding in puppy mills. German shepherds are often used as bait for dog fighting."

Dad wrapped his arms around Tori and pulled her into his chest. She buried her nose into the rough cloth of his denim shirt and inhaled his warm, sweaty, sawdusty scent. "You are the most important thing in the world to me, Tori. I love you," whispered her dad.

"Love you too," whispered Tori. She couldn't remember the last time she and her father had been so close. Maybe it was Mom's funeral. A lifetime ago.

Nick scrambled to his feet and squirmed his way between them. *Nick's like a bridge,* thought Tori. *He built a bridge between Dad and me.*

Laura's parents held their daughter close too. Her mother spoke. "What about the house? It's been empty for years, we thought."

"Marion arrived in Maple Valley about six months ago," said Malik. "She was living on the streets or in her car for a while. Then at some point she broke in and began squatting in this house. She told the neighbors she rented it."

Malik turned and studied the house. "Used to be a nice old place, just a few years ago. Now it's falling apart and full of junk leftover from the previous owners." He placed a strong, weathered hand on his son's shoulder. "Good thing you kids didn't get hurt in there."

"I'm sorry, Dad. The situation just sorta . . . got away from me," Mike said. He kept his eyes on Chase.

"It was all my fault. I left Nick alone in the backyard. And it was *me* who went into Marion's house first." Tori spoke directly to Malik and Mike. "I couldn't wait. I just *had* to find Nick."

"It's over now," said Dad, his long arms still encircling Tori. "And you're OK. That's the main thing."

"Even though I can't say that you kids did the right thing by confronting Marion and going into the house, we wouldn't have known about her without you," said Malik. "If she knew we suspected her, she probably would have cleared out, taking the dogs with her to who-knows-where."

"So she needed money? Is that why she stole the dogs?" Laura asked. Her mother and father kept their arms around her shoulders.

"Well, yes, that's what she told us. She has mental health issues. She's had a hard life and it's difficult for her to get a job and support herself. And she got involved with the wrong people. She'll have to pay for her crimes, but wherever she ends up—prison or maybe a hospital—there are programs to help her."

At one time, Marion was a girl, maybe like me, thought Tori. *Just a girl who loved her dog.* "I hope she does get help," she said. "Underneath it all . . . I think there's a good person . . . struggling to get out."

CHAPTER 44

Tori and her father drove straight to the emergency veterinarian, who examined Nick thoroughly. The scrapes and cuts on his back from Marion's crate weren't too serious, the vet said, and he gave Tori some salve to put on them.

Tori walked Nick back to the minivan, and Nick trotted up the ramp and into the back. He circled and lay on the soft pad Tori had placed there. "You don't have to go into a crate for a while," Tori told him. She cupped a hand to his cheek, and Nick cocked his head, pressing himself into her hand. She massaged the loose skin under his floppy ear. Nick groaned, and his eyes met hers. The light that usually sparkled there was dim.

"I love you, Nick. No one will ever hurt you again, I promise."

That evening, Tori's family gathered in the living room: Dad in his overstuffed chair, Tori on the couch with Nick sleeping beside her, and her mother in her photo on the wall.

"How did you figure out that Marion stole Nick?" asked Dad. The exact events were all jumbled up inside Tori's head, but she did her best to explain how—and why—she and Laura had investigated the stolen shelter dogs.

Her father listened thoughtfully, then asked, "Why didn't you tell me about it?"

Why didn't I? thought Tori. "I guess . . . I didn't want to bother you," she said, "And no one was supposed to know about the missing shelter dogs. I just found out accidentally. We didn't do anything wrong or dangerous. Not *really* dangerous, anyway."

Dad leaned forward and rested his elbows on his thighs. "You could never bother me, Tori." His eyes drilled into Tori's. "Next time something like this happens, if there is a next time, you'll come to me right away. OK?"

Tori sat up straight, looked into his eyes, and nodded. "OK."

The next day, Tori and her father went to the police station and Tori told her story to the detectives. Mike's dad told them more about Marion.

"Marion said she targeted the shelter because she thought no one would miss those dogs or post lost-dog notices online about them, since they don't have real owners yet," said Malik. "The dogs you found were a mix of dogs stolen from the shelter and from homes in Maple Valley and nearby towns. Marion stole several other dogs from the shelter and homes in the past few months and has sold them. But she's agreed to help us try to track them all down. She had a buyer for German shepherds, so when she saw Nick, she followed you home and saw that she could get into the backyard. Then she came back the next morning and lured him away."

Tori imagined friendly Nick following Marion out of the backyard and hopping into her car to get a treat, as Tori napped in the house. She shivered and shook her head. Nick might have ended up in a lab or in a dog-fighting ring. The whole experience didn't seem real anymore. It was more like a horrible nightmare.

She spent the rest of the day at home with Nick. When he wasn't fast asleep, Nick followed Tori wherever she went.

To fill the time while Nick rested and healed, Tori watched some of the dog movies she had always enjoyed. The ones where dogs understand complete sentences in English and pull babies from wells and win prize money so their owners can save the farm.

But now, knowing the reality of living with and training a dog, the movies seemed silly and childish.

She found herself talking to the TV screen. *Hey, that's not how you should teach a dog! Reward, reward, reward! Keep your training sessions short!* Nick lifted his head from the couch and eyed her. *Ha! I sound like Min!* thought Tori. She picked up the remote and surfed some other channels. A local news show caught her attention.

"A ring of thieves targeting purebred dogs has been uncovered in Portland, with at least one member operating in Maple Valley." The news video showed police cars in front of Marion's house. "Police became aware of the criminal activity through the brave actions of three teenagers, who located and identified the suspect arrested Sunday afternoon. Some of the dogs were stolen from the Franklin County Animal Shelter. Sergeant Malik Armstrong was first on the scene." And there was Mike's dad on TV!

"We made the news!" Tori called to her dad. He rushed into the living room.

"Unfortunately, unscrupulous dog breeders and dog fighting rings create a market for stolen dogs," Sergeant Armstrong said. "We urge anyone with information about these crimes to contact the Maple Valley Police Department."

During the next couple of days, Tori and her dad answered lots of phone calls, texts, and emails. Somehow, her agility classmates found out about Tori's and Nick's part in rescuing the stolen dogs. They each called or wrote to wish Tori and Nick well.

Min called to ask if everyone was all right. "Take some time off lessons. Wait until Nick wants to play agility again. There's no rush," Min advised Tori.

Gisele and her other school friends—even Abby!—texted her. They wanted to hear all the details. "Later, OK?" Tori wrote back. "Still processing."

Tori called Mrs. Johnson to reschedule her walks with Francois. She had seen the newscast too. "No problem, Tori. You take care of Nick! We—I mean Francois and I—are so proud of you! I don't know what I would have done if *my* dog had been stolen! I've told some friends about you, and they are interested in hiring you to walk their dogs . . ." She talked so long and so fast, Tori wondered when she breathed.

Jordan phoned with good news. The poodle and beagle stolen from the shelter were doing well and lots of people were asking about adopting them. The TV news story had ignited interest in the shelter, and donations to the building fund were pouring in. It turned out that Jordan's money problems were related to the shelter's fundraising efforts. "Juan sends his best wishes too," said Jordan. *It seems like a hundred years have gone by since I confronted Juan at the shelter,* thought Tori.

The next call was a bit odd. "Hello? T . . . t . . . Tori?"

"Yes. Hi?"

"This is . . . Cole. Mike said it would be . . . OK t . . . t . . . to call you."

Tori wasn't sure what to say to Cole. She hadn't been very nice to him when they had met before. "Of course. It's fine."

"Just wanted to say . . . g . . . g . . . good . . . job. Rescuing the d . . . dogs."

"Thanks, Cole. Hey, I'm curious . . . why do you have a tattoo of Mac'n'Cheese on your arm?"

"My last name. MacChesney."

"Ha! Good one!" Tori chuckled. "Thanks for calling, Cole."

Between phone calls, Tori mixed the ingredients for Nick's favorite salmon dog treats. Soft guitar music drifted into the kitchen. Tori used to think that her dad's music kept them apart. It sent Dad into his own world, where she didn't belong. Now it comforted her; it was the sound of home.

As she slid the baking dish into the oven, the doorbell rang. "I'll get it!" she called.

Laura and Mike stood on the front steps. As Tori opened the door, she saw them untangle their interlaced fingers. *OMG*, thought Tori. *They were holding hands!* Mike cleared his throat and abruptly turned his attention to a very interesting shrub in the front yard. Laura suddenly needed to brush some invisible dog hair from her new teal blouse.

"Hi!" Tori stifled a giggle. "C'mon in." She held the door open as her friends entered.

"We just stopped by to . . ." Mike's deep voice shot up into the stratosphere. He coughed. ". . . to see how Nick is." He looked straight into Tori's eyes. "You two are an amazing team."

Tori felt her cheeks heat up. "Thanks." She lowered her eyes and nudged her glasses. So far, only she and Mike knew all the details of their escape from the old farmhouse. She gave Mike a quick, secret smile. "Nick's getting better. He'll be fine. C'mon into the living room and say hi to my dad."

Mike's black baseball cap read *Flea*. Tori hoped the word referred to some band, not the insect. "Hey, Dad, look who's here."

"Hi, Mike," Tori's father stopped strumming the guitar and stretched his long arm toward the boy. Mike blinked, pulled his cap off, then stepped toward Dad and shook his hand. Dad said, "Nice to see you again. I'm glad it's under different circumstances."

Dad turned to Laura. "Hey, Laura. Why do dogs make terrible dance partners?"

"I don't know. Why?"

"Because they have two left feet!"

Laura fake laughed. Tori rolled her eyes and sighed. She leaned toward Laura. "See what I have to live with now?"

Mike surveyed the shelves of CDs and vinyl records and the vintage stereo equipment. "Wow. You like jazz?" He gazed at Tori's dad with a new level of respect.

"Yeah. And I'm starting to listen to some indie rock bands too," said Dad. "How 'bout you?"

Tori and Laura eyed each other and sneaked off to Tori's room, leaving the two musicians to talk. Nick sprawled on his side across Tori's bed, surrounded by his chew toys.

"Nick! How are you?" Laura said. She petted his shoulder gently. With sleepy eyes, Nick raised his head a few inches to greet Laura and thumped his thick tail against the quilt. The golden feathers waved up and down. The corners of his mouth turned up into a grin.

"The cuts and scrapes on his back are healing pretty fast. He's getting more like himself every day. We'll be back at the DSC soon." Tori picked up her journal from her desk and flipped through it—a hundred pages that detailed her and Nick's agility career, from their first agility lesson all the way through the fun match. Both she and Nick had learned and grown so much.

Tori found the entry she wanted. "Ya know, I've been thinking a lot about something you said a while back. I wrote about it in my journal." She cleared her throat, glanced at Laura, and read.

In dog sports, it's best not to focus on winning. Running the course perfectly isn't always the goal. The most important

thing is to make sure that your dog is healthy and happy. That has to come first. An agility trial is just a way to test your training. To see how far you've come. To explore the connection and communication and trust you've developed with your dog. And to celebrate your partnership after each run. If you can do all that, you and your dog have won.

She sat down next to Nick and gently traced the soft black V on his forehead. "Isn't that right, Nick? Scarfing down the celebration treats is your specialty."

Laura smiled at Tori and nodded in agreement. For once, she had no words. She petted Nick's side in long gentle strokes.

Nick had helped her win in a lot of ways, thought Tori. She had won friends and a better relationship with her dad. Stolen dogs would be reunited with their families. Marion was getting the help she needed. The animal shelter was raising the money it needed. And, not least of all, both she and Nick were still in one piece after their training and bond with each other were tested to the limit in Marion's house.

Nick stretched out his legs, extended each toe, then relaxed and shimmied his body deeper into Tori's quilt. As the girls petted him, he lifted his head and began to chew gently on a soft pink elephant.

CHAPTER 45

AUGUST

Maple Valley Town Park had been transformed into a dog agility trial site. Volunteers had built two competition rings and set up several big white shade tents to keep the hot August sun off the dozens of dogs and their handlers who gathered for the Maple Valley Dog Sports Center Summer Trial.

A gaggle of teenage girls perched on the sunlit bleachers. Their voices filled the warm summer air.

"Yay, Nick!"

"Good luck, Tori!"

Gisele struggled to hold on to a fidgety Jack Russell terrier puppy, who nipped at her DSC t-shirt. Abby sat beside her. She tossed her long black hair, crossed her arms, and lifted her nose, but her eyes followed Tori and Nick. The sun glinted off the shiny new braces on her teeth.

"C'mon, Gunnar. Do your business! I want to watch the next team." In the waiting area, Harry held a plastic bag and followed his yellow Lab as the dog searched for the perfect place to poop.

"I'll be right back," Jordan told his volunteers at the shelter information table. "I want to see this team run." He hurried to the agility ring, craning his tattooed neck to see over the crowd of handlers and spectators.

Mike paced back and forth near the bleachers with Chase and Onyx. He glanced toward the agility ring every few seconds. "Good luck, crazy girl," he murmured, just loudly enough for the two dogs to hear. They pricked their ears and looked at him curiously.

Min walked Zen past the in-gate to check the gate sheet posted on the whiteboard. "Four more dogs, Zen. Then you get to run." She smiled and nodded at Tori as Tori and Nick got ready to head into the ring.

Dad, as the volunteer gatekeeper, stood at the whiteboard. He checked the gate sheet, then turned to Tori and gave her a private grin. "Good luck. I'm proud of you," he told her quietly. Then he called to the nearby group of handlers, "Tori and Nick are next! Dog on course!"

Laura stood just outside the orange plastic fence that surrounded the ring, where she had a clear view of the entire course. She aimed her phone at the girl and dog entering the ring.

With long, sure strides, Tori walked to the start line. Nick trotted gracefully at her side. She surveyed the array of colorful agility obstacles and mentally reviewed her plan for running the course. *We can do this.*

"Sit," Tori said lightly, and Nick settled beside her. She looked down at her best friend, and he locked his golden eyes onto hers. "I love you, buddy. That's what matters. Whatever happens, that's what matters." Impulsively, she leaned over and kissed the soft black fur between his floppy tan ears.

The trial judge flashed Tori a thumb's-up.

Tori tossed the leash behind her and strode forward, her left arm extended back. Nick quivered in anticipation, his shining eyes fixed on Tori. She looked over her shoulder and pointed at the jump in front of him. Nick focused on it. He shifted his haunches, readying himself for a powerful start.

"Break!" called Tori.

She took off running, and Nick leaped into the air—and soared.

Tori's Glossary of Dog Agility Terms

Obstacles

A-frame: Full height is about five feet. The ramps are three reet wide and nine feet long. My cue is "climb!" I usually have Nick do a running contact for the A-frame.

Contact: The A-frame, dogwalk, and see-saw are called contact obstacles or just contacts. They all have a yellow area at both ends of the obstacle (only the down end of the see-saw) that the dog must touch with at least one foot before exiting the obstacle. The yellow area is called the contact zone. The rest of the obstacle is a contrasting color, usually blue.

Dogwalk: Full height is about four feet. There are three planks, and each one is about twelve inches wide and twelve feet long. For practice, you can lower it so that the middle plank is anywhere between one foot and four feet above the ground. Nick can do either a stopped or running contact on the dogwalk. My cue is "climb!" (I use the same cue for the A-frame and dogwalk.)

Jump: Also called hurdle. The cross bar—that's the pole that the dog goes over—can be set at many different heights, depending on the size of the dog. Nick jumps sixteen inches at trials, but sometimes lower in practice. The bar will fall if the dog hits it hard enough. Jumps are usually made from PVC poles. (PVC is a hard plastic, usually white.) My cue is "jump!"

See-saw: A twelve-foot plank about twelve inches wide that sits on a triangular support called a fulcrum. It stands about two feet high in the middle. Nick does a stopped contact on the see-saw. My cue is "seeeesaaaw!"

Tunnel: Made of heavy flexible plastic. The opening is 24 inches wide. They come in different lengths: ten, fifteen, or twenty feet, for example. You can curve them into different shapes, and they are held in place with weighted bags that sit on both sides of the tunnel. My cue is "tunnel!"

Weave poles: PVC poles attached to a metal base, set two feet apart in a straight row. Usually there are twelve poles, but sometimes only six. My cue is "weave!"

Terms

Collect: Imagine you are running full speed, and suddenly you see a fence ten feet ahead of you. You would shorten your steps and slow down—collect yourself—to prepare to stop or jump the fence. Dogs must collect themselves often while running agility—for example, when entering the weave poles or preparing to stop at the end of the dogwalk.

Discrimination: Two or three obstacles are set so close together that the handler must give a clear cue to the dog about which one to go to. The most common discriminations consist of a tunnel and dogwalk or a tunnel and A-frame.

Fault: When competing, the judge gives faults for mistakes such as the dog hitting the jump bar so that it drops, not entering the weaves correctly, or not touching the contact zone on the contact obstacles. A perfect score for a standard course is 0. If you get faults, your score would be 5, 10, or 20, for example.

Leadout: When beginning a course, the handler leaves the dog at the start line and walks (or runs) to a place on the course, then releases the dog to begin running. This strategy allows the handler to get ahead of the dog right away, making it easier to direct the dog as they enter the middle part of the course.

Off-course: On most agility courses, all or some of the obstacles are numbered and the handler and dog must run them in that order. If the dog takes a wrong obstacle, it's called an off-course. For example, your dog runs to obstacle 5 (a tunnel) instead of the correct obstacle, number 3 (a jump). The tunnel in this case is called an off-course, and the judge would give you an off-course fault.

Running contact: The dog runs across the yellow contact zone without stopping. I use a running contact for the A-frame. My cue is "run, run, run!"

Stopped contact: The dog stops on the contact zone. Often, dogs are trained to stop with their front paws on the ground and their back paws on the obstacle. That's called a 2-on, 2-off stopped contact. I use a 2-on, 2-off stopped contact for the dogwalk. My cue is "target!"

ABOUT P. J. RICH

Dog on Course is a story I've been thinking about since adopting my German shepherd mix Emma in 2006. I was honored to share my life with her for 17 years, and she is the model for Nick.

I live in a small city in Oregon with a sweet, hilarious dog of many breeds who loves agility as much as I do. Her little brother, a poodle-border collie puppy, is having a blast learning about life and has confided in me that he is eager to learn about agility too. I volunteer as a dog walker at my local animal shelter, where I especially like to help the German shepherds and shepherd mixes learn their manners.

I've worked at many different jobs: nonfiction editor at a publishing company, biological technician for the National Park Service, scuba diving instructor, veterinary technician, paralegal, musician, and substitute teacher in public schools, to name a few.

Dogs are my passion; writing is my dream. I'm lucky enough to be able to combine the two in *Dog on Course: A Tori & Nick Adventure.* I hope you enjoy it. Look for another Tori & Nick Adventure book coming soon.

I would appreciate your review on Amazon, Goodreads, and any other place where you find my book. You can also *like* others' reviews on Amazon. Reviews help readers discover the book, and that means more people can learn about kind, positive dog training, the sport of dog agility, and the wonderful pets available at animal shelters. I promise to read what you write.

Visit me at pjrich.com.

Note From The Author

Thanks for reading my book! All the information about dog training is based on the teachings of experienced, professional, positive reinforcement dog trainers and on my own more than twenty years of experience training and competing in agility with my dogs.

There's a lot more to training dogs than what you read in this book! The scenes about dog training are not complete lessons, and it can take much longer than a few months to teach agility to a dog. I included just enough examples to fit the story and give readers an idea of what it's like to educate a dog. You can find more information at your local library and online by searching for *positive reinforcement dog training*.

If you are interested in playing agility with your dog, search for positive reinforcement trainers and dog agility clubs in your area. You might go to a local agility trial and ask the competitors who they train with. To find a trial, check the Events pages on these websites:

American Kennel Club: AKC.org

Canine Performance Events: cpe.dog

North American Dog Agility Council: NADAC.com

UK Agility International: ukagilityinternational.com

United States Dog Agility Association: USDAA.com